RunaMok

RunaMok

A NOVEL ABOUT
THE
REALITIES
OF SMALL
BUSINESS

TOM
PARK

PETERSON'S/PACESETTER BOOKS
PRINCETON, NEW JERSEY

For my Dad, one of the world's greatest guys,
and for Janie, my best friend.

Visit Peterson's Education & Career Center at
http://www.petersons.com

Copyright © 1996 by Tom Park

Library of Congress Cataloging-in-Publication Data

Park, Tom.
    Runamok : a novel about the realities of small business / Tom
Park.
      p.   cm.
    ISBN 1-56079-662-6
    I. Title.
    PS3566.A67472R86   1996
    813'.54—dc20   96-4550
                                                         CIP

Editorial direction by Andrea Pedolsky   Composition by Gary Rozmierski
Production supervision by Bernadette Boylan   Creative direction by Linda Huber
Copyediting by Kathleen Salazar   Interior design by Cynthia Boone
Proofreading by Marie Burnett

Printed in the United States of America

10 9 8 7 6 5 4 3 2 1

Acknowledgments

Thanks to Andrea Pedolsky, one of the few people more stubborn than I am, and to Stephen Frankel who patiently led both Andrea and me into the world of fiction. And thanks also to all the John Walpolds out there that inspired this book.

Preface

It is not the critic who counts; nor the man who points out how the strong man stumbles or where the doer of deeds could have done them better. The credit belongs to the man who is actually in the arena, whose face is marred by dust and sweat and blood.

—Theodore Roosevelt

*W*hat follows is not a how-to manual for small-business owners but a novel about a typical small business, Walpold Enterprises. The company and its employees are fictitious, but anyone who has been involved with a small business will recognize most of the people. Likewise, most small-business owners and managers will be able to empathize with John Walpold as he wrestles with dwindling cash reserves, betrayal by his partner, key employees with their own agendas, and the pressure exerted by his financial backer who begins taking steps to replace him—in short, a company running amok. Couched within the framework of the story, however, are the methods and procedures necessary to eliminate the chaos—the fundamentals of professional management.

Because of the variety of issues the small-business owner faces, it is easy for him or her to lose sight of a fundamental fact: The same management techniques that work in large companies are also crucial to the success of small, growing companies. Learning how to apply these techniques will result in a company in control of its destiny, rather than one constantly whipsawed by the events of each day.

—Tom Park

T*h*E Pla*C*e

Walpold Enterprises, a three-year-old company located in Orlando, Florida, that manufactures high-resolution display interface cards.

T*h*E P*E*oPL*e*

John Walpold, CEO and cofounder of Walpold Enterprises, 38 years old. Married for 18 years to his wife Beth; they have two sons, Andy and Zach, and a dog, Barney.

Dan Killian, head of R&D and cofounder of Walpold Enterprises, 36 years old. Married to Liz; they have no children.

Joan Richardson, office manager of Walpold Enterprises, 40 years old. She is in the midst of a divorce from her husband Bill; they have two children, Jennifer and Paul.

Pete Delaney, head of technical support, 28 years old. Dating Rita Gonzalez, head of purchasing.

Jerry Wilson, head of production, 43 years old. Married.

Phil Jackson, head of sales (but calling in "sick" a lot lately).

Scott Nichols, assistant head of sales, 27 years old. Single.

Marie Manning, bookkeeper, 33 years old. Single.

Rita Gonzalez, purchasing agent, 25 years old. Dating Pete Delaney.

Rick Devereux, small-business consultant, 45 years old.

Herb Chandler, venture capitalist and silent partner/financier of Walpold Enterprises, 60 years old. Married to wife Arlene.

Leonard Wasserman, works for Herb Chandler, 27 years old.

Phyllis "Phyl" Stapleton, works for Herb Chandler, 28 years old.

Mike Smith, Walpold's attorney and longtime friend of John, 38 years old.

Beth, John's wife, 38 years old. Works as a dental hygienist.

Sean Davis, John's nephew. Works in Receiving and attends college at night.

Wendy, receptionist, 19 years old.

Marty Dorsey, Walpold's banker.

Cal Reilly, Walpold's accountant.

FRiDAy

July 28, 1995

$a$nother typical Florida morning," John thought, one hand on the steering wheel and the other holding a mug of lukewarm coffee, as he turned his aging Dodge van into the gravel parking lot in back of his office. The Orlando sky was hazy from the heat, and the humidity was so thick you could reach out and touch it. The current of warm air that had rushed through the open windows as he drove had bathed him in it. Beads of perspiration had collected on his forehead and stayed there. "I've gotta get the air-conditioning fixed in this crate," he muttered to himself. He pulled into his usual parking spot, drained the last of the coffee, and balanced the mug precariously on the undersized cup holder in the van's center console. Then he rolled up the windows, grabbed his notebook and a stack of papers from the seat, slid out of the van, and locked it—a holdover from the days when the van or its contents could be considered valuable.

He glanced at his watch—it was only 6:55 a.m. Just as he got to the office door and inserted his key into the lock, he could hear the phone ringing. He threw open the door, ran to the receptionist's desk, and grabbed the phone, tossing down his notebook with last night's "homework." Trying to catch his breath, he said, "Good morning, this is Walpold Enterprises. Can I help you?"

"Yeah, this is Al Williams from the San Francisco office. I've been at First United the whole damn night, trying to get them up and running. What the hell happened to the spares I requested? Joan told me she would send them yesterday morning so I'd get them on the four p.m. Delta flight. Do you know how far it is from downtown San Francisco to the goddamn airport? Well, I drove out there yesterday afternoon, and guess what? No boards. By then, you clowns in Florida were already gone for the day, and I had to rob parts from another client to get First United running, which just happened an hour ago. You guys are killing us out here!"

"Al, this is John Walpold. I just got here, but I guarantee you I'll personally look into this, find out what happened, and call you back within two hours. Will you be at the office?" he asked, trying to throw a little oil on the troubled waters.

"Are you kidding? It's four o'clock in the goddamn morning, and I've been up all night because you guys screwed up again. I'm going to bed. I'll call you this afternoon, if I can convince myself there's any reason to," he snarled, and slammed down the phone.

John shook his head, picked up the notebook and papers he had hastily dropped, and walked to his office. He often called himself a closet nerd, but it was no secret to the people who knew him. John was thirty-eight years old, six feet tall, with light brown hair, hazel eyes, and an engaging smile. Lately, he had been worrying too much about business to think about his appearance, and he had begun to look pale, overweight, and out of shape. His eyes, which once displayed an impish gleam, now appeared almost glazed over, and under them were the beginning traces of the insomniac's telltale dark circles. He had been talking about joining a health club, but so far it had just been that—idle talk; he was convinced that he should be focusing all his energy on the company until things were under control.

He knew that as president he should project a professional image, but he hated wearing a suit and opted instead for a more casual outfit of sports jacket, slacks, pastel shirt, and a nondescript tie. At least he didn't jam a plastic pocket protector into his shirt pocket every morning the way he did when he was a journeyman design engineer, although he probably still would if he hadn't been teased about it so much. He owned three sports jackets. Today he was wearing the beige one. He took it off and hung it on a hook behind his door and began looking for his coffee cup.

John's office was as cluttered as his thoughts. Like the other eight offices in the building that the company occupied, it was crowded with secondhand furniture that had been purchased three years earlier when he and his partner, Dan Killian, started the company. With lots of enthusiasm but a limited budget, they had gone to used-furniture stores and garage sales and picked up a mismatched collection of slightly worn pieces that by now looked pretty shabby. In the middle of the room, facing the door, was his gray metal desk, covered with papers. One corner of it was taken up by a set of black plastic "In" and "Out" baskets stacked one on top of the other. This was John's failed attempt at organization, for each of them was stuffed with dozens of papers about a variety of topics, the urgency of which had long since expired. With the baskets full, dozens more papers were in several haphazardly arranged piles that covered the rest of the desk, except for a small area that he managed to keep clear right in front of him. These piles contained items he had at one time tried to prioritize, but he had lost track of which pile contained the highest-priority issues.

Behind his desk was a table with his computer terminal and a few more piles of papers. A few feet in front and to the right of his desk was a long brown metal worktable that also doubled as a conference table. Papers from some of the most recent meetings hadn't been removed and were still scattered about the surface in no particular order, along with a half-dozen Styrofoam coffee cups, some half filled. One cup was tipped over, and its contents had dried on several adjacent papers. The table was surrounded by armless metal chairs of various colors: three green, two gray, two brown, and one black—John referred to them as his attempt at equal-opportunity employment.

The thin wall-to-wall carpet was of a color that defied description—sometimes it appeared gray, other times brown, sometimes even light green. John had figured that this would be advantageous, since it wouldn't show dirt easily; in reality, it just always looked dirty. The walls were painted off-white and contained a random assortment of unframed posters displaying various travel scenes: a bullfight in Mexico, the mountains of Austria, a sailboat regatta, and a view of the Great Wall of China. John's wife, Beth, chided him about having the world's tackiest poster collection and threatened to upgrade it by adding a velvet painting of Elvis, but John just ignored her—the office decor had never been one of his priorities.

Spying his coffee cup half buried under the miscellany on his desk, John grabbed it and headed out to the break room to start the morning pot. "I wonder what happened with Joan," he muttered to himself, pondering the early morning call from Al. "She's always so reliable."

John entered the break room and found the lights already on, not because someone had beaten him to work, but because they hadn't been turned off the previous night. He rinsed out the leftover coffee from the coffeepot, dumped the used filter and grounds in the garbage, grabbed the can of coffee and spooned the proper amount into a new filter, and turned on the automatic coffee maker. Before he put the plastic lid back on the can of coffee, he paused to inhale the pleasant aroma. "Not exactly stopping to smell the roses," he thought to himself, "but as close as I can get." The break room was a large, centrally located room where people relaxed during their breaks and ate lunch. In addition to a sink and a counter where the coffeemaker resided, it contained a large refrigerator and several tables and chairs that looked like they came from 1950s dinette sets, which they probably did, and a bulletin board.

John glanced at the board and was surprised to find that it was empty. It used to be an infinite source of entertainment— filled with everything from garage-sale announcements to requests for roommates, serious and tongue-in-cheek. "I guess everyone's as busy as I am," he thought. The coffee had not quite finished dripping into the pot, but John couldn't wait. He jerked the pot out and quickly filled his cup, hurrying to put the pot back under the dripping filter so that only a minimum of drops would land on the heating element. He opened the refrigerator to get the cream, but there wasn't any. "I wonder whose week it is to pick up the supplies," he grumbled. He didn't much care for black coffee, but it would have to do.

Returning to his office with the coffee, he sank into his desk chair with a sigh and glanced over the stack of unreturned phone messages from the day before—from his lawyer, his accountant, his banker, three vendors, his broker, and three people he had never heard of, probably wanting to sell him something. John had spent the entire previous afternoon with a potential customer who had flown in to check out the operation. John marveled at the stack of messages that had accumulated in such a short time. He wouldn't be able to reach anyone at that hour of the morning, so he decided to tackle the mail.

He turned on his computer to see if any E-mail was waiting for him. There was a computer in the office of each of the key people in the company, and all the computers were networked together. Ultimately this was supposed to help them operate more efficiently, but so far it had only been useful as a means of communicating via electronic mail. The concept seemed silly to John, who felt that the company was still small enough that anybody could talk with anybody else just by walking from one office to the other, but everyone else seemed to like it. He found a message from Jerry, the head of production, asking him about a purchase order for some printed circuit boards he needed, and a cryptic message from Dan, his partner. Apparently Dan, who was also head of R&D, had had a midnight revelation about some new product he was working on, but the message didn't make much sense—Dan's midnight messages seldom did. He missed the days when he could work with Dan well into the night, but now that John was the CEO, he felt that his presence was necessary during the day, and he couldn't do both.

He turned back to his desk. In addition to mail, John's "In" basket contained several memos and contracts for his review. He rummaged through the stack and pulled out yesterday's mail. Joan had already opened it for him, and he could see three bills that were stamped in red ink "Final Notice" and an official-looking letter that said something about turning over the account to a collection agency. He got a sickening feeling in the pit of his stomach, so he tossed them aside. Next were a letter from his banker asking for an updated personal financial statement, a flyer from a consultant with the headline "Are You Running Your Business, Or Is It Running You?" and a cheery letter informing him that he was a finalist in the Publishers Clearinghouse Sweepstakes. Noticing that the latest issue of *Computer Weekly* had also arrived, he happily shifted his attention from the stack of mail.

Leaning back in his chair, John flipped open the magazine to the lead article about the most recent drop in computer prices and why prices would continue to fall under the pressure of intense competition. "Great," he thought, "we're barely surviving now, but we're going to have to cut prices again as soon as our customers see this stupid article or else run the risk of losing market share to all our competitors." This further depressed him, since he didn't have any idea how they could cut prices and still make a profit. He sighed again and began chewing on the skin around his thumb.

As he was pondering pricing, he heard the outside door open and a few seconds later saw Joan drop an armload of files on her desk outside his office. "Good morning," she offered breathlessly, obviously a habit rather than an opinion.

"What are you so glum about, Joan—it's Friday!" said John.

"I guess you've forgotten that Friday is also payday, and I haven't figured out yet if there's enough money in the bank to pay everybody, to say nothing of the four calls I got yesterday from Sue at Consolidated telling me that they're withholding any more shipments until we bring our account current. I spent all day yesterday dealing with vendors wanting money and didn't get anything solved." It was only 7:30 a.m., but she already looked harried. Joan was barely forty years old, and her face had the pinched look of someone with more than her share of life's problems. Her light brown hair was cut short in an "easy to maintain" hairstyle. She wore a tailored white silk blouse with a straight hunter green skirt and low heels, an outfit that neither emphasized nor hid her shapely figure. It was one of several versions of the "uniform" she had resolved to wear when she took the position as John's assistant. She used to have rosy cheeks and a smile on her face but not anymore—her vitality was being sapped.

"How are the kids?" asked John, aware that her stress was more than job related lately.

"Terrific," she answered sarcastically. "Last night I walked into the den where Jen and her boyfriend were watching TV, just in time to see him slip his hand into her blouse," she said, referring to her fifteen-year-old daughter Jennifer. "I told him that was inappropriate and asked him to leave but not exactly in those words. Jen was really pissed, and as she stalked off to her room, she told me that maybe if I'd been a little sexier, she'd still have a father. Like I want to compete with Bill's twenty-three-year-old sex kitten," she said, trying unsuccessfully to hide how deeply her daughter's remark had hurt her.

"Speaking of yesterday," offered John, changing the subject, "Al Williams called this morning and asked about a shipment you promised him."

"Oh crap!" she said. Still standing outside John's door, she reached under a pile of papers on her desk and found the note she'd written the day before on a torn piece of paper. Waving it in the air, she said, "I remember what happened. Just as I got off the phone with Al, Jerry came in and said he was almost out of blank printed circuit boards and that if the order he placed two weeks ago couldn't be expedited, he was going to send the assembly people home because they wouldn't have anything to do. So I called Rita and asked her to check on the status of the order. She looked everywhere and couldn't find the purchase order, but she finally came across a copy of it and told me that the original was probably on your desk awaiting approval and that as soon as you signed it, she would place the order. You were in your office with the door closed and were in the middle of a meeting with that Buzz guy from New York, and I didn't want to interrupt you with something like this in front of a potential customer. I had to meet Bill at the attorney's office to go over the property settlement, and we got into a big fight over who would get the kids for Thanksgiving and Christmas. I was so upset when I got back that I completely forgot about Al's order," she said breathlessly, wringing her hands and looking contrite.

"On my desk?" John asked with a quizzical look. "I thought I had signed everything that was on my desk. Is that what Jerry's E-mail message was about? Hmm, let's see," he mumbled as he shuffled through the papers on his desk. "Oh here it is, clipped together with this purchase order for new workbenches. Why do we need new workbenches?"

Joan, glancing quickly at her watch, answered, "How should I know? What I do know is that if I don't figure out how much money we have, I can't let Marie issue the payroll checks, and that'll be great for morale. Of course with Jerry sending everyone home, it probably won't matter. I'm not sure they'll release the boards at Acme anyway until we bring our account current—I think I put a copy of their note on your desk. You said we were profitable, so why do we owe everybody so much money?"

"Receivables, I guess. Doesn't *somebody* owe us some money? I could swear both First United and National owe us more than thirty thousand dollars. Why don't you call them and see what's up. Maybe since they're late paying, we can get them to wire us the money."

"Should I do that before or after I call Al and apologize, or should I figure out how much money we have so we can process the payroll, and which one of us is going to tell Jerry about his boards?"

"Receivables," John said forcefully, "Let's collect some damn money to get us out of this cash squeeze. If we had some cash, we could get back to running the business and not be distracted by all this crap. You, Wendy, and Rita get started calling our deadbeat customers, and I'll call Marty at the bank and see if we can get some bridge money to get us through the next couple of weeks." Feeling in control again, he added, "And get me some more coffee while you're at it, if you won't sue me for asking. And find out who screwed up on coffee supplies—we're out of cream again."

"Right, chief," Joan said saluting, feeling better with John starting to take charge again. She grabbed his cup and started to leave for the break room but then stopped. "John, this is your week—you were supposed to check the supplies." Then, before he could respond, she quickly added, "Don't worry about it; I'll take care of it," and headed off toward the break room.

Terrific. John had gotten tired of always being the one to get the supplies, so he had set up a weekly schedule that rotated among his key managers. The lucky person of the week was responsible for keeping the break room supplies in stock, using money from petty cash. With everything else that was happening, he had simply forgotten.

John picked up the phone, dialed the bank, and was connected immediately with Martin Dorsey, his personal banker— a term that made him chuckle. "Hey Marty, this is John Walpold. How are things?"

"Hi John, it's good to hear from you. Things are fine over here. How's business?" said Marty amiably.

"Too good, I guess—that's why I called. I really need some extra cash to get me through this bind I'm in right now. Everything should be sorted out in a few weeks but, until then, I could sure use thirty-five or forty thousand dollars to ease the crunch."

"Well John, that might be a problem. I was going to call you today to discuss your credit line. It's been maxed out at two hundred thousand for several months, and it's supposed to be cleared for thirty days each year before we can renew it. The loan committee is suggesting that maybe it needs to be turned into an amortized note, so we can predict the paydown. That's why I left the message yesterday that we'll need the latest personal financial statements for you, Dan, and Herb, as well as the company's financials."

"Marty, we've been doing business with you for two years. Are you telling me that you're cutting off my credit?" John's hands started to sweat, and the sickening feeling in the pit of his stomach returned as he wondered what he would do if sufficient cash wasn't available to make the payroll.

"Not exactly John, but with the new restrictions that we're having to deal with, we don't have the latitude we used to have. All the t's have to be crossed and all the i's dotted, and everything has to satisfy an impartial committee. It's all standard stuff, nothing to worry about if everything is in order, John."

"Let me get this straight—there are no conditions under which I can get a bridge loan this week?" John asked. He began to sweat and nervously drummed his fingers on the desk.

"Well John, if your credit line weren't maxed out, you could certainly draw from that. But it is, and with your inventory and receivables already pledged against that and your building pledged against its mortgage, I don't see how we could approve any more debt without a thorough review of your business. Do you have a current business plan?"

"Are you kidding me? What about the fact that my inventory and receivables are a lot higher than when we established the credit line?" said John, feeling like he might have found an area for negotiation.

"That might be worth pursuing. What's the current value of your receivables?"

"Well, I don't know exactly, but I'm sure it's higher than it was ten months ago," he said, realizing that he really wasn't prepared to answer questions about his company's finances. Managing receivables was Joan's responsibility. He had delegated the task to her, and by not meddling he was merely letting her do her job. That's what all the management books said: You have to avoid micromanagement or the company can't grow. At least, that was how he justified not knowing the status of his receivables, but the logic was beginning to seem less sound as the conversation continued.

"Do you know how current they are, and whether they are all collectible?"

"I'll ask Joan; she keeps track of that stuff. But the inventory is also higher than it was ten months ago."

"Okay, what is your current inventory level, and what is your inventory turn rate?" asked Marty, starting to regret that the discussion had even gotten started.

John paused before answering. Inventory was Jerry's responsibility and since he didn't bug him every day about it, he didn't know these answers either. He pulled a half-finished roll of Tums from his pocket, popped two into his mouth, then grabbed a new roll from the supply he kept in his desk drawer and put it in his pocket, along with what was left of the other roll. "I'll check with Jerry; he should know that," said John hastily. "Is that what you need to know before we can increase the credit line?"

"It would be a good start. Why don't you put together a plan describing what your current condition is, what you need, and how you'll be able to handle the debt? Then maybe we can get together next week and discuss it. How does that sound?"

"Terrific, and in the meantime, I guess I'll have to get a mask and gun to solve my payroll problem today. See ya," he said as he slammed the phone down. "Swell. Now what am I going to do?" he wondered. He was feeling less and less in control. He unconsciously reached into his pocket for his Tums but then realized that he'd just had some, for the taste was still fresh in his mouth. The thought of losing his company was starting to frighten him. Lately he had been considering cutting the payroll as a way to ease the cash shortage, but every time he thought of having to lay people off, people that had all become his friends, he broke out in a cold sweat.

John decided that as much as he hated it, he would have to call Herb Chandler, his and Dan's silent partner, who had helped them put the financing together to start Walpold Enterprises. Herb had always been very supportive of John and Dan, but at the most recent meeting of the board of directors, he had begun to ask some rather pointed questions about sales and potential profits. John dialed Herb's number, and after a single ring, Herb answered.

"Hello."

"Hi Herb, this is John Walpold. How are you doing?"

"Oh, hi John," he said, rather coolly. "What can I do for you," ignoring John's pleasantry.

"Well, we're in sort of a cash crunch, and the bank's stonewalling me. I was wondering what you would think about a short-term note to tide us over until we collect some receivables."

"What I would think about being your *banker,* you mean?"

"Not exactly." Herb's blunt response made John realize that things with Herb were not the way they once were. Herb sounded distant and confrontational. He told Herb, "We have the sales, but some of our customers are stringing us out, and we need some cash to run things for a couple of weeks. When First United pays us, we'll pay you back."

"So you want me to start factoring your receivables?" he asked. "How much are we talking about?"

"First United owes us about thirty thousand dollars for the order that we shipped them last week. They usually pay in thirty days."

"Okay. I'll give you ninety-three percent of the order price. You sign a note agreeing to give me a hundred percent of the payment when you receive it in thirty days. It'll cost you seven percent."

"Seven percent for one month is eighty-four percent annually. I can get better terms from the Mafia!"

"So call the Mafia. Don't forget, you called me, I didn't call you. And before we do anything, I want to send Leonard and Phyl in to look things over and maybe give you a hand. After they've had a look around, we'll discuss the details. Okay?"

"Great, with everything else going on, I've got to entertain houseguests."

"They won't get in your way; they're very resourceful. You're not trying to hide anything, are you? I'm a board member, you know, and I'm entitled to know what's happening. Consider this a form of 'due diligence.' "

"No, I'm not *hiding* anything. Send them in, and we'll show them what's going on. I'll talk to you later," he said flatly, hanging up the phone. "A couple of shadows," he thought. "Just what I need."

He wondered if it would be simpler after all to get the money from the bank and decided to see what shape his personal financial statement was in. He swiveled around to face his computer, turned it on, and began to search in the directory that contained his personal financial information. As he reached for his coffee cup, he realized that Joan hadn't returned with it yet. Just then, Joan, Jerry, Rita, and Marie filed silently into his office. They looked grim. Joan closed the door.

"What's this, the Grand Inquisition?" asked John.

No one even cracked a smile. They pulled chairs from the conference table, set them in a row in front of his desk, and sat down. Jerry Wilson, the balding head of production, finally said, "John, we need to talk about a few things."

"Okay, so talk," said John. The somber expression on everyone's face worried him, but he tried to hide it. He thought, "The call from Al, the stack of dunning notices, the banker's outright refusal to help, Herb's coldness—how much am I going to have to take? What else could happen today?" He sighed and slumped back into his chair, tried to look pleasant, and said, "Go ahead. What's the problem?"

After a short pause, Jerry started. "We kinda need to know what's happening. I don't have parts to keep production running, Rita says our suppliers won't ship until they get paid, and Marie says she can't write *any* checks for *anybody* because we don't have any money. I thought we had plenty of orders, so what the hell's going on? Are we going out of business? Are you trying to sell the place? Have you lost interest—or what?" he asked, disgusted.

John had always considered Jerry a staunch ally, so his tone was very unsettling. "We do have plenty of orders," John said defensively. "Joan, get Phil in here to give us an update on our order backlog," he said, referring to Phil Jackson, the head of Sales.

"He's out sick today," said Joan. "Actually, I think he's out interviewing. Scott's been taking up the slack in his absence. I'll go get him." She got up and went to find Scott. Everyone else sat fidgeting silently until Joan came back with Scott. He pulled up a chair and sat down. Scott Nichols was blond, wore wire–rimmed glasses, and looked even younger than his twenty-seven years, more like a grad student than part of a management team.

"So, Scott, how's Sales?" asked Joan.

"Last week I thought everything was fine," he answered. "We had an order from First United for forty new systems. But Wednesday, their purchasing guy called me and said the order had been placed thirty days ago, and that if we couldn't ship by the end of the week, they were going to cancel it. I checked with Jerry, and he said he wouldn't have parts until next week. I called First United back and tried to get them to extend their deadline a week, but they said they'd done that before and it was a waste of time. So I guess we lost it. That's when Phil started staying out 'sick' and told me I was in charge of Sales while he's away." Scott used the first two fingers of each hand to emphasize the quotation marks around the word sick. "And Pete told me yesterday that General Medical was so pissed about their downtime they're canceling their order," he added. Pete Delaney was the head of technical support.

"You might as well go get Pete too, Joan," said John. "Is there anyone else who ought to be here?" he asked the group. "Where's Dan?" He suddenly realized that his partner and head of R&D hadn't shown up yet.

Before anyone else could respond, Pete stuck his head in the door. "What's happening? Am I missing something?"

"Pete, Scott says we're losing orders because of unhappy customers. What's going on?" asked John.

"Yeah, they're unhappy; I'd be unhappy too if I was promised spares that didn't arrive," said Pete, glaring at Joan about yesterday's San Francisco foul-up, "and when they finally did arrive, half didn't work. Don't blame me—I've turned in the orders to Jerry. Ask him why we don't have spares."

"Now wait a minute," said Jerry quickly, his face beginning to redden. "I build the products that are specified on the forecast. You can't expect me to jump through hoops when you come in with last-minute orders. I don't even have the parts I requisitioned, much less the extra parts I need for your midnight requests. Then, the mix of boards that we actually sell never matches the mix on the forecast, so we run out of one model and have plenty extras of others. If we could get a decent forecast from sales and get our purchase orders processed on time, I'd have everything anyone needed." Jerry's face was now very red, and the veins in his forehead were pulsing.

"Of course our sales forecast is screwed up. The deals we have in the bag get killed by tech-support problems," said Scott defensively. "Then we have to scramble for more sales, and naturally they're different from the forecast. But they're not that different, for God's sake." Being the youngest and also newest to the company, Scott was not about to be too confrontational. But he wasn't going to take all the heat for the problems either. "Why don't we keep a stock of our most popular stuff? If we did, we'd have a smooth flow with our customers, assuming that the boards worked when they got there," he added.

"No one told me we were having DOAs," John interjected, referring to boards that are found to be Dead On Arrival. "What about that, Jerry?"

This was the last thing Jerry wanted to hear. In his younger, less experienced days, he would have really let loose. His temper had gotten him into trouble before, so he took a deep breath and counted to ten. "That hardly ever happens," he said as calmly as he could. "Last week Dan gave me a modification to incorporate for some special customer he had talked to. I didn't have any way to test it, but he said to go ahead and ship it, 'cause the customer needed it and would know how to get it to work. And that's in addition to throwing some boards together at the last minute for some hot order that Sales created so they can make their weekly quota—which happens all the time. But even with those last-minute requests, we'd be fine if we could just get the parts I order in a reasonable time," he concluded, obviously near the boiling point.

"Where is Dan, anyway? Didn't I just ask that a minute ago?" asked John, deciding to divert the attention from Jerry before he completely lost his cool.

"It's only 10 a.m.," said Pete. "He probably worked late last night, forgot to set his alarm, had an errand to run, decided to go sailing, went to Bermuda—"

"I process the orders the day I get your purchase order, Jerry," interrupted Rita. Her testy tone belied her small stature. She wouldn't sit back and take the heat for someone else's screw-up. "The vendors used to ship when I called them, but now they want prepayment and that has to be approved by John, and the check then has to be written by Marie," she said, as if daring someone to blame her.

"Well, I can't write the checks until I get the approved purchase order," said Marie with frustration, "and only if we have enough money in the bank to cover them. Lately that hasn't been the case, so I have several on my desk right now waiting to be processed."

John had finally heard enough. "Okay, let me get this straight. The correct boards can't be built without an accurate sales forecast, which doesn't exist because we keep losing forecasted orders because of tech-support problems that result from production not building the correct boards. This sounds like some stupid Abbott and Costello routine, not a business!" The room suddenly went quiet. John's outburst angered everyone in the group, but they held their tongues. He looked at them, wondering what he should say. He certainly couldn't give them an old-fashioned "rah rah" pep talk; they were beyond that. He felt utterly alone. The company that they had all worked so hard to build was slowly crashing down around them, and he didn't have a clue why. At one point he had felt that if he just worked harder, things would get better, but they only got worse. He found himself working from seven in the morning until after six every night and then taking home work that he hadn't finished. His weekends were shot, because even when he was home, he was worrying about what to do next.

In the early days, everyone was enthusiastic and no one minded working long hours. Now everyone was always exhausted and unhappy. He couldn't plan a vacation, even if he had the money, because he was certain that the company would fall apart if he left. They were always short of cash, and customers that he had personally signed up in the early days were beginning to drift to his competitors. His banker was cutting him off, and probably rightly so, because he didn't have any idea how he would pay off any more debt, let alone the existing debt. His silent partner was becoming less silent and was sending someone in to check up on him.

He remembered that last year his CPA had congratulated him on the tidy profit they had managed to make. "What a joke," he thought. "We made a profit and have no cash—imagine how desperate the companies must be that didn't even make a profit. Maybe I ought to just shut the place down and go back to a nice five-day-a-week job, where someone else would figure out how to find the cash for payroll every week. Or maybe I could sell it. But who'd buy this mess?" John suddenly felt his heart pounding and thought, "I've got to get my blood pressure checked." The pounding spread to his head, and the thought flashed through his mind that if his head suddenly exploded, at least his problems would be over.

He sighed deeply, shifted forward in his chair, and folded his hands together in front of him on the only clear area of his desk, empty of everything except the consultant's flyer. He began tapping his thumbs together as he looked at each of his employees soberly and slowly began to speak. "Okay, I'll tell you what we're going to do. We've let things get out of control. It's time to take stock of where we are and where we're going. I know other companies have gone through this, and I'm confident that since we got things this far, we'll figure out how to get past this. I'm going to get someone with experience in these situations to give us some help." Then, with a gleam returning to his eye, he added, "In the meantime, don't everyone look so glum. We've been through worse than this. Don't you remember our first computer show, when our displays got shipped to Salem, Oregon, instead of Salem, Massachusetts, and we spent three days making shadow figures on the wall? Come on, lighten up!" It wasn't much, and he could see it wasn't very effective, but John always counted on humor as his first and last line of defense. After everyone left his office, John called his accountant.

"Winston & Reilly, CPAs. How may I direct your call?"

"Yeah, this is John Walpold, and I'd like to speak to Cal Reilly."

"I'm sorry, Mr. Reilly is not available right now. Would you like to leave a message?"

"I suppose so," said John, wondering why he could never get through to his CPA. He always had to leave a message and then wait several hours for Reilly to call him back. "Tell him I'd like to talk to him before lunch, if possible," he said glumly.

He hated to call a consultant without knowing anything about him. Picking up the flyer and reading through it again, John remembered that he had met this guy briefly at a Chamber of Commerce function, but just as he had started to talk to him, some clown interrupted and started talking about workmen's comp rates, so he had escaped and left early. As much as he hated to talk to Marty again, John decided to call him at the bank and see what he knew about this consultant.

"Marty, this is John Walpold again. I'm thinking about giving Rick Devereux a call to see if he could help us put together a cash-flow forecast, and I was wondering if you knew anything about him."

"Yeah, John, I do. I think he has a pretty solid background in financial analysis, and I'm sure he could help you out. Sounds like a good idea. Be sure and shoot me a copy when it's ready. By the way, I think I saw your name on my list of delinquent accounts. Did we miss it, or did you forget your interest payment last week?"

"Oops, you're probably right, Marty. I'll check into it and send it out this afternoon if it isn't already mailed," John said, hanging up. "I've got to quit calling that guy," he thought.

He picked up the phone again and called Devereux, who agreed to stop by after lunch to meet John and assess the situation. John whiled away the rest of the morning reviewing contracts, and shortly before noon, still waiting for a return call from Reilly, he left to meet his attorney for lunch.

J ohn arrived at the restaurant first, as usual, and took a seat at a booth where he could watch both the door and the parking lot. Mike Smith, his corporate attorney and longtime friend, was always late. Mike had joined the most influential local firm right after law school and was now a partner. John and he were the same age and had attended college together. Although John's hair and complexion were a little lighter than Mike's, the two men were the same height and had similar features and were sometimes mistaken for brothers. On the weekends, John and his wife, Beth, frequently socialized with Mike and whoever—Mike hadn't married and was always with someone new. During the week, John and Mike had been meeting each other for lunch at least twice a month for years, as much for pleasure as for business, and took turns paying the bill, with whoever paid deducting it as a business expense.

Finally, John saw Mike's new Range Rover glide into a parking space, but instead of getting out, Mike stayed in the car another five minutes, talking on his cellular phone. When he finished the call, he folded up the phone and brought it with him into the restaurant. He immediately spotted John and slid into the seat across from him. Mike wore a dark blue blazer, gray slacks, a white shirt with narrow gray stripes, and a loosely tied dark blue tie with bold red "power" stripes. His expensive tasseled shoes looked like they had just been shined, and his fingernails were manicured. He noticed that John looked tired and that he had the forced smile of someone trying to look cheerful. "You look terrible, John. What the hell's wrong?"

Instead of answering him, John said, "You've turned into a real dandy, you know that? You've got your preppy Range Rover, your hi-tech cellular phone, your fancy custom-tailored clothes—hell, you've even gotten a manicure!"

"Hey, I'm dating a manicurist, and I get special treatment—so sue me," he responded lightly. "You're avoiding my question. What's wrong?" He knew his friend must be in trouble.

"Just your typical day at the counting house. That jerk Cal Reilly won't return my calls, Marty's capped my credit line, I've got mad creditors out the kazoo who won't ship the parts we need to fill the orders we already have, my employees are all turning hostile, and Herb wants to send someone in to look over my shoulder." He smiled again weakly. "Just a typical day," he repeated, and his smile quickly faded.

Mike considered this. Wanting to soothe John's feelings, he said, "Hey, Trixie and I are leaving tomorrow on a cruise to Nassau. Why don't you and Beth join us? It'll do you good to get away and relax and take your mind off things." Mike's manicurist wasn't really named Trixie—that was just a generic name he used when he was talking to John about whichever girl he was dating. Mike's idea of a meaningful relationship was one that lasted more than a month. During his younger days he devoted most of his time to his job, maximizing his billable hours and avoiding relationships that might jeopardize those numbers and what he called his "quest for a partnership." When he finally made partner, he discovered that the women his age were either already married or divorced with several small children, so he ended up leading the life of a playboy by default. He didn't see any other viable option and, in fact, he seemed to enjoy his life of ever-changing bedmates, social partners, and travel companions for his frequent pleasure trips.

When the waitress came to take their order, Mike asked for a bacon double cheeseburger with everything, an order of fries, and a Michelob, and John opted for a turkey breast sandwich, no mayo. After the waitress left, Mike said, "Boy that sandwich sounds yummy. You're really living on the wild side, aren't you?"

"I've got to lose some weight," said John defensively. "With all the stress I've been under, it's going to give me a heart attack or a stroke. In a meeting this morning, the blood vessels in my head were pounding so hard I thought they were going to rupture. Don't you realize what that cheeseburger's doing to your arteries?"

"I'll just work it off at the club. I thought you were going to join. It would do you a world of good. You'd get rid of some of that flab you're collecting around your waist, and you'd be surrounded by girls in tight exercise outfits."

Normally his lunch with Mike perked John up, but today it just further depressed him. He looked at his good friend and had to admit that he was jealous. Mike was physically fit, tanned, making plenty of money, well respected in the business community, and free to leave town on another pleasure trip with his sex kitten *du jour*. In comparison, John was out of shape, scraping to make ends meet financially, and saddled with the responsibilities of his wife and two teenage sons. John also realized that if he had stayed at his former company rather than risking everything to start Walpold Enterprises, by this time he would have been a department director, and, like Mike, would be well respected, making plenty of money, wearing custom-tailored clothes, and would be able to take his family on wonderful vacations. "What have I done?" John thought with a sigh. He spoke again. "Remember when I left R.S.S. to start this company, how eager everyone was to lend a hand? Remember all the lunches I told you about with CPAs, bankers, insurance agents, brokers, and vendors, all enthusiastically offering their services? It's hard not to be cynical when I think about that and see how they've all disappeared now that cash is short."

"Anything I can do to help?" Mike offered.

It was hard for John to resent Mike. In spite of his slick appearance, he was anything but ostentatious around John. He was still his good friend, eager to help. Unfortunately, John's problems were beyond Mike's help.

"Thanks. If I can think of anything, I'll let you know. I've called a guy named Rick Devereux to come by this afternoon. Know anything about him?"

"Hmm, I think so. Wasn't he involved with the takeover of Stan's company? I thought he worked mostly for some v.c. vultures out of New York. Are you looking for additional financing?"

"Not really, I'm just trying to figure out how to get things back under control. I met Devereux a few weeks ago, and he sent me a flyer that piqued my interest. I hope he's not just trolling for acquisitions," John mused. "That's all I need— another player with his own agenda."

"You've built a multimillion-dollar company, and you've read almost all the management books there are. What happened?"

Before he could answer, the waitress returned with their lunch, refilled their water, and left to bring Mike another beer. Mike slathered catsup on his fries and cheeseburger. John looked at his dry turkey sandwich and the macaroni salad that had come with it, which, if he ate it, he realized, would defeat the purpose of his low-fat entree. "I should have just ordered something good for a change and enjoyed it, rather than subjecting myself to this torture," he thought. He reached across the table and selected a particularly plump-looking French fry from Mike's plate, smooshed it in the catsup, and popped it into his mouth but not before dropping a splot of catsup on the table between them. The French fry was golden and crispy on the outside and almost hot enough inside to burn his mouth, but not quite. He wistfully savored the taste.

Enough self-indulgence, he decided, and began eating his sandwich. After a few bites, he finally responded to Mike's question. "What happened? I suppose nothing. We've always had problems, but they seem to have taken on a life of their own and become the norm, rather than the exception. Sure, I've read all the management books, but every time I get ready to do something to improve things, I get derailed by another crisis. Yeah, I know what I need to do—I just can't find the time to do it," he said, his misery and frustration apparent in his voice. "I'm not even sure I'll have enough in the bank to cover payroll this afternoon. According to the books, I suppose you could say we're financially insolvent."

"Big deal, so are a lot of companies, if you look just at their working capital. By the way, have you brought your legal bill current? Just thought I'd ask."

"What a guy. I just hope I don't have to spring for lunch today—it could be the difference between surviving another week and Chapter Eleven," said John, shaking his head.

"Seriously," Mike interjected, "why don't we roll up our sleeves this weekend and see if we can't sort things out? The planning we did in the early days not only helped convince Herb to get on board but got things going in the right direction. Maybe a few hours of brainstorming could help—it always did before."

"And you think Trixie might come up with a few good ideas during this powwow?" John had gotten into the habit of using Mike's nickname for his girlfriends.

"Oh yeah, Trixie. I forgot about the cruise. Well, maybe the weekend after," he offered sheepishly.

"Yeah, maybe," John sighed. For the rest of the lunch, they talked about sports and politics, topics about which the two had few disagreements.

When he returned from lunch, John was not surprised that Cal Reilly had failed to return his call. His situation reminded John of an old joke: The Lone Ranger and Tonto were hopelessly surrounded by Indians, whereupon the Lone Ranger turned to his trusty companion and asked, "What should we do, Tonto?" and Tonto replied, "What do you mean *we*, White Man."

As John sat as his desk, virtually paralyzed by everything happening around him, he couldn't help but wonder how things had gotten so screwed up. Things had started out so great. . . .

T*h*REE YE*a*Rs E*ar*L*ie*R
Monday, August 24, 1992

Hurricane Andrew was raging through South Florida. The storm didn't deviate from its course as it headed directly for the town of Homestead, much to the relief of the residents of Central Florida. Orlando seemed a million miles away from the destruction that was occurring just one hundred and eighty miles south, in spite of the overcast sky and the bumper-to-bumper northbound interstate traffic.

John and Dan were oblivious to the brewing storm, having worked most of the night on their first prototype. They had both already quit their former jobs and were working without salary, but neither of them cared—they were convinced that their revolutionary product would soon be paying dividends.

They had rented a four-hundred-square-foot office that doubled as a lab. Actually, it looked more like a lab than an office; along the rear wall were three workbenches containing two computers in various stages of disassembly, an oscilloscope, a logic analyzer, a signal generator, and a variety of test fixtures that they had built. Near the front door was a desk and a phone, but the desk seemed to have no function other than to provide a location for the phone. Working at two side-by-side homemade drafting tables in the middle of the room, John and Dan made the technical drawings that served as blueprints for the hardware they built on the workbenches along the back wall.

"Where the hell is my coffee mug?" asked Dan of no one in particular, as he poked around under a pile of papers and folders on the workbench.

"Hey, don't mess that stuff up," said John sharply. "That's part of tomorrow's presentation—I mean today's." He looked at his watch; it was almost 6 a.m. "Forget the coffee. Let's go to Harold's for breakfast and plan our strategy for the meeting. The prototype is working perfectly, and it should knock Herb's socks off."

They gathered up their briefcases, stuffed several folders in each, and headed out the door. "I hope Joan has time to clean this mess up a little before the meeting," John said. "Is she working today?"

"I hope so. I think she said something about taking one of her kids to the doctor, but I wasn't paying much attention. Maybe she was talking about tomorrow. Of course, since we're not paying her any salary yet, I don't know why she works for us at all. You two sleepin' together?" Dan asked jokingly.

"Yeah, right. You know that she's betting on this thing succeeding, just like we are."

John and Dan walked to their cars in the shadows of the deserted parking lot. The early morning sky, still pitch black in the west, was just becoming light enough in the east to deactivate the sensor-controlled lights. "See you in a minute," said John as he threw his briefcase into his car.

They arrived at Harold's and walked to a booth without waiting to be seated. A waitress approached them with a pot of coffee and menus as they began pulling papers from their briefcases.

"You guys working late again?"

"Hi, Iona," John replied absently, continuing to spread papers out on the table.

"Iona couple acres south of town," said Dan, enjoying the ritual of telling the same lame joke every time he saw her.

Iona rolled her eyes. "I think you guys oughta add a little protein to your diets. The gray matter seems to be deteriorating. How about that hurricane—it sounds pretty bad, doesn't it?"

"What hurricane?" asked Dan.

"Are you kidding? Hurricane Andrew. The weather forecasters are saying it may be one of the worst of the century. The eye should be passing over South Florida right about now. The authorities have ordered a million people to evacuate. You didn't think it was a little strange that we're packed at this time of the morning? All these people have come up from down there to flee the storm," she said.

"I guess we've been distracted by other things, Iona. This is a big day," said John. "Today we pitch the money man. If we convince him to back us, it'll be smooth sailing. Keep your fingers crossed."

"As many mornings as you've dragged yourselves in here after working all night, you certainly deserve it. What kinda chance do you think you have?"

"Beats me. He's got a ton of money, we've got a great idea—seems like a match made in heaven. You never know."

They ordered breakfast and began discussing preparations for the meeting. By the time they finished, the table was covered with dirty dishes and haphazard piles of charts, drawings, and tables of numbers. They quickly gathered everything up and rushed to their respective homes to shower and change clothes for the meeting.

Shortly before 10 a.m., John and Dan returned to their office and were pleased to find it in better shape than they had left it. Joan was puttering around in the back, putting the final touches on the area they would use for their meeting.

"When did you get here?" asked John.

"Just after you left, I hope, since you forgot to turn off the coffeemaker. It was behind a pile of drawings, and it was still on. I wish you guys would turn it off before you leave—it's a bitch to scrape the sludge off the bottom when you let it smolder like that. Anyway, I thought I ought to set up a conference area. Is Herb bringing anyone with him?''

"Hmm, I don't know—he didn't say. It doesn't matter though, I suppose."

Just then, the door burst open and in strode Herb Chandler, all two hundred pounds of him, accompanied by two young associates. At only five feet eight, the poundage would have been too much if he hadn't been an amateur weight lifter all his life. He wore a plaid short-sleeved shirt that seemed a size too small; it showed off his bulging biceps but appeared to restrict the movement of his upper body. It was easy to overlook the fact that he was almost sixty years old, despite his thinning gray hair and the wrinkles around his penetrating light blue eyes. His face had the ruddy complexion of someone who either worked outdoors, or, as was the case with Herb, participated in a variety of outdoor sports. The shirt was tucked into well-worn but obviously expensive Pierre Cardin blue jeans. On his feet were loosely laced purple Nike Air-Max running shoes, also well-worn.

His two companions were in their mid-twenties, thin, and nattily dressed—the antithesis of Herb. John approached them and extended his right hand toward Herb. "Morning Herb, glad to see you."

Herb gripped John's hand firmly and shook it, and then made the introductions. "John, meet Leonard Wasserman and Phyllis Stapleton, two recent M.B.A.'s I'm introducing to the real world." Then to his two young charges, "And this is John Walpold and Dan Killian, the two geniuses I told you about."

As they exchanged handshakes, Phyllis said brightly, "Just call me Phyl."

"And call me Leonard," Leonard said curtly. At six feet two, he was half a head taller than Herb and a full foot taller than Phyl. He had dark brown hair; wore a charcoal gray suit, white shirt, dark blue tie with bold red stripes, and shiny black loafers with tassels; and his face was pale and impassive as if he were made of stone. Phyl, blonde and perky, wore a white silk blouse, a straight black skirt, and simple black patent-leather flats. Their serious attire contrasted sharply with John's and Dan's sport jackets and slacks and Herb's even more casual outfit.

"We can sit over here," John said, directing them to the area Joan had set up. He introduced them to Joan as they sat down and started opening a folder with the presentation material.

"How did you find this place?" Herb asked, waving his hand around to encompass the office.

"Just lucky, actually," said John. "Martin Dorsey, a banker friend of mine, steered me to the building's owner. This is the back half of the unit left over when he shuffled space around for one of his other tenants. No one wanted it because it's worthless for a retail operation, but it's perfect for us. At least for right now."

"Dorsey's the one who suggested you call me, isn't he?"

"Yeah, he is. I've shown him our plans, but he says since we have no track record, the bank couldn't touch it. He said that when we're a little farther along, we might consider the SBA, but right now, it would be a stretch."

"Having read your business plan, I'd have to agree," Herb said. "So how have you financed things up to now?"

"By working without salary. How else?" answered Dan with pride and shame in equal parts. "But it's not so bad; at least we don't have to pay that damn FICA stuff."

"Working without pay, and borrowing. Marty Dorsey calls it familial funding," John added. "I probably never would have considered asking a relative for money if he hadn't suggested it. He said that if we were really convinced we were going to make it, and we had the balls to ask a banker for money, we should be willing to tap any resources we could find. It's my savings and the money I've borrowed from my uncle that have kept us going this far, paying for our rent, utilities, and supplies. But we're not totally reckless," said John, getting more and more animated as he spoke. "We tried to minimize our financial exposure until we were sure that the idea we had in the middle of the night would result in a viable product. The prototype that we want to show you vindicates all our effort and risk. There's nothing on the market that can match its performance. Let's go over to the bench and—"

"Wait just a second," said Herb calmly, "there's plenty of time for that. If I didn't already think you had a viable idea, I wouldn't be here. Right now I'm more interested in some of the background. Like this business plan—did you two prepare it yourselves?"

"You're just engineers, aren't you?" asked Leonard. "What did you do, buy a 'Build a Business Plan' computer program?"

Before answering, John stared at Leonard. Herb seemed so agreeable, and Leonard was so brusque. "An attorney with Wellbourne, Smith and Stein helped."

"They're rather pricey," said Herb. "How can you afford them?"

"Another freebie. Mike Smith is a college classmate of mine. His partners aren't real happy about it, but he's been donating his time. Needless to say, he's been very helpful."

"Who's going to run the business?" asked Leonard coolly.

John was starting to get annoyed by Leonard's attitude. He peered around the room as if looking for someone, then said, "We asked Joan if she wanted the job, but she declined, so I guess Dan and I will have to do it."

Phyl looked at Leonard quizzically and said, "That information is right here in the business plan's organization chart, Leonard."

"I know that, Phyl. But neither of them has any management experience at all—it doesn't make sense to me."

"We'll get to that later, Leonard," Herb interjected. "Let's take a look at the product demo now."

John and Dan took the group to the back of the room. In spite of Joan's attempts to straighten things up, the workbench was still a hodgepodge of circuit boards and test equipment.

Leonard eyed the conglomeration of electronics and said, "What a mess. Which part is the board you've designed?"

John flipped a switch to turn on the power to the workbench as he began to speak. "This is a garden-variety computer with its cover off, exposing the interface slot where our board is plugged in. This is our creation here," he said, pointing to a board roughly three by seven inches. "Of course, at this stage it's still hardwired, but when we have funding, we'll have artwork generated so a printed circuit board can be fabricated by one of the local PC board companies. Then we'll install the components, plug it into a test fixture to guarantee that it works, and it'll be ready to ship." John turned on the monitor and ran through a demo of the product, which displayed graphic images that he had selected to show off the features they had touted. He started to go into a technical explanation of how the system operated, but when he noticed Herb's eyes start to glaze over, he quickly wrapped it up.

"That's remarkable," said Herb when the demonstration was over. "The clarity and speed is everything you said it would be. I'm impressed."

"Naturally," Dan added, "we'll be designing versions for several other platforms, like the Mac and Sun workstations. This version just verifies the concept."

Leonard looked skeptical. "If it's so good, why didn't R.S.S. want it?" he asked, referring to John and Dan's former employer.

"Because they're putzes," said Dan quickly.

Before Dan could continue, John added, "We presented the concept to them, but they decided it didn't quite fit in with their other products and would require different distribution techniques, different—"

"Speaking of which," Leonard interrupted, "the business plan was rather light on the topic of distribution channels. What makes you think—"

"Actually, I've got another meeting early this afternoon," Herb said quickly, breaking in on his young associate. "Why don't we continue this discussion over lunch? It'll give us a chance to get to know each other better."

"Great idea," said John, glad that Leonard had been prevented from finishing his interrogation. "We'll just grab our coats."

Dan followed John to the corner of the room where they had left their coats and said under his breath, "Where did that creep Leonard come from? Are things going good or bad?"

"It's too soon to tell. Herb seems impressed, but Leonard seems to be looking for reasons to turn us down. But don't worry, Dan—just be cool. Everything should be fine."

As they put on their sports jackets and returned to the group, John asked Herb, "Where would you like to go for lunch?"

"Someplace simple," Herb answered. "We don't need to be wined and dined; we're aware of your financial situation. Have you been to the little diner down the road—I think it's called Harold's?"

"Not for a couple of hours," said Dan. "Good idea."

Herb turned to Joan and asked, "Won't you join us?" He looked back at John and said, "Do you mind?"

"Of course not. Come on, Joan," he said, ignoring the look of apprehension on her face. "You can ride with Dan and me."

When they arrived at Harold's, still crowded with hurricane refugees, they were seated at a table in the back. The waitress who came to pour their water and take their orders was Iona, just an hour from finishing her shift. John looked up when he heard her voice, and Dan muttered, "Iona cattle ranch in Wyoming."

"What?" said Phyl.

"Oh nothing. Hi Iona. Long time no see."

After they placed their orders, Herb said, "You guys must come here often."

"Actually, we were here this morning," said John. "We've gotten into the habit of stopping by for breakfast at three or four a.m. when we leave work. Then we go home and crash for a few hours and return after lunch to start again. We haven't been working what you'd call conventional hours."

"What do your wives think of that schedule?" asked Herb.

"My wife, Beth, is tired of it," said John, "but she's willing to put up with it if there's an end in sight."

"And is there?"

"I hope so. If we get funding, we'll be hiring more people, and I'll be able to go back to more reasonable hours. I think the company's president should be around during the day. Quite frankly, I'll miss the excitement of development, but you gotta do what you gotta do, I guess."

"My wife has her own career, and we don't have any kids," added Dan. "I've always been pretty much of a night owl, and we've learned how to deal with it. We get away frequently together, and although John didn't mention it, we're always home for dinner with our families. Then we come back to the lab in the evening. It's not so bad once you get used to it."

"And what about you, Joan? Do you work all night too?" Herb asked.

"Nope, strictly eight to five for me. My two kids are a handful, and I'm not blessed with an understanding spouse like they are. Besides—they're the engineers."

"So how do you know John and Dan?" Herb continued.

John wondered why he was so interested in Joan.

"I worked for John at R.S.S.," she said. "He was the R&D engineering manager, and I was his secretary. But John was unusual. Since he advanced through the ranks, he worked very closely with the design engineers and didn't just rule from an ivory-tower office. He's the only boss I ever had that seemed to know what was going on. When he decided to leave R.S.S. and start his own company, he had a constant stream of people in his office offering to come and help. If he had wanted to, he could have decimated the engineering team at R.S.S. by hiring them all. It might seem risky, my leaving a secure job to work without pay at a start-up company, but I'm not worried. I'm sure John and Dan will succeed."

Herb seemed to be considering this response very carefully before he spoke. "You might wonder why I'm asking so many questions. Well, I'm not a venture capitalist in the traditional sense. I don't make ten investments and hope that at least one is successful. My success rate is much higher, and I attribute that to my being much more selective when I evaluate potential deals—and a little luck."

"Uh-oh," thought John. "He's going to turn us down. He'll tell us, 'Yeah, you have a great idea, but . . .'"

"I hire talented support people like Leonard and Phyl here to make sure I don't miss anything obvious," he continued, "but I also have to feel comfortable with several other factors. For example, how committed are the principals? Are they planning to use my money to continue living the way they were when they had high-paying jobs, or are they willing to sacrifice a little? What level of 'sweat equity' are they willing to invest? Will they be able to hire a quality staff or have to settle for whatever they can find? And how easily will they be distracted by nonbusiness-related issues? Do you know what I mean by that, John?"

"Nonbusiness-related issues? I'm not sure. I do have a family," he said, a bit testily, "and if you're saying you expect me to neglect them, I'm afraid we have a major problem. I've already invested all I have and all I could borrow, and both Dan and I have been working without salary to get things this far. We could never have done this without the support of our families. I'm not planning to take time off to coach my son's Little League team, but I'm not planning to miss any games when I'm in town either," he declared with emotion. "In fact—"

"Wait a minute," Herb interrupted, holding up a hand as if to physically stop him. "I'm not saying you need to neglect your families—quite the contrary. I'd be worried if you *didn't* have stable families. And the distraction I'm referring to is of an amorous nature. That's why it's reassuring to know that you have a good relationship with your family. Because if you didn't, someone might think there was an extracurricular reason why Joan is working without pay. You might think that it's none of my business, but hey, when you start using my money, it *becomes* my business. Am I too nosy? Maybe. If you don't like it, then we shouldn't be partners. But if it doesn't bother you, I'll tell you right now that I'm satisfied with everything I've seen and heard, and I'm ready to start talking about the structure of a deal."

"But Herb," interrupted Leonard, "I think we need to—"

"It's all right, Leonard. I've already done my own personal due diligence. I've talked to people about both of you," he said to John and Dan, "not only about your technical capabilities but about all the other aspects I've been discussing here. Today's meeting was just to make sure our chemistry was okay." He turned to Leonard and Phyl and said, "This might seem unusual to you analytical whizzes, and you might not believe it this early in your careers, but I'll wager that more business failures result from ignoring the intangibles than from incorrectly assessing the market or underestimating the cash requirements."

John was shocked at Herb's announcement. He had expected this to be a much more difficult task. Still waiting for the next shoe to drop, he asked, "What type of deal are you considering?"

"Well, as I mentioned, it's not my plan to make you rich while you're building your business. You should be counting on making your fortune later, when you either build the company to the size that can afford high-priced talent or when we all decide it's time to find a buyer. So we need to agree on only two things."

"Uh-oh, here it comes," thought John.

"First, my maximum exposure and when it occurs. Leonard here has taken the financials from your business plan and put together a forecast of your monthly cash requirements. The single largest expense for a company such as this is usually payroll; if both of you will limit your personal salaries to a little less than you forecasted in your plan, your monthly cash requirements shouldn't exceed what we show here," he said, pulling out a single sheet that had been folded up in his shirt pocket. He spread the paper out on the table for John and Dan to see. "If you can live with this amount for your monthly salaries and expenses, then I'll guarantee a line of credit, and you can draw the money from it each month until you turn cash-positive, then start paying it back. I'll have the right to examine your operation whenever I want. If all goes well, the bank provides the money, the company grows, and we all live happily ever after. If not, I'll pull the plug and be left with whatever debt has accrued."

John and Dan examined the monthly cash numbers and realized that their salaries would be significantly less than they had been making at R.S.S. Neither would be starving, but the difference was a little hard to swallow. Of course, it was more than they had been making recently. Dan was the first to speak. "You said we need to agree on two things. What's the second?"

"Ownership. What percentage each of us gets."

"Great," thought John. "This guy's not putting up a nickel, and he probably wants to own the whole damn thing." He spoke again. "So what are you thinking?"

"I'll take thirty-three percent, and you and Dan split up the rest."

"What?" exclaimed Leonard, his tightly controlled manner momentarily breaking into steely anger. He couldn't believe what he'd heard. "If you don't have control, Herb, God knows what can happen. I thought we were talking about—"

"Nope, that's what's right in this situation. If all goes well, I'll own thirty-three percent of a company without having spent a penny. Naturally, when the legal eagles write all this up, it will include a clause that will give me the option to increase my ownership if the financial goals aren't met and my exposure increases. But the reason I'm willing to do this without gaining majority control is that I believe you have to have the incentive not only to sacrifice a portion of your salary to make the company succeed, but to bust your asses to do it. At the end of each day, I don't want you to feel that your efforts are just to make me rich. I rarely invest without gaining control, but I think that in this case it's justified. So what do you think?"

"Naturally we'll have to see what it looks like when the lawyers are done with it, but it sounds fine to me. What do you think, Dan?"

"Sounds good to me. I was hoping my scrimping days were coming to an end, but I suppose I can hold out a little longer. It's actually a better-sounding deal than I imagined we'd get," he said candidly.

John was finding it hard to believe his good fortune. "I'm curious," he said. "In this day and age when people are so cunning and distrustful, I'm almost shocked to run into someone who seems genuinely interested in helping us succeed. Or am I just too naive to recognize how we're about to get screwed?"

"Leonard accuses me of making too many decisions with my gut. If I were investing someone else's money, I might be more conservative; but it's my money, and I'm betting that your character and ability are up to the task. Also, I remember what it was like in my early years to be strapped for cash."

"You do?" asked Joan, unaware of Herb's background.

"You bet I do. In the Sixties, when my wife, Arlene, and I were first married, we decided to buy several acres on Highway A1A south of Cocoa Beach. This was long before Disney World was built, bringing on the population explosion in Central Florida, so we got it at rock-bottom prices. We tried to finance our investment with a bank loan but had the same success you've had trying to get Martin Dorsey to lend you money. I finally convinced the owners to carry the mortgages. For more than ten years we struggled to make the payments; I worked as a teacher and part-time in construction, and Arlene worked as a waitress, until the early Seventies when the land prices started to skyrocket. We sold a single acre and retired the remaining mortgages, and the bankers suddenly became more agreeable to accepting the land as collateral for other loans. That's how we were able to build our house on the water. If it hadn't been for the appreciation of the land, I'd probably still be working two jobs and struggling to make the mortgage payments."

"So you've lived a life of leisure since you paid off your land?" asked Joan.

"Well, not exactly. It allowed me to buy a boat and learn to play golf, but that got boring, so I got my M.B.A. at UCF and started getting involved with small companies and helping those with promise get going."

"The only thing that bothers me about this deal, or potential deal," said Dan, almost apologetically, "is that I've heard some stories about how you've looted small companies after investing in them. Rather than dance around the issue, I'll ask you directly. You mentioned the clause the lawyers will add to increase your ownership—are we just being set up for a future takeover?"

Dan looked at John and shrugged his shoulders as if to say, "I'm sorry," but John had been thinking the same thing and was relieved that Dan had raised the issue.

"Yeah, I've heard the stories too," responded Herb. "In my opinion, I've never looted anything—I've just taken steps to protect my investment. My mode of operation is to give managers total control but to monitor their performance closely. Yes, there have been times when I've felt it essential to insert or remove people. And when things go awry, and I have to increase my exposure to bail a company out, I expect my ownership to increase. I didn't get where I am by being a fool. But let me assure you, my intentions here are just as I stated them; if you achieve the goals you've set, my exposure will be minimized, and you won't have to worry about the ownership changing. If it appears to me that things are getting really screwed up, then look out—I'll do whatever is necessary to protect my investment."

"Fair enough," said John. "No reason to dwell on the downside. It sounds like we should have no trouble living with the deal you've proposed. How long will it take your lawyer to draw up the papers?"

"A couple of weeks, I suppose." They set a date to meet again and review the documents, and Herb, Leonard, and Phyl left for Herb's next meeting. Watching the trio walk out the door, Dan looked at John and Joan and said, almost to himself, "I wonder if we're getting screwed."

"I think he's a nice guy," said Joan.

"Well, he's made a lot of money, and it didn't all come from his land on the beach," John responded. "We'll just have to trust Mike to make sure we're not stepping on a land mine."

*a*s they were getting into the car, Leonard shook his head in disbelief and said to Herb, "I can't believe you're going to give those yahoos control of the company."

"I was a little surprised myself," Phyl added.

"So what's the problem?" Herb asked, with a slight taunt in his voice.

"Zero management experience for one thing. Walpold may have been an engineering manager, but he's never had P&L control. At R.S.S. he just managed the budget they gave him. And what experience does he have setting up a distribution network? They could have the greatest product in the world, but if they don't know how to sell it, it won't matter. And how do you know he'll be able to hire decent people? Sure they might be able to design a good product, but they also need to be able to buy the parts and produce it, sell it, collect the money, motivate the workers—"

"Peace," Herb said, holding up his hand. "I know all that. But this isn't a business-school case study—this is the real world, and what you find in the real world is real people. John and Dan have been working unsalaried in surroundings only acceptable to someone genuinely interested in long-term success. I've discussed their product with industry experts who believe that if it works as they say it will, and as we have just seen demonstrated, it will revolutionize the computer display market. Can they pull it off? Well, I'm betting that John is up to the task, and it won't cost me much to find out. If he is, all is well. If not—well, I'm not ignoring the possibility. As I told them, I won't hesitate to take whatever measures are necessary to correct the problem. You might get your first opportunity to come out of the classroom and run a real business," he said to Leonard. "So give it a rest—I know what I'm doing." They continued the remainder of the trip in silence—watching the hurricane winds whip and bend the palm trees.

Two YEaRs EarLieR
Monday, August 23, 1993

John had hired a staff of very capable people. And as he had promised his wife, he had begun to work more reasonable hours, at least when he was in town. He had been willing to share the day-to-day running of the company with Dan, but Dan preferred to focus solely on R&D. Now, instead of working in the lab, John spent every available moment out in the field trying to sell his product, traveling from coast to coast and racking up frequent-flier miles three or four days a week. Herb was right when he had suspected that John wasn't one-dimensional, for he turned out to be just as effective in sales as he had been in R&D.

Sales had taken off as Herb had expected, too. John had a gift for instilling confidence in his prospective buyers and very soon had a large and rapidly increasing number of very happy customers. It hadn't hurt that Herb had used his influence to get a major computer magazine to evaluate one of the first production boards, and the reviewer had written a glowing report. With no competition and a product that everyone seemed to be clamoring for, the company turned cash-positive in the eighth month and appeared on the verge of actually beginning to pay down the debt.

John was sitting at his desk stuffing product literature into his briefcase when Jerry frantically entered his office. Pulling out his handkerchief to absorb the beads of perspiration that were forming on his balding, freckled forehead, he said "John, we've got a problem with the Computer Independents order. I thought we had plenty of parts, but apparently we used them to fill the Winthrop order last week. We're not going to be able to fill C.I.'s order 'til later in the week.''

"You've got to be kidding! I promised them the boards by tomorrow. They've got a big demo at the New England Computer Show the day after. If they don't have our boards, we're going to look like schmucks. Come on, Jerry, that's the single most important customer we've got right now. If we blow it, it'll affect God knows how many orders down the road. What'll it take to fill the order like I promised?''

"Well, I suppose we could rob from other orders that are already boxed up and ready to ship, but—''

"Great, then do it," John said quickly. "I've got to get to the airport—my plane's leaving in thirty minutes," he announced, rising from his chair and collecting his sales materials. As he passed Jerry heading out the door, he added, "I'm counting on you, Jerry. Ignore everything else until C.I. is taken care of—it would be catastrophic to lose them as a customer." He walked out of his office and down the hall.

"Okay John, I'll take care of it. Have a good trip," Jerry muttered to the empty room. "Ignore everything except C.I.?" he thought. "Oh well, he's the boss.''

Before John reached the front door, Pete Delaney caught up with him. "Hey John, before you go, I need to ask you about—''

"I've gotta run, Pete. My plane's about to take off without me. If you've got a technical problem, talk to Dan; if it's about parts, check with Jerry. See ya," he said, abruptly walking out and closing the door.

Pete looked around and saw Jerry leaving John's office. "Hey Jerry, I need some replacement boards for Entro. Can you—''

"I've got to take care of C.I. first—it's the most important thing right now 'cause they're showing our stuff at a trade show this week. Gotta run," he said, scurrying back to the production area.

Pete thought, "Most important thing for whom? Maybe for you, but my number one problem isn't C.I. But if that's what they want to do, so be it."

T*h*REE DA*y*S laT*e*R
Thursday, August 26, 1993

When John traveled, he normally returned on the last flight of the day, around 10:30 p.m. That night, his flight into Atlanta from Cincinnati had been on time, but the connecting flight into Orlando had been delayed due to bad weather in upstate New York, so he didn't land until after midnight. The interior of the plane was ghostly quiet as the passengers rubbed the sleep from their eyes and began to rummage around in the overhead compartments for their belongings. Eighty percent of the passengers were returning from business trips. The men had loosened their ties, and most wore suits that were now wrinkled from hours of sitting. Few of the frequent fliers checked their luggage, in order to avoid the delay of fetching it from the baggage-claim area (or the possibility of the airline losing it), so they all carried their hanging suit bags, briefcases, and computers with them. John stood in the aisle bleary-eyed, waiting for the door of the plane to open and the people ahead of him to start moving. The sour taste in his mouth reminded him that he hadn't had anything but peanuts to eat since lunch, and the brandy on this flight had only made him hungrier.

"Hey John, where you been?" came a voice from behind him. John looked around and recognized the speaker. "Hi, Jim. Chicago and Cincinnati today. Minneapolis and Detroit earlier in the week. I'm beat. How about you?" Because of the camaraderie that develops among those that endure a common ordeal, many of the business travelers knew each other and had also become familiar with the flight attendants. He didn't remember Jim's last name but knew that he worked for one of the local defense contractors.

"D.C., as usual. I just went up for the day, so my car's in the lot. Need a ride home?"

"Thanks, but I called Beth from Atlanta and told her I'd be late, and she said she'd pick me up." John yawned and shook his head, trying to revive himself.

Most of the passengers walking out of the airplane and down the jetway looked like zombies. They stumbled through the terminal toward the doors, then either continued on to the long-term-parking lot or stopped at the curb to wait for their ride. A few read books while they stood by the curb, but most just stared blankly into space. When Beth saw John emerge from the terminal, she pulled the internal switch to pop the trunk open; John saw her, tossed his baggage into the trunk, and got into the car. "Hi hon," he said, leaning over and kissing her on the cheek.

"Hi. How was the trip?"

"Great. I signed everyone I talked to. How's everything here?"

"Pretty normal. Little League practice or games almost every night. Andy was disappointed that you weren't at the game tonight to see him pitch," she said, referring to their older son. "He struck out the other team's players in one of the innings, but his team ended up losing. The big guns were silent, or so the coach said. Everything is fine with Zach, but Barney mopes around when you don't come home for dinner." Zachary was their younger son and Barney their small, very spoiled terrier—much more spoiled than they would ever tolerate with either of their kids. "Everything okay at the office?"

"I guess. I talked to Joan this afternoon, and except for being rather frantic, she seemed fine. Frantic seems to be the name of the game these days. But we have plenty of money coming in, so I guess no one can complain."

"Who's in charge when you're out of town, anyway?"

"Dan I suppose, but he tries to avoid everything except technical issues. It's never been a problem though; everybody is too busy to worry about things like that. I read an article about staff meetings this afternoon in the airline magazine. I think I'll try having a weekly meeting where we can hash out any problems that are occurring and make sure everybody's singing from the same hymnal—at least that's what the article said."

"How long are you going to continue traveling like this? I thought you brought in Phil to do the selling. What's he doing, anyway?"

"He should be up to speed in a couple of weeks. I'm taking him with me to New York next week to introduce him around. Once he knows the accounts, I should be able to cut back on the travel."

"I talked to Liz the other day," she said, referring to Dan's wife, "and she said Dan misses having you working with him."

"I miss the R&D work too, but what can I do? If I hadn't been out setting up all these accounts, where would our sales have come from? But even when Phil is doing the selling, I still won't be able to work in the middle of the night the way Dan likes to do. I'm afraid those days are over."

T*h*E NE*x*T d*A*y
Friday, August 27, 1993

That Friday morning, John busied himself writing follow-up letters to the people he had just visited, thanking them for their orders and confirming shipping commitments. When he asked Joan to schedule a staff meeting, she suggested doing it that afternoon and set off to inform everyone. A few people attempted to talk to him during the morning, but he told everyone they could resolve whatever needed resolving at the staff meeting after lunch.

At 1:15, John began cleaning up his desk, since Joan had told him that she had scheduled the meeting for 1:30. He also stacked up the various piles of papers on the conference table into one big pile in order to make room for the meeting. When Joan walked in, he glanced at his watch; it was 1:30 on the dot. "So where is everybody?" he asked, taking a seat at the end of the table.

"On their way, I guess. It's a pretty busy day." She sat down at his right with a blank pad of paper.

The rest of the staff wandered in during the next few minutes, making idle chatter with each other until Dan wandered in at 1:50. Once everyone was finally seated, John started the meeting. "Welcome to the first of what I plan to be a regularly scheduled staff meeting, a meeting where we can discuss problems and share information. I suppose the first order of business is to set a regular time—does one-thirty on Mondays suit everyone?"

"Not me," said Dan immediately. "I usually work late, come in mid-morning, take a late lunch, and return around two. Two o'clock would be fine."

"Not for me," said Jerry. "I have a regularly scheduled status meeting with the assemblers every Monday at two. Why not three o'clock?"

"That's too late," said Marie. "I'm only working here part-time, and I have to be somewhere else by three o'clock. What's wrong with a working lunch? That would suit me."

"Anytime is fine with me," offered Rita, brushing a wrinkle out of her skirt. "As long as I know ahead of time, so I don't schedule anything else."

John gazed at the group, expecting other objections, but no one else said anything. "So how about it, Phil and Pete? Want to suggest a midnight meeting or something?"

Phil was much too new to make waves, so he sat mute while Pete added, "Hey, you're the boss. You tell me when the meeting is; I'll be there."

"Well, that's refreshing. I guess Joan will have to figure out a suitable time and tell us about it later. Now that that's out of the way, let me give you a brief summary of what's going on. I just got back from a Midwest trip, and I'm happy to say I signed twelve new accounts. Our products are being shown at three trade shows during the next few weeks, so we can expect additional orders from those. Our current customers seem to be happy, or they wouldn't be paying their bills. So that's the news I've got. Now let's hear from everyone else. Jerry, how are things in production?"

Jerry's right hand went nervously to his head, making sure that the few remaining strands of his light brown hair were still stretched out over his bald pate. At five feet nine and probably thirty pounds overweight, his pear-shaped body resembled a child's plastic blow-up clown that rocked back and forth and finally righted itself whenever it was punched. "Well," he began, wrinkling his brow, "we got the C.I. order out like you wanted. We had to delay some other orders, which slowed us down a little, but we'll recover."

"You got the spares order out for Entro didn't you?" asked Pete.

"Hopefully they'll go out this afternoon," he responded.

"Jeez," said Pete, rolling his eyes. "I told them they'd have their parts by today. On Monday you told me there was no problem."

"That was before we had to stop everything to get the C.I. order out."

"And that was important," John added. "They could be our largest single customer if the trade show goes well."

"At the expense of Entro?" Pete asked.

"Losing the C.I. order would be a disaster. I told Jerry to do whatever he had to to get them their boards. It was my decision," John insisted.

"Whatever," Pete said, folding his arms and sliding back in his chair.

"So, Rita. How's everything with purchasing?" John continued.

"Fine, I guess. I have a never-ending stack of orders to process, but Jerry keeps getting his parts, so I guess I'm keeping up."

"No problems?" John probed.

"Occasionally when I call someone to place an order, they tell me we owe them money, but when I mention it to Marie, she sends them a check. I don't think anyone has held up any shipments yet."

"Pete, what about the field? Are the customers happy?"

"The main problem seems to be normal set-up problems. The boards seem to work okay once the switches are set right. Nothing earth-shattering. I'd like to be able to get spares out faster, but there isn't much I can do about that."

"The wave-soldering machine I've been asking for would help solve that problem," said Jerry.

"I've seen the purchase order for that," said John. "It's pretty expensive, isn't it?"

"Sure, but we can certainly justify the cost. If it allows us to increase our production, won't that generate more cash? It seems like it would pay for itself in no time."

"Okay, you're right—order it. Now, what's next?" asked John.

"Pa-*tchew*," said Pete, mimicking the sound of a gunshot and pointing his index finger like a gun, then raising it to his mouth and blowing on the end of it.

"What's that all about?" asked John.

"Just shooting from the hip. Don't mind me," said Pete cynically, as everyone looked at him.

"My turn?" asked Dan. "I've come up with a really neat way of interleaving the retrace that looks like it might improve the Sun resolution even more than we thought." He got up, walked to a white board attached to the wall, picked up a marker, and began drawing a timing diagram. In a few minutes, the board was covered with squiggly lines, and Dan was in the midst of a very detailed technical discussion with John.

"Do you guys need us?" Marie asked, rising from her chair. "I've got a lot to do and can't imagine how I could add anything to your discussion."

John, suddenly aware once again of his employees sitting there waiting for him to finish, apologized to them. "Sorry. I guess that's about it. We'll meet again next week. Joan, don't forget to settle on a time." Then, as everyone exited from the room, John and Dan resumed their conversation, oblivious to everything around them.

*L*ater that evening when John got into bed, he selected a book from the stack of paperbacks on the nightstand, opened it to the first page, and set it in reading position on his chest as he mused about the events of the day.

"What are you reading?" asked Beth as she entered the room and crawled into bed.

"I'm not, actually. I'm just thinking about the day." He closed the book. "It was frantic as usual, but everyone seems to be getting a lot done," he said, stifling a burp.

"Our lovely dinner backing up on you? Just be glad they ran out of chili before you got your hot dog. I swear I don't know where they find that stuff." Beth was referring to their dinner at the Little League game.

"It beats the peanuts I had on the plane last night. But I don't mind dinner at the ballpark; I miss seeing the games when I'm out of town. I just wish I'd get to see Andy pitch," he added plaintively.

"That's why he was disappointed you missed last night's game. They can only pitch every fourth day, which means when he pitches again next week you'll be out of town. By the way, did you have your staff meeting today?"

"Yeah, we had it."

"You don't sound very enthusiastic about it. What happened?"

"I guess nothing. It just seemed like a waste of time. Everyone was busy, and they had to take time out of their day for it. I'm not sure I really understand why a weekly staff meeting is so important. Maybe if we had major problems to deal with, we could get together to hash things out. But to be perfectly honest, the company seems to be running itself."

"Running itself?"

"Yeah. Dan takes care of R&D, Jerry has production covered, Rita supervises purchasing, Pete directs tech support, Marie pays the bills, Joan acts as the den mother, and Phil and I sign up the customers. Maybe I should just stay out of the way."

"That doesn't sound like management to me," Beth offered skeptically.

"I suppose not. But look at the results—business is booming. Sure, life is a little hectic, but so what? Everyone is doing a great job, or we wouldn't have happy customers and plenty of money. I think the most important thing a manager can do is hire competent people, provide a suitable environment, and then leave them alone."

"That's three things."

"Whatever. 'Night honey," he said with a yawn, returning his book to the nightstand and turning out the light.

B*a*cк T0 *t*He Pre**S**e*n*T
Friday, July 28, 1995

Shortly after one o'clock, Rick Devereux arrived at the Walpold Enterprises parking lot in his green Jeep Cherokee. Rick was in his mid-forties and kept himself trim by jogging and playing racquetball. He was almost six feet tall, had sandy-brown hair and a deep tan, and was dressed casually in a plaid sports shirt, gray slacks, and black Bally loafers. During the summer in Florida, he rarely wore a jacket. He carried a notebook-size leather organizer that contained his appointment book, calculator, notepad, and pencils.

An independent consultant for ten years, Rick had started out calling himself a financial consultant, because his work relied heavily on information that was gleaned from a company's financial statements. Unfortunately, when he introduced himself as a financial consultant, people instantly thought he was trying to sell them a mutual fund, insurance policy, or annuity. So then he started calling himself a management consultant, and people thought he carried around a stopwatch so he could do time-and-motion studies and improve worker efficiency. Finally he settled on business consultant, which only slightly differentiated him from the hoards of out-of-work middle managers and engineers who brandished that title until they found another job.

Rick had been a senior-level manager at a large company, but he became disillusioned with the bureaucratic inefficiencies and politics that plagued the workplace. It was much more exciting and rewarding to analyze the professional management techniques used by successful large businesses and apply them to emerging small businesses. At a small company, decisions to change things can be made without getting the approval of a large steering committee, and the complications of office politics were manageable. Most small businesses are run by people who genuinely want to improve things but become bogged down in the day-to-day details and lose sight of the big picture. It is not uncommon for a successful small business to outgrow its operating methods, getting by at first with just a few people handling everything, but as the flow increases, information starts getting lost and details overlooked.

He recalled meeting John Walpold briefly. He had tried to set up a subsequent meeting to describe and explain his services, but John was always too busy, so he put his efforts to sign up Walpold Enterprises on hold and periodically sent them a marketing flyer. He wondered about John's call. With all the talk about how ineffective direct mail is becoming, could it be possible that his latest marketing flyer had been the impetus for John's call?

When Rick walked through the entrance into the front office of Walpold Enterprises, he found no one there. As he stood looking around, he noticed stacks of papers and files haphazardly strewn over several desks around the room. In the center of the room were two filing cabinets, each with a drawer partly open. On top of one of the filing cabinets was a very tired-looking fern, partly brown and in desperate need of care.

He was about to yell "Hello" to get someone's attention when a young blonde appeared at the back of the room from the hallway leading to the staff offices. She was wearing black patent-leather heels and a little black dress that clung to her figure. Her nails were perfectly manicured, her skin emanated a hint of delicate jasmine perfume, and she'd put on just the right amount of makeup to highlight her flawless complexion. Just as he opened his mouth to speak, she popped the bubble gum she'd evidently been chewing and shattered the image, which changed in an instant from that of a goddess to a mere cheerleader. Before he could say anything, she said, "Hi"—not "May I help you?" or "What can I do for you?"—just "Hi."

Rick responded, "Hi, I'm Rick Devereux. I think John Walpold's expecting me."

"I'm Wendy. John's office is the third door back," she said, pointing to the hallway behind her.

Rick waited for her to show him to her boss's office, but it became obvious that she had no intention of doing so. With a slight frown, he zigzagged his way through the furniture and made his way down the hall to John's office, where he stopped and looked in through the open door. Seated behind the desk was John Walpold. Rick rapped lightly on the door frame and said, "Hi John, remember me? Rick Devereux."

"Oh, you startled me," said John, looking up quickly. He had been deep in thought. "Sure—of course I remember." He got up and came around his desk to shake hands. "It's good to see you again, Rick. Glad you could make it on such short notice." John shut the door and offered Rick a chair facing his desk, and then returned to his own chair behind the desk.

"You look like you've been spending some time in the sun," said John enviously. It occurred to him that he hadn't spent any time outdoors in weeks.

"My son Eric was in town visiting last weekend, and we spent most of it windsurfing on the Indian River over by Melbourne. The wind was great, so we zipped up and down the river until our forearms were so tired we couldn't make a fist. I find that after a week of office duty, I need to get out and be active."

"This company seems to be my hobby," said John. He extended his arms out in front of him as evidence. Even the beige shirt he wore was darker than his pale skin. "I used to play a little golf, but it takes so long to play eighteen holes, I felt guilty about taking the time away from work, so I quit. Maybe I should start again. But I've been talking about joining a health club, and I still haven't found time for that."

"From what you told me in our phone conversation, it sounds like you've had your hands full. What kind of help are you looking for exactly?"

"Nothing major. We just need a good cash-flow forecast so we can figure out how to get ourselves out of the bind we're in. And if you see anything along the way that might help us get better control of our operation, I'd be interested in that too."

Rick thought, "The typical unfocused businessman's nebulous statement of purpose." When he arrived at a small company for the first time, he was seldom presented with a clear picture of what was needed; he usually had to ferret it out. "You're in a cash bind? Caused by what?"

"Receivables, I think. But I guess part of the problem is that I'm not really sure. Maybe our expenses are too high, or possibly we've just had a momentary dip in sales. I'd be interested in your opinion after you've had a chance to look around. Is this within your area of expertise, or do you just focus on large companies?"

"Small is my specialty. But they require the same management techniques as large ones. Sure, I love to get involved with companies that have cash problems. It's such a challenge to figure out where my fee will come from! But we can worry about that later. Here's how I'd like to start. First, I'd like you to tell me a little about yourself and Walpold Enterprises. Then, I'll ask you a few questions and spend some time with each of your key people. I'll donate the first hour or so; then we'll discuss my terms later if it looks like I can help. Okay?"

"Sounds fine to me," said John, relieved that the guy didn't pull out a multipage consulting contract. He sat back in his chair, folded his arms in front of him, and considered how to begin. "I was a design engineer with R.S.S. before I started this company with Dan Killian. Dan and I figured out a different way to interleave graphics data to create an ultrahigh-resolution display for computer monitors, which is important in graphic design and some special scientific applications. We founded Walpold Enterprises a little over three years ago to manufacture the circuit board for this high-resolution display. We increased our product line by adding several special-purpose interface boards that our customers requested.

"In the beginning, we could charge a premium price. Unfortunately the concept isn't patentable, so now we have about half a dozen competitors, driving the price down. We still have plenty of orders, but we don't seem to have enough money to buy the parts to fill the orders. In the beginning, everyone worked real hard and accomplished a lot. Today, everyone is working just as hard, but things are constantly getting screwed up, and our customers are mad, our vendors are mad, and our bank's cutting off our credit. We're always short of cash. Every time we schedule a planning session, we end up having to reschedule it because of some crisis. When I saw your postcard, it struck a chord—we're not running the company anymore, it's running us."

Rick was pleased that his flyer had generated the intended response. "What about your initial financing. How did you get the money to get started?"

"I forgot to mention our silent partner, Herb Chandler. I used my own savings and some money I borrowed from a relative, but Herb arranged for most of the initial capital in the form of a guaranteed credit line. As soon as we had a track record, we got an additional credit line from the bank, backed by our equipment, inventory, receivables, and the strength of Herb's considerable wealth. Herb and Dan each own thirty-three percent, I own the other thirty-four percent, and we are the only three directors."

"Have you kept up with your federal tax deposits and sales tax payments?"

"Not very well, actually. We never seem to have the cash to make the tax deposits, so we're behind a couple of months. We're okay with sales tax because most of our customers are resellers, so they're exempt."

"Do you know how current your receivables are?"

"Martin Dorsey, our banker, asked me the very same question this morning. That's Joan's area; you can ask her later."

"What about your payables?"

"Based on the number of calls and letters we get asking for payment, probably not real good. But Marie can give you the details."

"Do you have a revenue forecast?"

"Well, we keep a forecast for production purposes, but it's not too accurate. Every time we try to update it, something seems to come up."

Rick's line of questioning wasn't yielding much information, but John's answers clued him in to a significant fact: John wasn't on top of the details of his company's business. Rather than continue to probe, he decided to take a more innocuous tack. "Are you married?"

"Yes, for eighteen years. My wife, Beth, is a dental assistant. We have two teenage sons. One of them will be graduating from high school next year."

Just then the door to John's office burst open and in walked Leonard Wasserman and Phyl Stapleton, Herb's two "shadows." John bristled at the intrusion but stifled the impulse to hustle them out. "Don't you believe in knocking?" he asked.

"Hi John," Leonard said curtly, an arrogant smirk on his face. "Herb said you'd be expecting us. He also said you'd probably resent our being here, but that really doesn't concern us."

Over the three years that John had known Leonard, his distrust of him had been overtaken by distaste. In fact, he often referred to Leonard as Herb's pet scorpion. Phyl seemed less dangerous, but John was wary of her, too.

"And who might you be?" asked Leonard, looking at Rick.

"Rick Devereux," he replied, reaching into his leather organizer and pulling out a business card that he handed to Leonard.

"I'm Leonard Wasserman, and this is my colleague Phyl Stapleton." Leonard examined the card and said, "Business consultant, huh? Too little too late, don't you think?" He turned back to John and asked, "Where can we find a current set of financials?"

"Didn't Herb give you his set?"

"Yes, but they *aren't* current, and we need to see what they look like as of the most recent month. You do keep your financials up-to-date, don't you?"

"Joan can take care of it," said John, ignoring his question. "Tell her what you need, and she'll put it together." John wanted to say more, but decided not to be confrontational. "This guy is a rude bastard," he thought, "but I don't want to alienate Herb."

Leonard started to leave, with Phyl right behind him. When he reached the doorway, he turned and said to John, "If you haven't figured it out yet, you're going to be keeping us informed of every detail from now on. We'll chat again later." They walked out the door, leaving it open, and went to look for Joan.

"Who was that?" asked Rick incredulously.

"I talked to Herb this morning about providing some bridge financing, and rather than agreeing, he decided to send those little twerps in to 'check things out.' They're a couple of M.B.A.'s who Herb uses for his analysis work, or at least he has in the past. I can't stand Leonard, but Phyl seems okay. Anyway, don't worry about them. Where were we?"

"I was about to ask you to lend me your office for about an hour to talk to your key people, one at a time, and to leave us alone while I'm interviewing them, if you don't mind. They might talk more freely without you in the room."

"I suppose you're right. Dan Killian should be first, but unfortunately, he hasn't shown up yet today. He keeps odd hours. I'll start you with Joan Richards instead. She's forty and married, with two teenagers who cause her a lot of grief. She's in the process of divorcing her husband, a manager with Metro. It's getting kinda messy, 'cause he's going through a midlife crisis and is living with a girl almost young enough to be his daughter.

"Joan's brother-in-law, Ben, is a software whiz—he put together our computer network, inventory-control system, and a few other application programs we use. Joan's been with us since the beginning, and she's my right arm. We're not real big on titles here, but hers is probably Administrative Assistant or Office Manager or something like that. Nothing happens around here that she isn't aware of, although lately, because of her divorce, she's been missing more and more. She screwed up an order to one of our sales reps in San Francisco yesterday, and I'm sure it's just because she's distracted."

John left to get Joan and came right back with her. He explained to her that Rick was doing a preliminary evaluation of the company, told her to be completely open with him, and then left, closing the door behind him.

"First Leonard and Phyl and now you. What's going on?" she asked.

"I've never met them before today, so I don't know what they're up to. I may begin helping with some of the financial forecasting, depending on what John and I agree to. But it's too soon to say right now. John tells me you have a couple of teenagers. So did I, a few years ago. I hope yours aren't as much trouble as mine were," said Rick, trying to move the conversation to a less unsettling topic.

Before she could respond, there were two sharp raps on the door; it flew open and in strode Dan. He was casually dressed in clothes that were not inexpensive but appeared rather disheveled, and his shoes were scuffed. Part of the shirttail hung down over his pants from a shirt that was completely wrinkled, looking like it had come directly from the dryer, and the shirt pocket was stuffed with pens, pencils, and scraps of paper containing scribbled notes. His brown hair was too long, not by design but just because he hadn't taken time to get it cut recently. He looked confused at finding Joan and a stranger in John's office instead of John. Seeing Rick, he stuck out his hand. "I'm Dan Killian," he said, shaking Rick's hand, and asked Joan, "Where's John, and why are that weasely Leonard and his shadow poking around our offices?"

"I think John's talking to Jerry out on the production floor," said Joan, "and this is Rick Devereux, a consultant that John has hired. John's letting us use his office for a few minutes. As for Leonard and Phyl, Herb sent them. You should probably ask John about them."

"Thanks. See ya," he said, as he turned and left.

"The cofounder?" Rick asked.

"Yeah, that's Dan. He's actually quite brilliant. He and John designed most of the products we make. But he can be pretty hard to work with at times. He only sees one side of any situation, and he's pretty unforgiving when somebody screws up. Anyway, where were we?"

"Your kids—how old are they?"

Rick had inadvertently chosen a topic she would rather avoid. The mention of her children made Joan wince, as though bringing something unpleasant to mind. Rick noticed this, but it was too late. "Our son is seventeen and doing fine in school. Our daughter, fifteen, is driving me crazy. She and her boyfriend are moving much too fast—but that's another story. So what do you want to know?" Joan asked, looking uncomfortable.

"I'm interested in your perspective on how things are at Walpold Enterprises. How would you compare this past year with the first year, for example?"

"The first year was great," she said wistfully. "We started with nothing, and soon we had dozens of satisfied customers. We worked an incredible number of hours, which certainly wasn't easy for those of us with families, but it seemed worthwhile. Lately, when I'm driving home at night, I mull over what happened during the day, and I feel incompetent. I forgot to send a critical part to one of our sales reps in San Francisco yesterday—he managed to work things out, no thanks to me. It seems like we never deal with important issues anymore, because we're too busy fighting small battles."

"John says you manage the receivables. What sort of system do you have for keeping track of your outstanding accounts?"

"My brother-in-law is a software guru, and he put together a database system for us. It works fine, I guess, but it's not real easy to use and I never seem to get around to entering the data when we ship something or when we receive a check, so it isn't doing much for us right now. I keep a file on a word processor with a list of outstanding accounts that is pretty current, though."

"Aha," Rick thought, "beware the insidious software whiz." The world seemed to be full of such creatures who create application programs and confidently declare them complete after creating line after line of computer code and testing them under ideal conditions, seldom addressing the issues of efficiency of use, training, or support. "John also mentioned that you have a lot of vendors bugging you for money. Who decides who gets paid and when?"

"Marie keeps a list of bills and amounts. John and I usually go over it weekly and mark a priority number by the most important ones. Then, when enough money is in the account, she writes the checks and sends them."

"Do you have weekly staff meetings?"

"We try to, but we rarely have time. It seems silly for everyone to spend time getting ready for a staff meeting when there is so much else to do. But maybe I'm just tired."

To Rick, Joan seemed burned out. She looked exhausted and too whipped to fight anymore. "When's the last time you had a vacation?"

"I haven't had time for a vacation in quite a while, but every now and then I take a long weekend. We usually treat the annual Comdex computer show in Las Vegas as a vacation, but the last couple of years it's been pretty hectic. We spend all day in our booth, then all evening trying to catch up on the work we're missing during the day. Last year I never got to a single show, and I'd been looking forward to seeing Siegfried and Roy."

"What do you view as the company's largest single problem?"

"That's easy—lack of cash. If we had more cash, we wouldn't waste so much time dealing with our vendors, and we could keep more inventory, which would make it unnecessary for us to air-freight parts to fill a hot order. More cash would really help."

"Okay, Joan. Thank you for your time. You've been very helpful. Now I'd like to talk to whoever heads up production."

"That would be Jerry Wilson. He's a great guy but rather insensitive to our cash problems. He was a production manager with Avcom before he came here. I think he's real capable, but he doesn't look at the big picture often enough, and too many times when there's a problem he blames someone else. I'll go get him."

Joan left and returned in a few minutes with Jerry. She seemed anxious to get back to her growing list of tasks for the day. Rick thanked her again for her time, and she hurried out of the room.

Jerry sat in a chair next to Rick and looked at him expectantly. The sleeves of his white shirt were rolled up to his elbows. His pants were too tight, so his shirt blossomed out around and over his belt—he was losing the battle of the bulge. He wore a light green knit tie that was probably in style when he was in college, tied clumsily with the skinny end slightly longer than the wide end. With no tack or clip holding them in place, both ends flapped loosely whenever he moved. He fidgeted nervously as he waited for Rick to speak.

"Jerry, tell me a little about production. How many different products do you build?"

"Are you working with Leonard and Phyl?" Jerry asked.

"No, I've been asked by John to help with the financial forecasting."

"What're *they* doing here?"

"I guess you'll have to ask John; I really don't know. So, let's get back to my question. Tell me about Walpold's products."

Jerry relaxed a bit and started talking about the department he was in charge of. "Between the various graphics boards and the special purpose interface boards, we have about thirty different products, not counting the ones that Dan is probably dreaming up this afternoon. Several are just modifications of a single configuration, but always having the right ones ready is impossible, especially when sales gives us so little notice."

"How do you know what the production mix will be? Do you work according to some type of forecast?"

Jerry looked at Rick skeptically but decided that he had nothing to lose by telling him what was really going on. He was tired of being the fall guy. "John and Phil—he's the head of Sales—put together a production forecast that they update weekly, or at least they're supposed to. I haven't had an update in three weeks. When I don't get an update, I reuse the latest forecast. Lately, it seems like every time we finish a production run, we're missing some boards for some hot customer, and we have to drop everything and quickly build some more. And usually we have to FedEx some of the parts, since they didn't get ordered because they weren't on the production forecast. It would be simple if the forecast was right."

Rick recognized the frustration in Jerry's voice. "How do you handle quality control?"

Jerry wondered if someone had already mentioned last week's DOAs. "Leonard just asked me the same thing. We're very careful—our assemblers have been with us since we started. I've considered setting up a separate quality control department, but I just haven't had time to focus on it with everything else going on. We have test fixtures to make sure that everything works before it ships, but sometimes Dan makes a change in some boards at the last minute, and these products are shipped before they've been properly tested. There isn't much I can do about that."

"What one single change around here would be the most helpful for production?"

Jerry thought for a moment, and then said, "That would be a toss-up between a realistic sales forecast so we could build what is really needed and enough cash to keep the parts we need in stock."

Rick thanked Jerry and asked him about Phil Jackson. Jerry explained that Phil was the head of the Sales Department but that according to the company scuttlebutt, he was looking for another job and had been turning everything over to Scott Nichols lately.

Jerry went to get Scott and came back with him, quickly made the introductions, and left.

Scott had obviously been spending all his free time at the beach and was deeply tanned. Rick said to him, "My son Jim has a tan like that. He's a surfer. He practically lives at the beach. Do you surf?"

"Every weekend, whenever there're waves. I started when I was a kid and never stopped. I got my business degree at UCF here in Orlando and managed to hit the beach at least twice a month even then. I can't imagine not living near the beach. Listen, that Leonard guy was just asking me about the sales forecast and looking at me like what I said didn't really matter anyway. He mentioned that he knew a hotshot sales guy that he might give a call.''

Rick thought, "Leonard and Phyl are really making tracks.'' He asked Scott, "What's the source of the customer problems? Are the products late? Do they not work when they get there? Or is it a lack of support?''

"All of the above. I make promises to customers, and then Jerry can't build what I've promised. The boards were on the production schedule, but he claims they weren't built because he didn't have the parts. And when a customer gets a board that doesn't work, it's really a bitch. Our competition is getting fierce, and we can't afford slip-ups like that. What's your interest in this, anyway? Is John looking for a buyer?''

"Not that I'm aware of. He asked me to help evaluate the company's cash needs and to see if I thought anything else should be attacked. What would you recommend, if you were me?''

"That's easy. Get someone to straighten out Production and Tech Support. And do it fast, before all of our customers split.''

"Tell me a little about Tech Support.''

"That's Pete Delaney's area. He's a pretty sharp guy—he got his electronics training in the Navy—but he doesn't seem to be too responsive to the customers lately. Maybe he should spend more time worrying about the job and less time fooling around with Rita Gonzales in purchasing, though I can't say I blame him. Have you seen her yet?''

"Not yet. I take it Pete's not one of your favorite people?''

"He's not so bad—he just hasn't been keeping on top of things the last few months. The only guy I really can't get along with is Dan Killian. He contributes almost nothing, works whenever he wants, and acts like everyone should bow whenever he passes. We could solve a lot of problems if we just used his salary to buy parts.''

When he finished venting about Dan, Scott left to get Pete.

A few minutes later, Pete walked in. "Scott said you're looking for me. I'm Pete Delaney." He shook Rick's hand with a firm grip.

Pete was in excellent shape and had a rugged, "outdoorsy" appearance. He wore khaki-colored Dockers, a tight-fitting bright red Lacoste shirt, and Sperry Topsiders with no socks. He was handsome, with chiseled features, a clear complexion, neatly trimmed dark brown hair, and pale blue-gray eyes that could turn from sparkling to icy in a flash. He had a very self-assured manner, and he looked Rick directly in the eye.

"Hi. I'm Rick Devereux. John's asked me to help him get a handle on things. I wanted to get your take on what state the company is in and what could be done to improve things."

"I'm a technician. I can diagnose practically any problem related to our products, and that's all I want to do. I can only speculate on why we have DOAs and why spares don't arrive on time. I do my job, and I expect everyone else to do theirs. Why don't you ask Tweedle Dum and Tweedle Dee," he said, obviously referring to Leonard and Phyl. "They seem to know everything."

"A real team player," thought Rick. He suspected he wouldn't get much out of him, but there were a couple of points he would get him to clarify. "Do you have any formal procedure for tracking the problems that occur in the field?"

"Formal, no. Informal, yes, and it's worked pretty well in the past. I usually notice when a problem starts showing up, and I talk to Dan about it. He can usually figure out what's happening and either make a design change to improve things or help me put together a 'tech notice' to educate the customers. But mostly I just spend my time getting the right spares to the right location before the customers get too mad."

"If you could suggest any changes, what would they be?"

"Shorter hours, more pay, more holidays, shorter skirts on the women—stuff like that. Seriously, tighten the screws down on production and make them do what they're supposed to—no excuses, no whining about parts. Rita orders the parts they ask for, I'll guarantee you that. They just don't ask for the right parts."

"Okay, Pete, thanks. Now I'd like to speak to the bookkeeper next. Who would that be?"

"Marie Manning. I'll tell her you'd like to see her." They shook hands again, and Pete left.

Rick had seen his type many times before—single-minded about his goals, quick to accuse, and often not very loyal. His cause was personal, not corporate. As long as his direction happened to be the same as the company's, everything was fine, but it would be next to impossible to get him to change. "Oh well," thought Rick. "It takes all kinds."

Marie was a big-boned woman in her early thirties, not overweight but very solid-looking. She had a plain but healthy and youthful face, with high Nordic cheekbones, and she never wore makeup. Her once-blond hair was pulled straight back into a short ponytail for convenience, giving her a rather severe look. She wore dark blue slacks, a simple long-sleeved cotton shirt, and navy loafers. When she walked through the door, she stared at Rick for a few seconds, sizing him up. Marie was obviously a woman who didn't put up with any nonsense.

"Hi, I'm Rick Devereux—sorry to interrupt your day" he said to her cheerfully.

"Marie Manning. Pleased to meet you," she said as she approached him, with her hand outstretched. Rick stood up and they shook hands. Her grip was firm and self-confident. "But you don't have to worry about interrupting anything. Leonard Wasserman already did that a few minutes ago when he sat down at my computer and started poking around. What the hell is he doing here anyway?" she asked, as she sat down in a chair facing Rick.

"Beats me, but I'm sure he'll let everyone know eventually. You've probably heard by now that John has asked me for some advice and that I'm talking to key staff members to get an idea of how this company is run. You pay the bills and do the bookkeeping, right?"

"Yep, that's what I do," she said stiffly.

Rick waited a few moments for her to say something else, but she was apparently going to stick to name, rank, and serial number.

"What type of system do you use?" he finally asked.

"I use the checks with the carbon paper behind the 'pay to' line. I've purchased a computer program for paying the bills and keeping track of things, but I haven't had time to install it. Of course, we already have a system in place, courtesy of Ben, Joan's brother-in-law. It's a classic, I'll tell you," she said, rolling her eyes. "Anyway, I balance the bank accounts, write all the checks, and prepare the information for the accountants each month."

"How long have you been with Walpold Enterprises?" Rick asked, launching a harmless probe.

"From the beginning, although not full-time at the start. I used to do bookkeeping on a contract basis for several clients. Then I got involved here, and as things progressed, more and more time was required, so once I got some assurances from John that I would have a stable salary, I off-loaded my other clients to a friend of mine. Doesn't seem like such a great idea anymore."

"Why is that?"

"We're always short of cash, no one seems to know what's going on, everyone is accusing someone else of screwing things up—it's a disaster."

"Then why do you stay?" asked Rick.

"Too lazy to do anything about it, I guess," she said with a sigh, leaning back in her chair and folding her arms. "Are you the savior that's come to bail us out?" she asked skeptically.

"Beats me," Rick replied. "I suppose it depends on what the problems really are. Right now I'm just trying to get a sense of who's on first. What's your opinion—why do things seem so out of control?"

"That's the sixty-four-thousand-dollar question, pal. If I knew that, I'd be making what you are instead of the pittance I get."

Rick mulled this over and decided that at this point, he wouldn't get much more information from her. "I suppose I've bothered you enough. Would you mind asking the person who heads up purchasing to step in here for a few minutes? Rita Gonzales, I think Scott said."

She eyed him suspiciously and was on the verge of saying, "I ain't your servant, chum," but instead she just nodded, rose from the chair, and silently departed.

Rick waited patiently for Rita to appear and just as he was about to go look for her, she appeared at the door.

"I'm Rita. Looking for me?" Her lustrous dark brown hair hung down below her shoulders. She had large brown eyes, a cute upturned nose, full lips, and lots of makeup. She wore an ivory linen suit that looked more expensive than she could afford on her salary, but she had apparently put her wardrobe high on her list of priorities. She was in her mid-twenties and had the carefree look of someone not yet weighted down with the complications of Little League games and PTA meetings. He had to agree with Scott's assessment—she was definitely striking.

"Hi Rita. I'm Rick Devereux, and I'm working with John to help sort out what's been happening with the business. I think I've spoken with everyone else, but I wanted to get your ideas about what might be causing the problems that seem to be cropping up lately."

"Problems? Yes, they've been getting worse all the time. And the source is obvious—if everyone would just do their job, things would be fine. I prepare the purchase orders from information I get from Jerry. After that, things seem to break down. If the purchase order doesn't get signed, I can't order the parts. Even when it gets signed, the vendor withholds the shipment if they haven't been paid. If parts don't arrive in a timely fashion, it sure isn't my fault. When the parts finally get here, it's no wonder they're often wrong—Jerry's had to rob parts from other circuit boards in the meantime, so he needs more parts for replacements."

"So if you could get the purchase orders signed and your vendors would ship on time, everything would be okay?"

"It sure wouldn't hurt. There are probably other things going on too, but as far as purchasing goes, we'd always have the correct parts if everyone else in the process would just do their job. It doesn't take an M.B.A. to figure that out."

Rick decided that he had heard enough. As with everyone else, Rita was convinced that the problems originated in someone else's area. "Thanks for your time, Rita. Could you find John and tell him that I've finished interviewing everyone?" Rita, relieved that the interview was over so quickly, left to find John.

*i*t seemed to Rick that Walpold Enterprises had outgrown the procedures that had worked fine when it was smaller. Now, John had only the vaguest notion of what was happening in his company. Usually when an owner lacks specifics about the status of his operation, he isn't effectively managing it; that doesn't mean he must always know to the penny what his receivables are, but he should always have close at hand a status report listing the key operational ratios. Having such a report accomplishes two very important purposes; first, it forces his managers to prepare the data. Second, it gives the owner a "control panel" that can be utilized to implement changes. With such a tool he can direct that changes be made and then monitor the progress. Herb had apparently recognized John's lack of control, and that was why Leonard and Phyl were wandering around stirring things up. It might be a race against time: Could John regain control before Herb discovered how bad things were and took additional steps of his own?

At this stage of his analysis, Rick needed to discuss some specifics with John and see how he reacted. Rick tried to limit his consulting activities to operations where there was a reasonable probability of success. If John felt threatened, he might only halfheartedly endorse some of the concepts and thus almost guarantee their failure. If, however, John was willing to attack the problems enthusiastically, Rick believed that they could make significant improvements, assuming that they could react while John still had control.

As Rick was considering this, John entered. "So, what's the verdict? Are we salvageable?"

It would be easy for Rick to convince John that he was using poor management techniques, but this wouldn't serve any purpose. Hurting John's ego would only reduce the probability of success. "Maybe the best thing for you to do is to sneak out the back door, change your name, dye your hair, and start a new life in a new city," said Rick with a gleam in his eye.

"Don't think I haven't considered that," John said laughing, shaking his head, "but we've come too far to give up now."

"Actually, your problems aren't unique. Your company is displaying the classic symptoms of an operation that has outgrown its control systems and procedures. All companies go through this; companies that grow from nothing to hundreds of millions of dollars go through it several times. And it doesn't mean that you've done anything wrong. Two hundred years ago, horse-and-buggy technology was adequate to conquer the Western frontier, but it took different technology to get to the moon. If you wanted to stay as small as you were two years ago, you'd probably be fine. But as you grow, the amount of information that you must deal with grows, and better systems are required to process it efficiently."

"So we need to automate? Everybody already has a computer on their desk, but the only meaningful activity on the office network that I'm aware of is E-mail, and I have my doubts about its worth."

"Automation is a secondary issue. In all cases, before you can automate you must first have manual systems that work properly. Automating a screwed-up manual system doesn't cure anything—it just helps people screw up faster."

"But you said a minute ago that the manual systems were once fine. What happened?"

"Your manual systems are crumbling under the increased load. Joan doesn't have time to update the receivables report because she's too busy trying to collect receivables. Jerry is too busy trying to react to last-minute changes to make sure he is ordering the right parts. Pete can't recognize trends in customer problems unless they are blatantly obvious because he is so busy solving those problems. In all cases, more efficient methods are available to help these people manage their data so they can have meaningful information to work from. Does any of this make sense?"

"I suppose so. We used to be able to keep track of everything, probably because there wasn't that much to keep track of. Joan's brother-in-law set up a bunch of programs to help everybody keep track of everything, but it didn't seem to work, and I don't know exactly why. What do you suggest we do?"

"Home-grown database applications can be a good start, but without adequate training, discipline, monitoring, and feedback, they seldom solve any long-term problems. I don't want to sound like a psychologist who wants to sign you up to a never-ending stream of counseling sessions, but this can be a rather lengthy process. Each department should be evaluated, an operating plan formulated, changes implemented, and the results monitored. It will require several hours of my time each week, decreasing as the systems mature."

"That sounds rather open-ended to me," said John. "How will we know things are improving? Hook up a 'chaos meter' and watch the needle?" he asked ironically.

"Hey, that sounds like a good idea," chuckled Rick. "Actually, the way to begin is for me to prepare an analysis of the company from the financial statements, to give us a starting point. Then, as we implement the changes, we'll have a yardstick to measure their effectiveness."

"At the risk of sounding overly anxious, I don't think I've got much time. Herb has already sent his minions in to poke around, we barely had enough cash to cover today's payroll, the bank is becoming increasingly uncooperative . . . I doubt that I've got more than a week before things start to happen that are beyond my control."

Rick considered this before speaking. "That doesn't give us much time. Today's Friday. I can have the analysis done by Monday. You've got to get a firm grasp of what needs to be done to regain control over your company, and if you've got to do it by the end of next week, then you'll have to move fast. With the situation the way it is, the first week will be the most crucial. After that, I would suggest that I spend at least two to three days a week in here for a few weeks and then taper off when we see that things are beginning to settle down."

They were ready to talk terms. Rick told John the hourly rate he'd be charging, which was acceptable to John, and they hammered out an approximate schedule. John agreed to prepare a letter of engagement formalizing their arrangement and had Joan collect the monthly financial statements for the preceding six months for Rick to go over. As Rick collected the stack of financial statements, John mused that this was probably the first time anyone had even looked at the monthly tomes prepared by the CPA. To him, the numbers were incomprehensible and seemed to have very little to do with what was happening in the company. "I suppose that now I'll get another report I can't understand," he thought. "Just what I need."

*r*ick gathered up the papers and headed for the door. As he walked out of the building toward his Jeep, he looked up and saw someone watching him from an office window. "With those piercing eyes, who else could it be?" he thought. The face in the window turned away and disappeared.

In a few minutes, as Rick was driving down the road and mulling over what he had seen at Walpold Enterprises, his cellular phone rang. He picked it up and said, "Hello, this is Rick Devereux."

"Hello Rick, this is Herb Chandler. I understand you spent the afternoon at Walpold Enterprises, and I was wondering what you thought about the situation."

"Very interesting," thought Rick. He knew that Chandler was a director and minority stockholder of Walpold Enterprises and suspected that he would be playing a more active role in the future. Rick had to decide how to handle him. There was more than a remote possibility that this man, or someone under his direct control, would be running the company in the near future. Just in case it did happen, he wanted to keep on good terms with him to ensure the possibility of additional consulting with the company. However, he had no reason to paint a gloomy picture that would make John look bad. For the moment, he would stay noncommittal. "It's too soon to have any concrete answers, Herb. I'm going to spend some time with the financial statements and meet with John again early next week."

"Be sure to have Leonard and Phyl sit in when you go over the financials. I want Leonard up to speed on everything that's going on. He might be playing a more extensive role than I had envisioned. Keep in touch," said Herb as the connection was broken.

"How?" thought Rick. "He didn't give me his number." He wondered if he should tell John about the conversation he'd just had. After all, John was the client, not Herb. Or should he sit on the fence and wait to see who would emerge victorious? It would definitely be an interesting couple of weeks. He was so consumed by these thoughts that he almost missed the turnoff on the highway for the road to the town where he lived.

*L*ater that evening John flopped on the couch next to Barney, planning to relax in front of the Atlanta Braves baseball game on TV. Barney, a black terrier, rolled on his back, trying to get John to scratch him on his stomach. "No problems with you, eh Barn?" said John as he ran his fingers over the patch of white fur on the dog's belly. Barney perked his head up for an instant, then dropped it back down and relished the attention. A summer rain was beating on the window, and if it weren't for the other distractions in his life, all would seem very serene.

Steve Avery was pitching for the Braves in the bottom of the third inning. The Cubs had loaded the bases with no outs—things were looking pretty grim for the Braves. The base runners inched forward as Mark Grace approached the plate with a look of confidence on his face. After Avery struggled to a three-and-two count, Grace hit a fair ball high over the third-base line, and it seemed for a moment that the Cubs were going to score until Chipper Jones leaped straight up at exactly the right instant and caught the speeding ball, tagged third base, and threw the ball to Blauser at second for a triple play! Avery gleefully ran to the dugout with the look of a convicted felon who had suddenly been pardoned.

"Jeez," said John to no one in particular, "I wish my problems could all be solved that easily."

Beth joined John on the couch, even though she had little patience for watching baseball on TV. She recognized that something was troubling him. After almost two decades of marriage, none of John's moods were a mystery to Beth. He often tried to withhold information that he felt might upset her, but without much success.

"A penny for your thoughts," she tried.

"Just thinking about work, hon," he responded absently.

"What's going on? You seem more worried than usual."

"It was a crappier day than usual. Cash is really tight, and our credit line is maxed out, so the bank isn't willing to lend us what we need. I called Herb this morning to see if he would help, and his response was to send in that jerk Leonard and his partner Phyl to look around."

"And Leonard and Phyl—what are they doing?" asked Beth.

"Digging around and grilling everyone."

"Can they do that? It's your company, isn't it?"

"Sure, sort of. Herb only owns thirty-three percent, but under the conditions of our original agreement, he has the option to increase his ownership if his exposure increases. We might have to borrow more money to survive, and he only needs a hair over seventeen percent more to gain control. Then God knows what could happen."

"Are you sure you'll have to borrow more money?"

"I'm not sure of very much these days," he said glumly. "I called in a consultant, a guy named Rick Devereux, to help me figure out what's going on. Hopefully he'll have the cash forecast figured out early next week, and I'll have a better idea of where we stand."

"I'm sure everything will work out fine. Won't it?" she asked hopefully.

"Yeah, sure it will," said John, trying hard to believe it.

SATURDAY

July 29, 1995

*e*arly Saturday morning, John decided to go in to the office to try to catch up on his mail and the paperwork that had accumulated on his desk. As he drove into the parking lot, he noticed a car that he didn't recognize—a black BMW 325i. When he reached the front door, he turned the handle and found that the door was already unlocked. They had been rather casual about making office keys available to those that might need them, but he couldn't imagine who owned the BMW and had a key. As he approached his office, he saw a rectangle of light on the floor and wall outside his office and heard the faint clacking of keys on a computer keyboard. He walked in and found his chair occupied by Leonard Wasserman, who continued whatever he was doing at John's computer without even pausing at the interruption.

"What the hell are you doing?"

Finally looking up, Leonard answered, "Just trying to find the financial files Joan said were on the system."

"What's wrong with the office and computer down the hall that were you using yesterday?"

"Your office was closer, and I had no idea you were coming in today. Have I upset you? Yes, I can see you're upset." His tone of voice was that of a parent dealing with an unhappy child.

John could feel his neck and face begin to redden. He shouldn't have felt embarrassed, but Leonard had completely turned the situation around with a few words. It amazed John that Leonard showed no guilt whatsoever at being there. Through clenched teeth he said, "Get the hell out of my office, and stay out unless you're invited. And when my door is closed, knock if you want to come in. Unless something has happened that I'm not aware of, I'm still in charge of this place."

"For now," said Leonard, rising from the chair and walking past John and out of the office.

"Wait a second, Leonard," John said sharply.

Leonard stopped and turned around. "Yeah?" he said.

Ru**n**a**M**o**k**

"This office is closed on the weekends except to employees authorized to have a key, which you're not. Give me the goddamn key, and beat it."

Leonard, reaching into his pocket, retrieved the key and tossed it to John. "I'll mention your cooperation to Herb," he said and headed toward the door.

John watched him leave, then walked over to his chair, sat down, and shook his head in disbelief. Looking at his computer screen, he noticed that the directory containing his personal correspondence was open. He wrote a note to Joan, telling her to have the locks changed and to issue new keys only to department heads and managers, and to get a second lock installed on his office door.

John decided to check the E-mail traffic, as he did about once a week. He couldn't read the mail, but he could monitor the number of messages and their sources. In that way he could anticipate the amount of system resources to allocate for the various functions. From the time it was installed, the number of messages had grown rapidly to about forty per day, where it had stayed for the past several months. He noticed that each day of the previous week had also averaged forty messages per day, except for Friday, when it had jumped to seventy. And the primary source of new messages was the terminal that had been assigned to Leonard. He wondered what the hell the guy was up to. He would have liked to read some of the messages and see what was happening, but each terminal was "guarded" by the user's unique password, without which none of the message files could be opened. Besides, it would be unethical, like reading someone's mail.

As he thought about what Leonard might have been doing at his computer, he suddenly felt a fleeting wave of anxiety accompanied by heart palpitations. "I've got to quit drinking so much coffee," he vowed, hoping it was that simple. But his thoughts turned again to the possibility of losing his company. He envisioned himself packing up his belongings and vacating his office—and even worse, assembling everyone and informing them that the money had run out and that the company was being forced into bankruptcy by the creditors. He could see the look in their eyes, as they all wondered how they would make their next house payment or car payment or buy groceries. Very distracted, John picked up the first item in a pile of papers on his desk—the recent purchase order from Jerry that included a request for new workbenches. He sent a brief E-mail message to Jerry asking why he needed more workbenches, then slogged through his mail for a few minutes. He finally realized that he couldn't concentrate, so he went home.

MO*d*DA*y*

July 31, 1995

*b*ack in his office on Monday, John had spent half the morning trying to get something done, with no success. His mind just wasn't on it. The weekend had been lousy. After the confrontation with Leonard on Saturday, John had planned to spend the rest of his time relaxing and watching baseball on TV, but he couldn't keep his mind off the problems at work. "If I could just get my batteries recharged," he thought, "I could be more effective. I'm so drained I wouldn't recognize a good idea if it bit me. Maybe Beth and I should have gone on the cruise with Mike." He knew, though, that he couldn't afford the time or the money.

When he started Walpold Enterprises, John realized that there would be good times and bad, but he never imagined the personal toll it would take. He recalled looking forward to the challenges of running a company and, because of his competitive spirit, thought it would be exciting. But attacking problems in the abstract is much different than doing it in real life: The issues become intertwined with other problems, personalities, and even the effects of national economics. Who would have ever predicted that the economy would be this depressed? That in itself hadn't affected sales much, but it had choked his source of working capital once the bank stopped lending him money. He had great products and knew how to produce and market them, but the company was slowly going down the tubes for no reason that he could put his finger on.

For the first time in his life, he felt like a victim, unable to control any of the events occurring around him. It bothered him that he had no one to confide in at work. Joan was too distracted with her divorce. He and Dan seldom talked anymore; Dan simply wasn't interested in non-R&D issues and for the past several weeks had been even more noncommunicative than usual. If Rick Devereux worked out, it would be ideal. Rick could be the sounding board he needed and might come up with some helpful suggestions that would get John moving in the right direction again.

Rick had called and told John that he'd finished his financial analysis and would be stopping by late morning. John was concerned about what Rick might think about someone running a company who knew as little about finance as he did, but he decided to level with him. He could certainly hold his own in any discussion about engineering, but when it came to finance, he "didn't know squat," as his sons would say. John was somewhat apprehensive about having to review a financial analysis. He had never received anything from his CPA that he understood, and this was probably going to be worse. He swiveled around to face his computer, scrolled down the directory to a file of confidential financial reports and clicked on it. But when he attempted to load it into his word processor, the computer displayed the message "Access Denied—Sharing Violation," which usually meant that someone else was using the file. "Must be a system error," he thought, and tried again, with the same result. Puzzled, he walked out of his office and down the hall to see who else was using the network. Seeing a light shining in Phil Jackson's office, he entered and said, "Phil, I just—" and stopped as he realized that the screen on Phil's computer was displaying the file he had tried to access. "What the hell are you doing?" he asked incredulously.

Phil sputtered, "Uh, I guess I loaded it by accident. Sorry John. I didn't mean—"

"You've got no business looking at my personal files," John raged. "What the hell are you doing?" he said again. Then, looking down at Phil's desk, he realized that the confidential financial reports were only a part of what Phil was collecting. Already printed out were copies of the most recent financial statements from his CPA, several letters he had written to Martin Dorsey concerning financing, and a complete customer list and several pages showing summaries of sales records.

"I was just collecting sales information," Phil stammered, "to work on the forecast—"

"Bullshit," said John sharply. "This has nothing to do with the sales forecast. You're planning to jump ship, aren't you, and you're trying to take as much information as you can with you. Well, forget about it. You're fired. Get the hell outta here," he continued, standing with his hands on his hips.

Phil shook his head, sighed, and stood up. He opened his desk drawer and started gathering his personal items. John said, "I've got work to do, and I want you outta here *now*. Call Joan and set up a time to come get your stuff. She'll escort you while you pack your things up." Phil hesitated a moment, but then walked out of the office and down the hall; John followed him.

Just as he reached the front door, he turned to John and said, "You guys are going down the tubes anyway. It's just a matter of time." Then he opened the door and left.

"Yeah, yeah," John muttered as he returned to his office, sat down, and considered what had just happened.

*r*ick arrived a half hour later, in a cheerful mood. He breezed into John's office carrying a manila folder and his notebook-size organizer. "Happy Monday morning!" he said. Let's get down to work." After sitting down across from John, he took some papers out of the folder and set them in front of him on the desk.

"I just caught the head of my Sales Department, Phil Jackson, trying to print out some confidential files from my computer, and I fired him on the spot. Apparently, he's been interviewing all over town for another job. I guess he thought Walpold's financial and sales data would make him more valuable to one of our rivals."

"It's a good thing you caught him, then. Do you have someone to replace him?"

"Yes, Scott Nichols. He's the Assistant Sales Manager, but he's actually been running the department while Phil's been out.

I think he'll do a good job. Now, as you said, let's get down to work. I've got to warn you, though, I'm no financial wizard. In fact," he said, as he reached into his bottom desk drawer where he kept infrequently sought-after items, "this is my copy of the latest report from my CPA," holding up a manila folder containing a sheaf of pages. "I've thumbed through it, but I really can't make heads or tails of it. And even without keeping track of the money end of things, I've built a multimillion-dollar company. To be perfectly honest, I've always felt that the money I pay for accounting services only benefited my CPA and the IRS. I've certainly never gotten what I felt was any tangible benefit for the money I pay for financial statements."

"John, you're not alone. Many of the small business owners I work with have only a cursory knowledge of accounting. However, don't overlook the original purpose of creating financial statements—to give you information that will help you optimize your operations. You should consider them your business thermometer."

"Business thermometer?" John asked.

Just then there was a knock on the door, and Dan entered. "Hey John, what happened to the request for workbenches that I tacked onto one of Jerry's purchase orders?"

"So that's why Jerry didn't know why I was asking him about workbenches," John said. "What do you need more workbenches for, anyway?"

"I need a separate setup for the new project I'm working on. What difference does it make? Do I have to justify everything I do around here?" Dan added testily.

"You're right," John said calmly, wondering what was bothering Dan. "If you had initialed the order, I would have known it was yours and sent it right back to Rita. I really don't care why you need workbenches, I was just curious." Just then, a small pager hanging from Dan's belt started beeping. "A beeper? You have a beeper?"

Dan pulled the small device off his belt and handed it to John. "This is the new project I've been working on. I haven't mentioned it to you yet because I didn't know if it would really work. That was my computer beeping me, letting me know that the compiling-and-linking operation is finished. Pretty neat, huh?''

"Your computer can beep you?" said Rick incredulously.

"Yeah. And send a short message, too. See?" Dan took the pager from John and held it so Rick could see it. It displayed the message "C&L Done." Dan explained, "With software running in the background on a PC, you can have it do anything. For example, if the computer receives a fax, it can beep you and report 'Fax In.' Or it can beep you to remind you of an important meeting. What do you think? We could launch it next year!"

"Will you market it through your existing channels?" asked Rick. "It seems to me that your display adapters are aimed at an entirely different market."

"So what?" Dan didn't get Rick's point.

"Can your support staff handle the new product, or will you have to hire new people? Have you worked out a break–even analysis, so you know how much cash will be required before the resulting profit hits the books? In fact, have you determined what its manufacturing cost will be, and what you should charge for it? And if you did, what competitive products did you use as a basis for your pricing?"

"Hey, wait a minute. Don't you think it's a neat idea?" Dan wanted to be complimented on his brilliant invention, not bombarded with practical questions.

"What *about* the funding, Dan?" asked John. "Where the hell are we going to get the money to put it into production? We barely had enough cash to cover the payroll last Friday."

"If we were generating the cash we'd projected when we started this place, it would be simple," Dan shot back. "It sure as hell isn't R&D that's dropped the ball, John," he added. "We had a neat idea three years ago and because of it we started this company. This is another neat idea—maybe it'll justify the start of another new company."

"The world is full of neat ideas that have no market," Rick said. "The national computer shows are always full of solutions desperately seeking problems. Are you sure this isn't one of those?"

Dan had heard enough. "Jesus," he said in a very frustrated tone, "could you just find the goddamn purchase order with my workbenches and send it to Rita?" Then he turned and walked out, closing the door behind him before John even had a chance to respond.

"I wonder what the hell is bothering him," said John, more to himself than to Rick. Then he said to Rick, "I'm afraid that's rather typical of Dan's thinking—he focuses on R&D at the exclusion of everything else."

"What I see very often in small businesses is owners who are very good in one or two areas, but weak in others. That's fine for getting a company started, but success in the long term is jeopardized when any areas are given short shrift. It doesn't mean that every business owner must know everything—that's why he or she hires help. Dan may be very good at R&D, but if he isn't willing to look at the bigger picture, he shouldn't object if someone else does."

"I'm sure he'll come around eventually," said John, closing the subject. He leaned forward, clasped his hands together on the desk, and said, "Now, where were we?"

"Oh, before we start, I forgot to tell you," said Rick almost apologetically. "Herb called me as I was leaving last Friday to quiz me about what was going on. He just about demanded that Leonard and Phyl be involved in any discussions I have with you about the financials."

"No way!" said John. "As long as I'm in charge, I'll invite whomever I want to my meetings, and exclude whomever I want. Herb said he sent them to perform due diligence, but I think Leonard may have another agenda. So let's get on with it—school's in session. I suppose this will be Accounting 101?"

"In a manner of speaking, yes. And I think you'll finally see that you *can* benefit from accounting data and industry-standard financial ratios."

"That's hard to imagine, but I'll be open-minded. But there's no way I have time to learn accounting fundamentals in the midst of everything else that's going on."

"Let's look at the report. I doubt that you'll have any problems understanding it." Rick handed John a copy of the report. [*See full report on pp. 243-252.*] "Let's start at the top of the first page. Here I state a very important point—the purpose of this or any business is to make money for the owners. A secondary purpose is to maximize the owners' return in the event they decide to sell the business. Does that seem reasonable?"

"How could I complain about that? It's pretty easy to forget about that when you're struggling to survive, though."

"Okay. Let's skip over the Observations and Recommendations for now, since they just summarize some of the key points detailed in the report. Page two shows graphs for revenue, cost of sales, operating expenses, and net profit, with lines showing the calculated trends. This type of presentation is often useful for operations that are less mature than yours. Your revenue doesn't vary wildly from month to month and has increased slightly over the past six months. Did you realize that?"

"I felt like it wasn't getting worse but wouldn't have bet one way or the other on it. The way Phil's been talking, you'd think we were on the verge of going out of business."

"Well, you're obviously not. Your cost of sales appears stable too, but before we can believe that, we need to look at how the data is captured. Until we review that, let's assume that it's stable. Operating expenses are increasing slightly too, but almost imperceptibly. The most significant graph is the bottom one, showing net profit. Since it's erratic, no trend line is shown. The level is low enough that slight changes in the other components drastically affect the profit. I'll bet your bankers aren't wild about your profit picture, are they?"

"They're not real wild about anything right now. I think I told you that they capped the credit line."

"Later in the report we'll examine the reason why. But first, let's go to the next page and look at the components of your revenue. The graphs are pretty self-explanatory. In the future, if we can capture the cost-of-sales data separately for each revenue component, we can determine how profitable each component is. For example, is your gross margin the same for each component?"

"I don't know what you mean. I warned you I wasn't an accounting genius."

"No problem. Let me define a couple of terms before we proceed. Gross profit is the revenue minus cost of sales, or the profit before any operating expenses are considered. Gross margin is a percentage, defined as the gross profit divided by the revenue. If your gross margin is thirty percent, that means you're receiving as revenue one dollar for every seventy cents you spend on the product. Percentages are important for comparative purposes. Two companies selling the same products might have drastically different gross profits if their sales volumes are not the same, but their gross margins could be identical. In fact, it's not uncommon for companies that sell similar products to have very similar gross margins. I'll go into more detail on that when we get to the section on profit.

"At any rate, your various components appear stable, with only PC-OS2 showing a slightly negative trend."

"I thought the OS2 market was kinda soft. Fortunately, the others look okay."

"That's true, but without the cost-of-sales data for each component, we can't tell how profitable each one is. Let me give you an example. Retail tire stores sell more than tires. They also do tune-ups and sell batteries, mufflers, and shocks, and many work on air-conditioning systems. In a typical tire store, the majority of their revenue will come from tires, but the service work will be the major contributor to the gross profit. Usually the gross margin for the service work is twice that of the tire sales. If you own a tire store, you might want to expand your service staff, encourage your sales people to sell more of your other products and persuade customers to bring in their cars for servicing, and do as much as possible while the car is on the rack. Do you see what I mean?"

"That makes sense, but what does it have to with our products? We don't sell a wide variety of products, and we don't do servicing."

"Well, even though your products have similar production requirements, don't you use different marketing methods for your Mac and Sun products?"

"You're right. We have to advertise in different publications, and we send out much more literature for the Mac products. Does that mean we should be charging more in one market than another, even though the products are very similar?"

"There's a simple rule of thumb for setting prices: Always make the price as high as you can. That may sound crazy, but think about it. Every dollar you save your customer comes out of your pocket. The marketing books have detailed analytical cases describing how price affects volume; higher prices result in lower volume and vice versa. But Madison Avenue has proved that certain price increases can be compensated for by other methods. A well-known manufacturer of TV sets based a very successful advertising campaign on the slogan 'More expensive, but darn well worth it.' Also, what if you have a captive market? If you have the only product for a given market, you can certainly charge more than commodity prices. Your higher price will doubtless encourage a competitor to enter the market, but until one does, why should you leave money on the table? You need to determine if Walpold Enterprises should be charging the same price in all your different markets. I don't know the answer to that, but I think we should look into it."

"Now that you mention it, we make the only Sun-compatible board, so I'm sure we could be charging more for it. I'll bet we could raise the price ten percent and not lose a single sale. What would that do to our profits?"

"Well, your Sun products represent sixteen percent of your total revenue, or two hundred forty-seven thousand dollars. A ten percent increase would add twenty-four thousand seven hundred dollars to your revenue, with no increase in cost of sales or operating expenses. If you had increased the price on January 1, you would have increased your net profit to thirty-eight thousand dollars—that's a hundred and sixty-three percent increase."

"A ten percent increase in the price of one product increases the net profit by a hundred and sixty-three percent? That's incredible!"

"Don't get carried away," cautioned Rick. "Part of the reason it results in such a large percentage increase is that the net profit is inordinately low. But we'll get to that in a minute. The point here is to realize the value of looking at the various components of revenue and the gross margin. Are you convinced?"

"Are you kidding? And you haven't even mentioned debits and credits yet," said John, feeling pleased that he was following the discussion. "What's next?"

"The asset review. Your assets are all the property that you own, such as cash, inventory, or claims against others, that may be applied to cover liabilities. Regardless of how you got them, you have total assets of slightly over $1.1 million. Dividing this number into your annualized sales results in the sales-to-assets ratio. Again, this is useful for comparative purposes, since the ratio allows us to compare your operations with other similar operations that aren't the same size. If they are more efficient than you, they will be generating more sales with the same amount of assets. In this case, Walpold Enterprises is six percent more efficient than the industry standard. This is good, but as you will see in a minute, it could easily be much better."

"Are you saying that our competitors are in deeper trouble than we are? We're really a little ahead of the game, and it won't take much to improve things? That's hard to imagine," said John, shaking his head.

"Not at all. Increasing the sales-to-assets ratio requires either increasing sales or decreasing assets, right? Well, let's look at two of your assets. The upper graph on page four shows your receivables collection rate in days. At the end of June, the average monthly revenue is two hundred fifty-seven thousand dollars and current receivables are four hundred fifty-one thousand dollars, resulting in an average collection rate of fifty-two days. That means each day represents eighty-six hundred dollars, or if the collection rate could be decreased to thirty days, receivables would drop by a hundred eighty-nine thousand dollars. If the resulting cash were used to pay down debt, the result would be a drop in assets, increasing the sales-to-assets ratio."

"Fifty-two days? Our receivables are fifty-two days old? I wonder if Joan knows that?"

"Fifty-two days on the average, meaning that some are more than fifty-two days. And does Joan realize that? Probably not the specifics, although she's likely to have a feeling that most payments are more than a couple of weeks late. Feelings are sometimes enough when you are a small company, but when you have almost half a million in receivables from sales to dozens of customers, it's easy to lose track of the details."

"Okay, so the receivables are too high. I knew that, I just didn't know how high. What else?"

"Your inventory is too high."

"According to the numbers, you mean. I hear every day about an order not shipping because of a lack of parts, and Jerry is constantly claiming he doesn't have enough parts. He threatened to send his assemblers home last week because of it. Couldn't it be just a statistical anomaly, and it's not actually happening?" asked John skeptically.

"I certainly don't claim to be an expert in your business, but let me show you how I arrived at this conclusion. Are you familiar with the term 'inventory turn rate'?"

"Yeah, it has to do with how many times the inventory turns over each year."

"Right. There are two ways people tend to look at it. The first, as you said, involves the number of times the inventory turns each year. The second, and the way I prefer to discuss it, is simply the number of days the current inventory would last if no more parts were purchased and the current sales level remained constant. This is obviously an unrealistic concept, since nobody's stock room would contain the exact right mix of parts to allow shipping to continue, but in any event, it's a simple way to envision the process. This term is calculated by dividing the inventory level by the average monthly cost of sales and multiplying by thirty days. Look at the lower graph on page four. It shows the results of this calculation for each month of the period. At the end of June, with inventory of five hundred thirty thousand dollars and cost of sales of a hundred twenty-four thousand dollars, your inventory turn rate was one hundred twenty-seven days. The industry standard, or the results of the same calculation for all of your competitors, was eighty-two days. That means you have a hundred seventy-two thousand dollars more in inventory than your average competitor, assuming that their sales volume is identical to yours."

"But we don't have any competitors that do exactly what we do."

"Ah, but you do have competitors, and they *could* operate as you do and offer only the products you do, and to do that, they would need a hundred seventy-two thousand dollars less in inventory than you have."

"Then why are we always out of parts?"

"There's only one explanation: You've got money tied up in parts you don't need. They're either obsolete parts you'll never use or extras of parts you already have."

"You make it seem like Jerry doesn't know what he's doing. Maybe he's not the right guy for the job."

"Let's not jump to quick conclusions. One of the challenges of management is using the available people effectively. Unless personality differences preclude reconciliation, I always prefer helping the existing people succeed rather than trying to find one that already knows how.''

It was clear to John that he was ultimately responsible for what had happened. How had he let things get so far out of control? Maybe he simply wasn't capable of running the business anymore. The concepts Rick was explaining certainly weren't difficult, but until this morning he had no idea that there was a simple analytical method to determine the proper inventory level. Here he was running a multimillion-dollar company, and he didn't even know the fundamentals of management. His people were failing, and he didn't know enough to help them. With a feeling of frustration, he looked up at Rick and said, ''Okay, so what should I do?''

''Do you have any reason to believe that Jerry isn't capable of doing the job? Is he on drugs, an alcoholic, always late for work, never around when you need him, or constantly making stupid decisions—anything like that?''

''No, not at all. In fact, I'd say that with his background and skills he should be perfectly capable of succeeding.''

''Then we'll simply fix the inventory problem. It's really no big deal, although it can feel like it at times. We'll put an effective system into place and teach everyone how to use it. That doesn't necessarily mean a computerized system; a system is merely a well-defined procedure. We'll define everything from who initiates the ordering of parts and how to who opens the parts shipments and where the packing slips go. But let's not get bogged down in that now.''

''Wait a minute. If it's so simple, then why is it so screwed up?''

''Inventory control on a macro scale can be a daunting problem, but looking at its components on a micro scale is much simpler. You either have an inadequate procedure or an adequate procedure that is not being scrupulously followed. When we analyze your inventory-control system, it will be simple to figure out which is the case."

Rick realized that John was feeling ashamed at his failure to stay on top of things and overwhelmed by the task now facing him. But Rick had found overwhelming the owner to be an effective approach when dealing with businesses where sweeping changes must take place. If the owner felt that a little tweaking here and there would fix things, it was much harder to implement the changes necessary to really improve things. However, there was no point in making him despondent.

"John, let me ask you something. If I wanted to know how long it would take a marble to hit the ground if I dropped it off the roof, could you tell me?"

"Except for wind resistance, yeah, I could figure it out. Why?"

"I want to illustrate something. How do you know you could figure it out?"

"Because I learned the principles in physics. It's simple mathematics."

"What about Joan? Could she figure it out?"

"Well, she's an intelligent woman, but she's never taken any physics or calculus courses."

"But she could if she'd learned the required concepts?"

"Sure, I suppose so. So what?"

"Just because you haven't been exposed to all the concepts required to optimize your operation doesn't mean that it's beyond your reach to succeed. The resources are at your disposal; you just have to take advantage of them. Years ago, when I was first promoted out of engineering into management at a large company, the event was described by a vice president as 'the loss of a really good engineer and the gain of a really mediocre manager.' At the time, I thought he was a jerk, but as I grew in experience, I learned just how perceptive he was. The skills are not difficult to acquire. Gifted managers don't start out that way. Until they learn the ropes, they can be really mediocre, just like I was."

John wondered if he would survive long enough to learn the fundamentals. He was starting to feel encouraged though, because the concepts Rick was talking about seemed very logical. In fact, he was starting to feel excited about getting things up to speed. Brightening up, he looked back at the report and said, "Okay, what's next?"

Before Rick could respond, the door opened and Leonard sauntered in. "I see you're going over the financials without me, John. Tsk, tsk—bad boy," he said, taunting him. "You know you should have informed me of this meeting."

"Get the hell out of here" said John. "I already told you to stay out if you're not invited."

Leonard ignored him and said to Rick, "Herb told you to include me in this discussion. Why didn't you?"

"I contracted with John for this assignment," said Rick, "not you or Herb—whom I have yet to meet, by the way. John's paying my fee, so I answer to John."

"Well, not for long. John, you're finished. You've misman-aged the company so badly that you've run it into the ground, worrying about trivia like workbench orders when you've got production disasters piling up like a demolition derby."

John couldn't believe what he'd just heard. It wasn't the insult that surprised him. How did Leonard know about the workbench order?

"You guys continue rearranging the deck chairs on the Titanic," Leonard continued. "Herb will not be pleased when I inform him of your continuing lack of cooperation."

"I told Herb you'd have access to any information you need, and you've had it," said John angrily. "What Rick and I are discussing is none of your business."

Leonard turned and left without another word.

"What was that about workbenches?" asked Rick.

"I'm not sure," John responded, mulling it over. "I can't imagine Dan or Jerry mentioning anything to Leonard about the request for workbenches that Dan added to Jerry's purchase order. Anyway, where were we?"

"We were just about to discuss your profit margin—it's too low. The industry standard is six point six percent, while you're below one percent. You probably already knew that, but do you know why?"

"I guess because our expenses are too high. What else could it be?"

"There are two types of expenses—fixed and variable. Which one do you think is the problem?" Rick asked.

"Hell, I don't know. How would anyone know?" said John with frustration.

"First, other factors could be the cause of your low profit margin besides expenses. For example, you could be paying too much for raw materials, not charging enough for your products, or a combination of both. To nail it down, we need to look at the gross margin. The industry standard is thirty-four percent, and you're at forty-nine percent. This seems to imply that you are spending less to make the products, hence your higher gross margin; however, since your profit margin is low, your operating expenses must be too high. Before we can say this with certainty, we need to examine the components of your cost of sales. For example, are you sure that the item identified as cost of sales on your financial statements includes all the expenses associated with the production of the products?"

"I thought cost of sales was just the parts—the components used to make the completed boards."

"That's not necessarily so. In theory, cost of sales should be the variable costs associated with producing the products. If labor is required, it should be considered a variable cost if it fluctuates with fluctuating revenue."

"I already know the answer to that," John offered. "All our labor shows up on our income statement as 'Payroll.' It never occurred to me that we should break out the separate pieces, but I can see now why we should."

"Good. Shifting the assembly labor to cost of sales will lower your gross margin and make it closer to the industry standard. Once we do this, we can examine the cost of sales and see if anything else is out of whack. I have a feeling that your product costs could be reduced, because I've heard some of your employees mention air–freighting parts in, which is much more expensive than the alternatives. Then we can examine your operating expenses and see how they look."

"So our gross margin is high, which is good, but it's because we're not reporting the costs right, which is bad. Is that what you're saying?"

"In a nutshell, yes. We need to shuffle the charges around to a more classical presentation. Then we can determine how good or how bad things are. Looking at the bottom line, though, we can say that somewhere you are losing about five point six percent, which translates to more than sixty thousand dollars annually. At this point, we can't identify the culprit or culprits, but we'll be able to soon."

"Do you suppose the bank knows this?"

"Banks use industry-standard financial ratios to normalize operations. You can bet that your banker knows your competitors are netting close to seven percent, and you are netting less than one percent. On annual sales of three million dollars, it's easy to calculate that you are making a hundred and sixty-eight thousand dollars less than your competitors. To your banker, even though your profit is positive, it feels like you had a loss of a hundred and sixty-eight thousand dollars. Would you lend money to someone who lost a hundred and sixty-eight thousand dollars last year?"

"But we made a profit."

"Again, if you were the banker, you look at an operation that should be making a hundred and sixty-eight thousand dollars more than it is, and you have to ask yourself why. Banks don't lend money to companies; they lend money to people. A failure of the company to produce the forecasted profit is viewed as a failure of the management team, and since that's who they lent the money to, the bankers get very nervous. Unless you are violating loan covenants, the only recourse the bank has to protect itself is to limit their exposure—which is why your credit line got capped, so at least you won't lose any more."

"But that just makes things worse," John mused.

"True, but they can't offer management advice, because they would be leaving themselves open to lawsuits. So even though it might precipitate even more disastrous results, they take the only action available to them—they close the spigot."

"You mean the reason they don't offer advice is that they are worried about getting sued?"

"In many cases, yes. Mostly, though, they aren't in the management-consulting business; they're in the money-lending business. I've known a few bankers who would offer informal advice, but they are the exception."

"No wonder Marty Dorsey is always asking me for information and never offering advice. He's just worried about getting burned. So the lesson is, my banker is my partner as long as everything is okay, but when things go bad, don't depend on him for help."

"Unfortunately, that's right. But from their perspective, it's logical, isn't it?"

"I guess. Depressing, but logical. What's next?" John asked, looking back at the report.

"Let's look at cash flow. You made a profit last year, though a small one. Why don't you have any cash?"

"Good question. I've quit asking Cal Reilly, my CPA, questions like that. He just shakes his head and acts like I must be kidding. But I'm not. It seems logical to me that if we made money, we should have money—but it doesn't seem to work that way."

Rick continued. "A company can have several sources of cash, only one of which might be an operating profit. But it can also have several uses for the cash, and when the uses exceed the sources, cash drops. That's pretty logical, isn't it?"

"Sure. But what are the uses besides expenses and new equipment?"

"In basic terms," Rick said, "anytime your assets increase or your liabilities decrease, you end up with less cash; anytime your assets decrease or your liabilities increase, you end up with more cash. First, let's look at actions that result in more cash, or the sources of cash. One way to decrease an asset would be to sell a piece of equipment; fixed assets would drop, and cash would increase. Similarly, decreasing receivables would generate cash. Another source would be drawing on your credit line—current debt would go up, and so would cash. The source most people can relate to is the increase in owner's equity, which is a fancy way of saying you made a profit."

"So the uses of cash," said John, picking up on the concept, "would be things like increasing receivables or decreasing the credit line. Or an operating loss."

"Exactly. Let's look at the report and see where your cash came from and where it went. During the six months of the analysis period, you had only two sources of cash: an increase in payables and an operating profit, which generated slightly over seventy-five thousand dollars. Now look at the uses: Your receivables increase consumed almost all of the cash resulting from the payables increase, and you increased your inventory and your fixed assets, for a net cash reduction of sixteen hundred dollars. So that's what happened to your cash."

"That's certainly simpler than I'd imagined," John admitted. "But so what? After it's gone, you can't do anything about it. I guess it's comforting to know at last why I don't have any cash, but it doesn't help me get more."

"No, but it helps you in your future cash planning. There are several reasons you need short-term cash. For example, your credit line needs to be cleared for thirty days each year. Where will the cash come from to accomplish that? Maybe you can stretch your payables or get some of your customers to pay early. The important thing is not to fall into the trap where you plan on using the next month's anticipated profit to buy something, only to find that the cash was already used for something else.''

John sat back and considered all of this. He felt as if he had just taken an entire accounting course in the past hour, and they hadn't finished going through the report yet. At least he was able to understand what Rick was talking about. The concepts were very straightforward, but he had never looked at Walpold Enterprises in these terms before. Although he felt saturated with the new knowledge, he was anxious to finish looking at the report. The next section was entitled ''Leverage.'' Maybe it wouldn't be as perplexing as it sounded. ''Okay,'' he said with a sigh, ''leverage. What's that all about?''

''Leverage means borrowing. If the majority of your financing has come from borrowing, your company is said to be highly leveraged. Debt financing is the borrowing of funds for which the company must pay a fixed cost. Examples are bank or stockholder loans, trade payables, and the sale of bonds. There are two basic types of debt: short-term and long-term.

''Short-term or current debt consists of debts that must be paid in the near term, usually within one year. A measure of a company's ability to service its current debt is its 'current ratio,' which is defined as its current assets divided by its current liabilities. The higher the current ratio, the more able a company is to satisfy its current liabilities. If its current ratio is higher than others in the industry and if the profit picture is bright, an increase in current debt could be considered to satisfy cash requirements. You can bet that your banker knows what your current ratio is and what the standard is for your industry. Has he ever mentioned this to you?''

''I seem to remember his saying something about a current ratio, but I thought he was talking about some ratio that had been recently updated. I didn't want to say anything, because he acted like I knew what he was talking about. But looking at the graph, it looks almost exactly equal to the industry standard. Increasing the current debt would just make it worse. No wonder Marty Dorsey capped the credit line," John added. "Is there anything we can do about this?"

"Sure, but first let's examine the other types of financing. Long-term debt refers to debts that don't require repayment in the near term, such as bonds and long-term loans. Owner's equity relates to the cash from operating profits and the sale of stock. Invested capital is defined as the total amount of long-term debt and owner's equity, and the debt-to-equity ratio is a measure of the relationship between the two quantities. If all of the invested capital is derived from the sale of stock, the company is underleveraged and will provide a lower rate of return to the owners than if a portion of the invested capital were derived from debt. However, the higher the debt, the more interest you will pay, thus decreasing the net operating profit. It's logical to maintain a balance, with the goal being to maintain a debt-to-equity ratio similar to the others in the same industry."

"So are you saying that we could trade our short-term debt for long-term debt?"

"Or pay it off by expanding owner's equity. In short, it means finding a partner. If you could convince someone to invest money, either in exchange for a long-term notes, which would increase the long term debt, or for shares of stock, which would increase the owner's equity, you could use that money to retire the short-term debt. And that's why it's important to look at your debt-to-equity ratio—so that you can decide under what terms adding a partner might make sense. Looking at yours, you are already overleveraged, meaning that your long-term debt is already higher than the industry standard. That means you should only consider adding an equity partner—finding someone to give you money in exchange for stock."

"But we already have a partner—Herb. Are you saying that we should sell stock to someone else?"

"A professor at the Harvard Business School used to say, 'The best time to sell equity is any time you can sell equity.' That sounds ridiculous at first, but when you examine it, it makes a lot of sense. But to be perfectly blunt with you, John, selling equity in Walpold Enterprises today would be tantamount to extortion. That's why I included the final section entitled 'Valuation.' Your cash flow would support a buyout, but the amount would be significantly below what you would consider reasonable. So a buyout is certainly not what you would be looking for. But if a complete buyout doesn't make sense, a partial sale of equity seldom does either."

"That must be why Herb hasn't exercised his option to increase his ownership."

"What option?" asked Rick.

"When we set this company up with the original financing, Herb got thirty-three percent for guaranteeing a loan, with the provision that if his exposure were to increase, his percent of ownership would also increase. At his insistence, we've kept his exposure from increasing by relying on the credit line secured by our assets."

Rick considered this a moment before saying, "If I were Herb, I probably wouldn't be wild about increasing my exposure unless it gave me majority control. And he must have determined that his cost to gain control would be too high, at least with things the way they are now. That's why he sent Leonard and Phyl in—not to find out what's going on but to figure out what to do." There was no point in upsetting John, but Rick was suddenly convinced that as far as Herb was concerned, John was history. The prospects for enough time for him to work with John to turn the company around looked bleak.

"Then we're already screwed," said John. "Herb isn't stupid. He probably already knows that our profit picture is erratic and that we're overleveraged, so we can't service additional debt. Our asset management and use of cash proves that we've screwed up, so increasing his equity position would be ridiculous. There's no way he would give us any more money. What the hell am I going to do?" he added, almost to himself.

"Good question," Rick thought. He told John, "I really don't think you have many options. You can throw in the towel and walk away, leaving Leonard at the helm, or you can scramble as fast as you can to get things under control and hope that it's not too late."

"That's a rather nebulous goal, isn't it? How do I do that? Shall I just line everyone up and holler, 'Organize, march!' and get out of the way?" John felt a pang of anxiety. Things were obviously screwed up, but if the advice he was buying was this vague, he was no better off than before he called Rick.

"I wish it were as simple as isolating a single problem, attacking and correcting it, and then living happily ever after. The key at this stage is to become a professional manager—one that anticipates and controls rather than reacts by the seat-of-the-pants. Just like we already discussed with inventory control, we have to look at each of the other areas and determine which procedures are lacking and what measures should be taken to modify them. On the positive side, it appears to me that the people you have are perfectly capable of succeeding; after all, didn't they get you this far? They were able to develop procedures that worked when the company was smaller. Now the company has grown, and they may have to alter some of the procedures rather than try to shore up the existing ones."

John sat up in his chair and said, "So we just push blindly ahead through a dark tunnel, hoping that we don't get flattened by an oncoming train?" Then shaking his head, he added, "I suppose you're right—I really don't have a choice. Okay, how do we get started, and how long will it take?"

"Everyone who is affected by a procedure should be involved in the process of improving it. Teamwork is the key. I can get the ball rolling, but no one knows more about the ins and outs of a process than the people who use it from day to day."

"Get the procedures fixed, and then everything will be okay? It still sounds rather simple. It's hard to imagine how that will solve my cash problems."

"Updating the procedures is just the first step. Then you've got to impose strict discipline to get everyone to follow the procedures, monitor their performance, and stay vigilant at the helm—but we can get into that more later. And your cash shortage probably isn't a problem, just a symptom of other problems. Like I said, your situation doesn't have a simple solution that can be implemented overnight. People's mind-sets will need to be changed as they accept the fact that Walpold Enterprises is no longer a small company with small problems. The result will be that you will regain control over what is happening. In that capacity, a cash shortage won't occur unless you let it. As to how long it will take, that's difficult to tell until we get started."

Rick was right, John decided. Instead of actively controlling things, he was always reacting to the problem of the day. He rarely knew what his day would entail until the phone started ringing or someone came in with his or her latest problem. He knew that this wasn't the way he should be running things, but until now he hadn't really stepped back to look at what could be done about it.

John had read books about management, but they never seemed to address the issues he had to face on a day-to-day basis. He had asked for biweekly progress reports in the past, but it had only caused grumbling. His staff meetings, which he had read were so important, always seemed to degenerate into a forum for petty quarrels. And it was no wonder that Marty Dorsey was no longer taking him seriously. Based on what Rick had said so far, John realized that his inadequacies resulted from being poorly prepared—he had entered the battle without all the essential tools.

Rick agreed to return first thing in the morning to help start the metamorphosis. After Rick left, John looked through the report again. He was surprised that financial analysis, when it was broken down into its components, wasn't such a mysterious topic after all.

As he was perusing the report, John suddenly realized that he hadn't yet informed Scott about his promotion. He wanted to deliver the news in person, so he left his office in search of Scott, who he found poring over a sales contract in his office. "Hi Scott," John said amiably.

Oh, hi John," said Scott, looking up. "I was just reviewing this latest contract that Telemax faxed over today. What's up?"

"How would you like to be the new head of sales? Phil is no longer with us," said John, omitting any details about Phil's departure.

"I can't say I'm too surprised about Phil. Where's he going?"

"Beats me," John said. "I just know I need a new head of sales, and you're the logical candidate." John explained Scott's new responsibilities and the salary potential with his enlarged territory.

"Fantastic," said Scott. "Thanks for your confidence in me—I won't let you down, John."

"I'm not worried. If you need information about any of your new accounts or any other help, just holler," John said, as he left Scott's office.

*L*eonard found Phyl working at the computer in the spare office they had been using. "What have you found, Phyl?"

"About what we expected. Lots of business—some good, some not so good," she responded, looking up from the computer screen. "What about you?"

"Terrible. The company is bleeding to death like a wounded animal. Herb waited too long before sending us in."

"Maybe," she said, pushing a strand of hair from her eyes and reaching for her coffee. "But the level of business might still be enough to sustain things for a while. Joan might not know exactly what the receivables are, but uncollected receivables can provide some quick cash."

"Yeah, if they know about it, and I'm afraid they might. Devereux has been with John all day going over the financials. He's bound to have stumbled onto something as obvious as that. What about their payables?"

"They've been dragging them out, paying only what they have to in order to keep new parts coming."

"Then it doesn't matter if they have receivables ripe for the plucking—the cash will have to be used to bring the suppliers current," said Leonard, smiling.

"Maybe." Phyl wasn't about to cave in to Leonard—she was confident in her own opinion.

"Look, Herb sent us in here to figure out the proper course of action. We already know that things are screwed up—that's a given. And it's clear to me that as long as John is running things, or thinks he is, the company is destined for failure. Do you have any doubts about it?"

"I'm just saying that with some assistance in getting things organized and systematized, they might be able to work their way out of the mess they're in. Wouldn't that be better than—"

"Are you kidding?" said Leonard curtly. "Aren't you forgetting the crisis of confidence the whole place has with John? Jerry knows more than John about manufacturing, and they both realize it. It's the same with Pete and tech support, Rita and purchasing, and Marie with the finances."

"I suppose that's true, although I'm not sure they've completely lost confidence in John's ability to ultimately run the place. After all, he got it started, and—"

"Yeah, he got it started, but that doesn't mean he can dig them out of the mess they're in now. Look, our allegiance is to Herb. Can you honestly say that leaving John in charge is the optimum approach for protecting his interests?"

"A management change can be very disruptive. A more conservative approach might be more prudent, given that—"

"Jesus, Phyl, pull your head out of the sand. Yeah, John is a nice guy," he continued condescendingly, "and he started the company, but if his key people have lost confidence in his ability to manage things, it would be much better to replace him quickly and get on with things."

"Herb sent us here to evaluate things, and I'm not convinced yet that John isn't capable of—"

"Phyl—"

"Would you quit interrupting me, for God's sake?" Phyl said sharply. "If we can determine that John has already lost his support, then I'll go along with you. But no one would ever confide something like that in you—you have the interpersonal skills of a viper. Fortunately Herb sent both of us. I'm going to poke around and see what I can find out. If you're right, then we'll do it your way. If not—well, then we'll see."

Soon after John returned to his office following the meeting with Scott, a slightly less frazzled Joan walked in and sat down in front of his desk. She held in her hand a folder with several pieces of paper peeking out.

"Boy, you've been busy—I haven't seen you all day," she said.

"Yeah, sit down and let's talk. How was your weekend?"

"Not bad, actually. The kids spent Saturday and Sunday with Bill, on a boat out in the lake. They camped on one of the islands, so Jen was separated from her scuzzball boyfriend for a couple of days. I went to several garage sales with a friend Saturday morning, then bummed around the rest of the weekend, reading a mindless romance novel and enjoying the single life. It was very relaxing. Of course, when the kids returned last night, I had to hear about what Tracy looks like in a thong bikini," she said, referring to her husband's girlfriend. "The thought of her cavorting around nearly naked with my children certainly spoiled a nice day. I can't imagine what Bill must be thinking, exposing his teenage children to that," she said, frowning. "Now, tell me what's been happening. How are things going with Devereux?"

"It's encouraging, maybe. I was just looking over the report he put together from our financials. He divides everything up into little pieces and compares each segment with industry standards that he gets somewhere. It seems a lot simpler than I thought. But I'm not sure what it all means yet. What did you think of him when you talked to him?" asked John, suddenly realizing that this was the first meaningful discussion he'd had with Joan in weeks.

Joan was more than just an administrative assistant for John. He valued her opinion—she was often able to provide a different slant on issues that neither he nor Dan would have ever considered. She was also tuned in to the pulse of the company—or at least she had been until she became so preoccupied with her separation from her husband, the looming divorce, and her teenage children.

"He seems like he knows what he's talking about. And he's certainly more personable than Leonard. But Leonard, Phyl, and Rick running around like they own the place is making everyone a little crazy. How would you feel if someone popped into your office and started quizzing you on what you are doing and why you are doing it that way?"

"How would I feel? How *do* I feel, you mean. I've been interrogated more than all of you put together. And if anyone should feel threatened, it's me. No one else's job is on the line."

"Come on, John. Everyone considers a threat to you a threat to them also, since whatever happens to you affects them. And anyway, this is their company too, and anything that upsets the status quo is unnerving."

"Well things are screwed up. What would you suggest?" asked John glumly.

"Just don't let anyone feel like you're throwing in the towel. If you've got a problem, don't feel like you have to solve it by yourself."

"If everyone knew how close to bankruptcy we are, they'd be paralyzed."

"No, that's not true. Everyone wants to help, no matter how bad things are. Does Rick have any suggestions? What does he think we should do? Borrow more money?"

"Actually, he says our cash shortage isn't a problem—"

"That's easy for him to say. Maybe we should assign our payables to him—that'll change his idea of how big a problem cash is."

"Let me finish. He said cash isn't a problem but only a symptom of other problems. He thinks our operating procedures need to be revamped, that we're bogged down trying to operate with systems that worked when we were a smaller company."

Joan considered what John was saying. The concept seemed to make sense, but how long would it take to make the necessary changes? What would they do for cash in the meantime, and would they even have time to implement any changes with Leonard on the loose? "What do we do about Leonard?" she asked.

"The first thing is to change the locks. I found him poking around on my computer Saturday. Who the hell gave him a key, anyway?" John asked.

"Sorry chief, I didn't think it was a problem—after all, he works for Herb, who could have a key if he wanted one. But anyway, I got your E-mail, and the locksmith should be here tomorrow," she added apologetically.

"Good, I guess the best thing to do right now is to move forward. I want to have a meeting with everyone tomorrow morning. Rick says they'll probably be defensive about the existing procedures, so we need to convince everyone that it's logical to consider examining them in detail. E-mail everyone—including Leonard and Phyl—for a meeting at ten. In the meantime, I'm sure I can find some menial task that I can busy myself with until then."

"Speaking of menial tasks, I dug through the purchase orders that were dying in your 'In' basket and pulled out the ones that seemed most critical," she said, handing him the folder she had been clutching. "This should make you feel useful for a little while."

RunaMok

*t*hat evening after dinner, John recapped the day's events for Beth. "And in the midst of everything else, I caught Phil Jackson printing out confidential files—files he had no business having access to. I was so pissed I fired him on the spot."

"What kind of files?"

"My personal financial statement, historical sales information, marketing literature, customer lists. Joan says he's been out interviewing for another job, so I suppose it could be called industrial espionage."

"And you fired him?"

"Of course I did. Confidential files, E-mail—all the information that we once locked in filing cabinets is now accessible to anyone clever enough to find it. Those documents and messages shouldn't be seen by anyone except the sender and the receiver—they're every bit as confidential as letters mailed through the post office, and a postal-system violation is a federal offense. Wouldn't you feel violated if you reached into our mailbox and found that all the letters had already been opened? Just because he was using a computer rather than physically rooting around in my desk doesn't mitigate his actions. He was robbing the company."

"I never thought of it that way, but you're right."

John continued, "Anyway, he's gone. One less problem to deal with."

T U e S D A y

August 1, 1995

*O*n Tuesday morning, John arrived at work a little later than usual. Late enough, in fact, that the coffeepot was already half empty, and everyone else was busy at work. As he poured his coffee, he mused over the events of the previous few days and wondered if today's big roundtable meeting would jump-start the process of attacking the problems that had crept into the company. Even with the uncertainty of the cash situation, Leonard's thinly veiled assault on his position as CEO and Dan's recent sullen and antagonistic behavior, he was buoyed by the thought that he was beginning to take action to improve things. Whistling a tune as he left the break room to return to his office, he heard the front door open, and Rick came in. "Hey Rick," he called brightly, "how about some coffee?"

"No thanks," Rick responded. "I'm coffee'd out already." They entered John's office together and sat down across his desk from each other.

"I've been thinking about how we should proceed with the meeting this morning," said John. "We have to explain that some changes need to be made and enlist everyone's support. But first we have to squelch any rumors about selling the company, bringing in new people, or having a layoff so everyone can settle down and help with the changes. Here's how I think we should do it: I'll start things off by giving a general idea of the situation and what we're going to do about it, and then I'll turn the meeting over to you, Rick."

"Okay," Rick agreed. "I've found that the best way to do these things is to have a roundtable discussion where we all talk in general terms about what should happen, and let everyone satisfy his or her own curiosity and voice an opinion about how to go about it. If it's done right, it can be a very positive session. Hopefully everyone will have a positive attitude, and we can get on with what we need to do."

John added, "I'll hold off until everyone's had their say. It'll be a good way to check their pulses."

The staff began straggling into John's office and sat down around the table, while Leonard and Phyl took positions in a corner of the room to observe the proceedings. A few moments later, Rick and John entered together. Dan appeared a minute after them.

John surveyed the group and began. "I know everyone has been frustrated lately. What we're going to do now is explore ways to deal with some of the causes of the frustration. Part of that comes from knowing that things are going wrong but not being able to do something about it. Well, that's about to change. We've just started a top-to-bottom analysis of the entire company, and we're going to figure out what the problems are and come up with the solutions—together. In fact, before you hear any rumors about Phil, I want you all to know that I had to fire him yesterday for trying to steal confidential financial records in my computer files. And I've promoted Scott to head of Sales.

"I want you to know that I consider everyone's input essential. That's why you're here. And that's why Rick's here. Rick Devereux has helped a lot of companies through times like these, and I've asked him to see what he can do for us," he explained. "He's going to run this part of the meeting."

Rick stood up, but before he could say anything, Pete asked, "What about Leonard and Phyl? I thought they were doing the same thing."

Before Rick could respond, John decided to confront the issue head-on. "Well, why don't we let Leonard answer that. Leonard?"

"Herb has been concerned about this operation for some time and has asked us to perform an independent evaluation. We've been involved in several projects with Herb, and—"

"Takeovers, you mean, don't you Lenny?" said Dan bluntly.

"It's _Leonard_, and yes, some of the projects have resulted in a major shift of stock ownership, but that's not necessarily what we're planning here." He paused, and then added, "But if a change in management is determined to be in the best interest of the company, shouldn't it occur?"

"Let me reassure you that nothing like that has been decided yet," Phyl added quickly. "We're just here trying to help."

John sat there thinking, "Good cop, bad cop," and trying not to appear riled. He stayed calm and just said, "Why don't we get on with the meeting."

"Yes, let's do that," said Rick. "Having spent a little time with most of you, it appears to me that you're still using operating procedures that worked fine when Walpold Enterprises was small but are now breaking down under the increased load. What I propose is an in-depth review of—"

"Wait a second," said Jerry. "Our purchasing system is almost identical to the one we used at Avcom, but Avcom is a hell of a lot bigger than we are, and it worked fine there."

"Yeah," piped in Rita, "I don't really see anything wrong with the procedure. It's not the procedure that's screwed up, it's—"

"If anything's screwed up," interrupted Jerry again, "it's the sales forecasting system. If we ever knew what to build, we'd know what to order, and we wouldn't be short of parts all the time—"

"Wait a minute," said Scott defensively. "Our sales forecast is one hundred percent accurate on the day that we generate it. It's not my fault if customers cancel their orders because of the problems they're having with our products."

"Problems?" said Dan, suddenly sitting forward in his chair. "I haven't heard about any problems. What's he talking about, Pete?"

"Yeah, what problems, Scott?" asked Pete. "If normal everyday customer problems cause your sales forecast to be screwed up, maybe you'd better reexamine your forecasting methods."

Scott took the challenge and responded, "Parts not arriving when promised are a normal customer problem? Products that don't work when they arrive are a normal problem? If that's true, I'm going to need a crystal ball to figure out which customers will be so desperate for our products that they'll be forced to place an order and which ones will cancel at the last minute.''

Rick had known that it wouldn't be easy, but he didn't think it would go *this* badly. It was clear why the few weekly staff meetings they'd had were so unproductive. He glanced over at John, who looked disgusted, and then at the rest of them. He was dealing with a group of strong-willed people, which was not surprising, since it usually takes a strong-willed group to create a multimillion-dollar company from scratch. But they seemed to be more interested in protecting their own turf and blaming each other than in working together. Rick decided to change tactics. "Wait a minute," he interrupted. "Let's step back a second and consider something. What would you say is this company's number one priority?"

Each of them looked around to see if anyone else was going to offer an answer. After a long silence, Rita said, "To make a high-quality product at a competitive price." Jerry and Pete nodded their heads in agreement.

There was another long silence.

"That's a good answer. A successful company needs to produce a high-quality, competitively priced product. Okay, anyone else?"

Marie spoke up. "Well, it may not be the number one priority, but I think at least one of the priorities is to provide good working conditions so that the employees can do their best. An unhappy, frustrated workforce is not going to deliver that high-quality product, and it certainly won't be competitive."

"We also have a commitment to the environment," added Scott. "We shouldn't make our products at the expense of natural resources. I think we should have some kind of recycling policy. I've read about some big companies that have full-scale recycling programs, where they sell all their recyclables to be used over again to make other products, and they print everything from their memos to their invoices on recycled paper."

"That's ridiculous," said Dan. "The environment is about the last thing we should be worrying about. In fact, I would say it's right below selecting the fourth topping on a pizza. Our number one priority is to stay number one. If our products aren't on the leading edge of technology, we won't have a company. Don't forget that the only reason we exist is that we had a better idea. If we lose our position as the industry leader, we might as well pack it in."

"I'd have to agree with Dan," said Leonard. "Being the industry leader has been a crucial factor in the company's success, and it's maintained that position in large part because of the R&D team."

Leonard's comment surprised everyone, especially John. After the friction between Leonard and Dan earlier, it seemed unlikely. And it was one of the few civil comments John had ever heard from Leonard.

"Thanks Len," responded Dan. "I'd like to show you the new product I've been working on. It's also state of the art."

"Let's get together over lunch and discuss it, Dan," said Leonard, in an even more surprising turn of events, and this time ignoring the license Dan took with his name.

John eyed Leonard incredulously. He wondered what the hell he was up to.

Scott continued. "It's because of antiquated thinking that the country's in the shape it's in now. Too many companies have been fouling things up, and somebody's got to stop the cycle by starting to act responsibly. This company needs to do better."

Dan shot back, "You've been spending too much time in the surf, Scott."

"Oh, come on, let's be civil," said Rick, realizing that he was again losing control of the meeting. "To sum up all of your comments so far, you believe that Walpold Enterprises should build products that are leading edge, of high quality, and competitively priced, without adversely affecting the environment, and should provide good working conditions for its employees. What about your customers—shouldn't they be somewhere in this list?"

After another long pause, Joan offered, "Well, if we made sure our customers were happy, we wouldn't lose any sales."

"Jeez!" exclaimed Dan, rolling his eyes. "If our products are the only game in town, they can be happy or unhappy, but they'll buy them anyway. Making leading-edge products is the key."

"Anything else?" As Rick looked around, he saw blank faces. "Well, believe it or not, you've mentioned many important things, but you've left out the number one priority. It's not building a leading-edge, high-quality product or taking care of the customers or providing a happy workplace or anything like that. Does that surprise you? In America, except for a few notable exceptions, our economy is based on capitalism, with a free market and open competition in which goods are produced for profit, labor is performed for wages, and the means of production and distribution are *privately owned*." He glanced from face to face, trying to see if he was getting through to them. "What does this have to do with Walpold Enterprises? Well, the first priority of any company in a free-enterprise system is to make a profit for the owners.

"Oh great," thought John. "Now he's alienating all my employees."

"Rick's right," said Leonard, deciding to make points with Rick at the expense of John. "Without happy investors, how far would this company have gotten? Many great ideas have died due to lack of funding."

"Absolutely," Rick continued. "And although many small-business owners may not have admitted it to themselves, the main reason they started their business instead of just working for someone else was that the potential reward was higher. Sure, there are other benefits, but without the possibility of making a lot more money, those other benefits wouldn't be enough for anyone to take the risk of starting their own business. If they could make the same amount of money working nine-to-five and letting someone else have the headaches, you might be surprised at how many business owners would just cash it in. Wouldn't you agree, John and Dan?''

"We started this company because R.S.S. was so screwed up. If they had agreed to let us develop our ideas, we'd still be there," said Dan. "I was perfectly happy working there until they—''

"Come on Dan," interrupted John, "you're forgetting about all the times we talked about the money we'd make calling our own shots, enjoying the fruits of our labors with more than just a biweekly paycheck.''

"All businesses need capital to start and grow," Rick continued, "and one major source of capital is people who have money to invest. If there is no potential reward, why would anybody give the company any money? If a company consistently pays its owners a suitable return, the owners will be content to let the company continue to use the money. If not, they'll find another place to put their money where their investment goals can more likely be met.''

"And when they get justifiably concerned," said Leonard, referring to his involvement, "they have the right to make changes to insure success. We're here because Herb wants to make sure that Walpold Enterprises is a success. If that means making a few management changes, so be it.''

"Aha!" thought John, as Leonard finally admitted what his real purpose was here. But John wondered if Herb was convinced that management changes were really necessary. What could Leonard have told him?

"So we should just ignore the quality of our products?" asked Rita.

"Of course not," said John. "What Rick is saying is that if we don't make a profit, we won't survive. All those other things are important but only if they enable us to make a profit.''

"Exactly," said Rick. "A master of understatement at Harvard Business School included in his commencement address to my class some concepts he had formulated over the years. One of the simplest but most powerful is this: Markets work. This concept governs all the different elements of your operation and explains why they all affect profit. Let's start with Dan's concerns. If yours is the only company that produces a certain widget and that widget is in demand, then it's possible for you to get away with poor quality and higher pricing. But because your widget is not difficult to copy, someone will eventually duplicate your efforts and create a competitive product."

"That's already happened," said Scott. "Many of the boards we produce, the ones that allowed us to get this far, are now being produced by several competitors."

"In fact," added Rick, "most of the products you make are offered by so many other companies that at this point they're generic and should be considered commodities."

Dan broke in to ask, "Then why don't we just drop production of items that become so-called commodity products when the competition picks up and shift our focus entirely to producing whatever leading-edge products we have and developing new ones?"

Jerry shot an angry look at Dan, realizing that this approach would effectively end his career at Walpold. He challenged Dan, asking him "And what if you can't come up with a successful new product, Dan? What happens to all of us?"

Rick cut the argument short. "Companies that only produce unique items are referred to as 'job shops' and are constantly struggling to come up with the next big hit. They are very vulnerable, since they have nothing to fall back on if the latest anticipated hit is a flop. Leonard, do you suppose Herb would have been interested in Walpold Enterprises if he thought it would be a job shop?"

"Too risky," responded Leonard quickly. "And the return is too low even if it succeeds for a while. Herb has always hoped that Walpold would grow into a multimillion-dollar company. You can't do that making one product at a time."

"Be honest, Dan," said Rick. "When you and John started Walpold Enterprises, you didn't really plan to develop just one product at a time, abandon it, and move on to the next, did you?"

"Well," Dan admitted, "we put together a spreadsheet showing how the revenue from the first product would fund the development of the next. That's what probably helped convince Herb to get involved in the first place."

"It definitely was," added Phyl. "I can attest to that."

"Well, with Walpold Enterprises producing both leading-edge and commodity products, each type can be handled differently," Rick explained. "That's the way markets work. You can afford somewhat lower quality while keeping prices high for a leading-edge product, but commodities require different marketing techniques. When you have only one product and it's a leading-edge product, you can be successful without competitive pricing, product differentiation, and high quality. But those things are crucial to the success of commodities. So you need to pay attention to commodity issues when your leading-edge product is only ten percent of your total offering."

John added, "The importance of a product's quality changes depending on market conditions. If all other factors are equal, a high-quality product will outsell a lower-quality product. And if two similar products are of the same quality, the cheaper one will sell better. So Rita, you're right—we need high-quality, competitively priced products."

Marie asked Rick, "But what about the way employees are treated? Are you saying that's not important?"

"No, not at all. Everyone will agree with you that happy employees are more productive than unhappy employees."

"In fact," said John, "a company is nothing without those people. Walpold Enterprises' products, service, and marketing didn't happen spontaneously—the people in this group made it happen."

"But without the funding," said Leonard, "Walpold Enterprises wouldn't exist; and without additional funding, it may cease to exist. So in spite of all that marketing mumbo jumbo, one fact remains: Since the bankers have lost confidence in you, and new investors are a remote possibility, Herb Chandler holds the key to the future. If he decides to pull the plug, Walpold Enterprises goes down the drain. If he decides that the current management should be replaced to instill new confidence, it would be in the best interest of the company.''

John looked around and saw that everyone was considering what Leonard had just said. Sure, the future of Walpold Enterprises was important, but for them the issue was their continued employment. They had always been very loyal employees, but would they remain loyal if they believed that their jobs were in jeopardy? "You make it sound like an either/or situation, Leonard, but it isn't,'' said John. "We've been through bad times before, and we've always prevailed. Don't forget, this is the team that took an idea and turned it into a multimillion-dollar company. Does anyone doubt that we've got what it takes to survive?''

Leonard smiled. "The biggest disadvantage of someone who has been successful is to believe that he is invulnerable,'' he said to John. "Just because you've been successful in the past in no way ensures future success. You may have pulled it off in the past, but even a cat has only nine lives; eventually, you run out of luck. Are you going to let pride destroy this company, John?''

John felt trapped. He didn't think that this was the right place or time for a confrontation with Leonard, but he'd been backed into a corner. To retreat would show weakness to all his employees. However, he needed some real ammo in order to fight Leonard and, unfortunately, he had nothing to retaliate with. Maybe Leonard was right—maybe he wasn't the right man for the job and should just withdraw as gracefully as possible. Although Leonard was supposedly just acting in Herb's interest, it was clear that he viewed himself as Walpold's next CEO. But John was a major stockholder and had a lot to lose if Leonard became CEO and then failed. No, it wasn't time to throw in the towel.

"Leonard," John began calmly, "we have recognized the problems, and we are taking steps to make improvements. It's only because of my relationship with Herb that I've given you access to my offices and my staff. If I find that your presence here is disruptive, you'll have to leave. As long as I'm in charge, I'll call the shots. Is that clear?"

"We'll see, John, we'll see," responded Leonard, smiling again. He had made his point and was sure that John's previously loyal staff was wavering. The fact that Herb lacked majority control of the stock was only a detail; it would be easy to solve that problem when the time came to act.

Wanting to move on, John said, "Let's get back to business, everyone. What we're trying to do here is come up with solutions to our problems. Let's not get sidetracked. Please continue, Rick."

"Thanks John. Okay, let's examine how we make decisions. One of the accounting principles used when analyzing the operation of a company is the concept of longevity—to assume that the operation will continue indefinitely. That means we should evaluate all decisions in a long-term context. We don't want to focus on short-term results at the expense of the future. So here's the deal. We want to examine each area and focus on changes that will improve the operation. And we will make trade-offs based on the question 'What is the best solution in the long run for Walpold Enterprises?' "

Before he could continue, Marie spoke up. "What you've said makes sense, but it sounds awfully abstract to me. We didn't inherit our operating procedures from someone else; we developed them ourselves. In fact, we spent a lot of time trying to figure out the best way to do things, avoiding procedures that hadn't worked at other companies and arriving at solutions through our own direct experience."

"Wait a second, Marie," said John quickly. "No one is saying that the procedures weren't adequate when they were created. But now that we're a bigger company than when we started, it's more than likely that we need to augment the procedures."

"John," Marie argued, "I don't think you're in much of a position to pass judgment on any of our systems, since you were traveling around the country when we were developing them. You weren't here."

"That's true," added Jerry, "I tried several times to discuss our inventory-control problems with you, but you were always too busy getting ready for your next trip."

Leonard whispered to Phyl, "See what I mean? They're not supporting him."

"Maybe," she whispered back. "I'll talk some more with Marie and Jerry and see how serious the problem is."

"I've worked at companies that were constantly changing things," Marie continued. "'Change for the sake of change,' we used to call it. And every so often they would pick an employee to take the blame for everything being messed up, and that person would be fired. I hope we're not starting down that road."

"No one will be pointing fingers," Rick responded. "The problems are natural for a company experiencing this growth. It's not illogical that procedures that work fine in a small company have to be modified to be effective as the company grows, is it? A good example is inventory control. A small company can do just fine with a set of index cards to keep track of parts and finished goods. As the company grows, the number of different parts and the rate at which they need to be restocked exceed anyone's ability to manage them. Before the technology was available to keep track of them, additional people had to be hired to accomplish the task. Now it's possible to implement computerized inventory-control systems that will accomplish the same purpose. Should you have an automated system when you are small? Probably not. Should you have a manual card-file system when you are large? Of course not. Walpold Enterprises is at the transition point in many areas. In some cases, more efficient manual systems can be used and, in others, automated systems are needed. But in all cases, we will decide on the solution that is best in the long run for Walpold Enterprises."

Pete was the next to chime in. "I have to agree with Marie. We spent a lot of time working together coming up with our procedures. I remember quite a few evenings around the conference table, and as each idea was considered, everyone else tried to shoot it down. Incidentally, John, Jerry's right—you were never around for those sessions. Most of us have worked at other places, and we've seen why some ideas work and others don't. You make it sound like all we have to do is throw a bunch of software at our problems, and they will magically disappear. Sorry, I just don't buy it," he said, settling back in his chair and folding his arms.

They were making their discontent clear. Rick hoped he could persuade them with logic. "If the procedures aren't the problem, then what is? Practically every Walpold employee I talked to said that lack of cash was the big problem, but in my experience, lack of cash is only a symptom of other ills. I don't know what the causes are yet. Some may be real, and some just secondary effects of other problems. But you have to agree that something is wrong, and for a company that has experienced this rapid growth, it's a good bet that a root cause is the inadequacy of systems that worked fine in the early days." He paused before making his next point. "I don't know if it's a contributing factor here, but something I've seen at other small companies is systems that rely too much on specific people and not enough on the procedures themselves."

"And what's wrong with that?" asked Pete. "It seems to me that if there's a glitch in one of our procedures, it wouldn't be the end of the world if someone figured out how to work around it instead of taking up a lot of the time trying to fix it."

"Sure, but let me give you an example of why that can be a problem," said Rick. "I recently helped a company that was doing fine until their office manager was out three months for surgery and convalescence. While she was there, all was well;

without her, it was chaotic. Why? Because there were gaps in the system." Rick walked to the white board, picked up a marker, and wrote the following in big letters:

1. DESIGN
2. TRAINING
3. DISCIPLINE

"These three elements are all essential for success. Without them, the system will eventually fail. When we examine each system over the next few days, keep these three points in mind."

"We're really still just a small company," said Pete. "You're talking like we're a big company. If you look around this room," he said, sweeping a hand through the air in a lateral arc to indicate his colleagues, "you're basically looking at the company. The eight of us run everything. And now you say we're going to start having training sessions so our procedures will work? This ain't the navy, pal." His handsome face hardened as he clenched his jaw. He could barely contain his impatience.

"Tell me, Pete," said Rick. "Do you have a formal procedure for examining the support calls to identify common problems that might be addressed by R&D?"

"I already told you I have an informal procedure."

"And if you got run over by a truck this afternoon," Rick continued, "would this informal system die with you?"

"Well, yes, but that's rather extreme, isn't it?"

"Is it? Do you ever plan to take a vacation? When the workload increases, are you planning to hire anyone to help?"

"Well—" Pete started to say, hesitantly.

"Then we've already found at least one procedure that's not adequate."

"Sure," responded Pete quickly, "and that's why things are screwed up."

Rick ignored Pete's comment. "What you really need is to train some of your people to serve as backups. That would enable the system to exist independently of any single person. A system that works great only because of one particular person is not only too risky for the company; it's seldom able to handle more than a fixed level of transactions, so it inhibits the company's growth."

"So we have to develop training manuals for all our systems?" asked Rita.

"Let me answer that with a question. Do you have a written procedure for purchase orders?"

"Well, for the purchasing system we have some notes that Jerry and I jotted down when we set it up."

"Many small companies often have very little documentation for their procedures. Why do completed purchase orders go into a particular file? Nobody really remembers; that's just the way it's always been. It doesn't take a huge amount of time to write down the details of a procedure. Writing down the procedure is intrinsic to the design, which is step one. If you can't write it down in a concise fashion, you don't have a comprehensive system design. Once it's written down, it can be tested against all the exceptions that anyone can dream up, to make sure all contingencies have been considered. After it has been examined, tested, and modified, it can be accepted as established procedure and can be used for step two—training. And if you hire a new person, you already have exactly what they need to understand how the system works. So in answer to your question, no, you don't necessarily have to develop training manuals—if you already have comprehensive written procedures for each system."

"Well, we don't," grumbled Pete, "so we're going to have to stop what we're doing and write procedures—great."

Rick continued. "Without a written procedure, it also becomes very difficult to establish the third step, which is discipline. A system usually consists of several elements linked together, and a weak link can result in the system breaking down. So, someone has to insure that each piece is being handled as defined by the procedure."

"Instituting all these systems is for a different kind of company," Pete protested, "not the low-key company I joined two years ago."

"Come on, Pete, things change," said John. "Don't be so negative."

Rick added, "It often happens that as a company grows and changes, some people find they don't like the way it's changed. I urge every one of you to approach this rationally—to wait until you have enough information to decide whether or not the new Walpold Enterprises is to your liking. Some of you who feel that you wouldn't like working in a larger company may find that you like it after all."

His advice was greeted with silence. Everyone was deep in thought contemplating the "new" Walpold Enterprises, whatever that was.

Rick looked around. "My point is: Never get so set in your ways that you ignore the possibility of new ideas, new ways of looking at things, new perceptions. Sometimes it takes new perceptions to succeed, where the old perceptions are no longer adequate."

John noticed Dan slowly shaking his head and muttering something to Leonard, who rolled his eyes. He decided that this was a good time to end the meeting. "Rick and I will be meeting with everyone during the rest of the week. Our purpose will be to examine all of the systems and procedures we have and determine which if any need revamping. And let's be open-minded— our goal is not to place blame for problems in the past, but insure the future of Walpold Enterprises. Thanks for your patience."

When everyone but John had left, Rick said, "You've got problems with several people—more than I imagined. How sure are you of everyone's loyalty?"

"I guess it's different with everyone. I'd trust Joan with my life. The others—I think they're okay. I have some problems with Pete, but I don't think he's particularly devious."

"Do you know that from experience or just hope it? You'd be surprised what people will do when money is involved. But other than that, what are your thoughts about the meeting?"

"I'm wondering if we have the right people to survive as we grow, whether we'll survive until we can make changes, why Leonard is courting Dan's favor, and how much influence Leonard really has with Herb. Just little details like that, that's all."

*a*s Phyl and Leonard were walking down the hall after the meeting, she quietly said to him, "Okay, you're right. But what should we do? You know as well as I do that Herb isn't going to ante up the money to obtain majority control. I could never recommend that—the cost would be far too high. Maybe we should just recommend that he cut his losses and pull the plug."

"No way. We have to think of some way to either gain control or somehow get John out of the picture. We should work on Dan—maybe his thirty-three percent is available." He looked up and saw Dan walking toward him. "Hey Dan, how about having lunch with us now?"

"Sure. Let's go."

They drove in Leonard's BMW to Harold's Diner. During the trip, Phyl began the assault. "So, Dan, what did you think of the meeting?" she asked.

"A big waste of time, as far as I'm concerned. Were any problems solved? Or even discussed?"

Leonard asked him, "John didn't consult with you before he contracted with Rick, did he?"

"Why would he?"

"You own thirty-three percent of the company. Don't you think you should be participating in making decisions that might have a major impact on the company?"

"Yes and no," Dan responded. "My area is R&D. I've tried to stay out of anything involving finances. That's John's area, and I trust him to do what's right—at least, I have up until recently."

"Do you think he's been doing a good job?" asked Phyl, trying to sound sincere.

Dan considered this question before he responded. "Something is wrong, there's no question about it. And I guess since John is the guy in charge, the ultimate responsibility falls on him. But I'm certainly not the one to throw stones—I wouldn't have been able to do as good a job as John did getting us this far."

They arrived at the diner and sat down, and a waitress took their orders. Leonard asked Dan, "So tell us about this new product you've been working on."

Dan pulled the beeper off his belt and placed it on the table.

Leonard looked at him and said, "Beepers have been around a long time, Dan. What makes this one special?"

"When it goes off, it's not a person beeping me—it's my computer."

"Your computer can beep you?" asked Phyl.

"Yeah. And it can send me a message. Like to remind me of meetings or tell me that it just finished doing something. So, what do you think?"

"Have you discussed this product with John?" asked Leonard hesitantly.

"Yeah, I showed it to John yesterday when he was meeting with Rick."

"And what was his reaction?" asked Phyl.

"John said he didn't see how we could afford to put it into production right now. Rick asked a million questions about how it would fit in with our current products, stuff like that. I don't think they're too wild about it."

Leonard took a few moments to think and then said, "It looks like it might have a lot of possibilities. Does it work?"

"Yeah, it works. This is the prototype, but we could put it into production right now. Of course, the other part of it is the interface board that plugs into the computer. I have a prototype of that also."

"Maybe it's different enough from the other products that it should be produced by a different company," said Leonard tentatively.

"Another company? Where would I find another company that wanted to do it?"

"Not find one, start one. Get seed capital and set up a separate entity, just like you did with Walpold Enterprises."

"I wouldn't know how to do that. John handled all the financial stuff to get Walpold Enterprises started. I don't have any money, and I sure don't know where to get any."

"We do," said Phyl quickly, realizing the direction Leonard was heading. "If you're not interested in running it, I certainly would be. I think it's a fascinating idea."

"And where would the money come from?" asked Dan skeptically.

"From Herb, where else?" said Phyl. "If Leonard and I do a feasibility study and it still looks good, I'm sure Herb would want in on the ground floor. You could do the development, and I could take care of the details—hiring a staff, putting together the financial forecasts, and all the other basics. What do you think?"

"And you think Herb would provide the funding? Just like that?"

"Herb is always looking for promising new ideas. You're in better shape than most entrepreneurs, since you already have collateral to pledge," said Phyl.

"I do?"

"Sure, your Walpold Enterprises stock. Once the new company is profitable, you could pay back the note, regain control of the Walpold stock, and be a major owner in both companies. How does 'Killian, Inc.' sound?" she asked, stroking his ego.

"I don't care what it's called, I'd just like to get the pager to market. And you really think it would be that simple?"

"Sure," Leonard chimed in. "Herb sets up new companies all the time. This one certainly looks less risky than many of them." Then, changing his tone, he added, "Why don't we keep this under our hats until we've had a chance to do our homework and talk to Herb. Okay?''

"I suppose," said Dan, feeling a little duplicitous.

When they returned to the office, Dan was eager to get back to the lab to resume work on his computer pager. Leonard and Phyl went to the break room for coffee. It was deserted.

"This will be easier than I thought," said Leonard. "You can tend Dan's little company, I'll run this one, and down the road we'll merge them. The cost to Herb will be peanuts compared to exercising his option to gain control. We're geniuses!"

"Let's get ownership positions in the new company at the outset," Phyl added. "That way we can trade it for Walpold stock, and when Herb decides to take it public, we'll make a nice killing."

Just then the door to the break room opened and Joan came in, so they quickly shifted to a safer topic.

*b*eth was puttering in the kitchen, adding the final touches to dinner when John got home that evening. He went straight to the liquor cabinet. "Want a drink?" he asked.

"Sure." She and John frequently discussed the day's events over a drink before their sons tore themselves away from their after-school activities and came in for dinner.

John grabbed two cocktail glasses from the cupboard and took several bottles from the liquor cabinet. He put some ice in each glass and then poured a small shot of vodka into one and filled it with tonic for Beth. He filled his about halfway with rye and added enough sweet vermouth to make a proper Manhattan—a very large one. He handed Beth her drink and leaned back onto the counter as he sloshed the ice around in his glass.

"I heard on the radio that Hurricane Erin's headed this way," said Beth. "It's expected to hit land near Melbourne sometime tonight and be here early tomorrow."

"Really? Remember Andrew in '92—when we were preparing the presentation to Herb? I hope it's not a repeat. Maybe we'll just get some high winds and ten inches of rain. So how was your day?"

"Nothing unusual, I guess. Did you have your big meeting with everyone?"

He nodded and said, "Yeah."

Beth waited for him to continue, but he just stared vacantly into his glass. "So how did it go?"

"Okay, I guess."

"Try to contain your enthusiasm," she said, trying to get a reaction, but without any success. "What happened—did the troops mutiny and make you walk the plank? Come on John, tell me what happened."

"The meeting wasn't too bad. It went about like I'd expected it would. In the middle of it, Leonard made it pretty clear that he's planning to take over as CEO."

"But how can he do that? I thought you said Herb's ownership wouldn't increase until you had to borrow more money."

"Yeah, but Leonard seems to be trying to win Dan's favor, and the only reason he would do that is to gain control of Dan's stock. If Dan sides with Herb, I'm finished."

"Can't you talk to Dan and convince him that he'd be making a big mistake?"

"He may have a real incentive to do it. He has a new product he wants to introduce, and I'll bet Leonard's been offering him backing for it. But I have to agree with Rick—it doesn't seem like a product that's logical for us right now."

"What is it?"

"A computer paging system, of all things. You can have your computer page you to remind you of meetings, tell you when it's finished with a specific task—things like that."

"Sounds kind of neat. What's wrong with developing it?"

"I'm sure we could produce it, but I'm not sure if it would be a hot seller or not. Rick says it might be just another solution desperately searching for a problem. And it would need a separate marketing strategy. I haven't had enough time to make up my mind about it." John set his empty glass on the counter and mixed another drink. "I'm drinking too much," he thought, but he poured it anyway.

"It sounds quite a bit different from the other products. You and Dan started Walpold Enterprises because R.S.S. wouldn't listen to your ideas about a product that was different from the ones they were making. But you put together an analysis showing that it was logical to move ahead with it. Why wouldn't you do the same thing with this one?"

"Hmm. Maybe you're right. Maybe I've got blinders on just like the management at R.S.S. did. It certainly complicates things, though. I would much rather not have to deal with it and concentrate entirely on getting things organized. But if I don't, and Dan jumps ship, I could lose control of the company."

"Sounds like a simple decision to me—you have to deal with it. Any other problem I can solve for you before dinner?"

WEdNESDAy

August 2, 1995

*J*ohn's forecast for Erin was wrong—the storm had reached hurricane force and hit land in the middle of the night and then proceeded directly toward Orlando. By morning, the streets were littered with debris, and the eighty-five-mile-per-hour wind and rain were raging at 6:30 as John was driving to work. The sky was still pitch black. It was a grim scene with great potential for destruction. "Reminds me of what's happening to my company," John thought as he swerved to miss a garbage can that was tumbling across the street.

He and Rick had agreed to meet at nine, and he'd wanted to get to the office early to go over the financial analysis that Rick had prepared and to think about Tuesday's meeting. At 7:30 he went to the break room to get a second cup of coffee and, upon returning to his office, found himself staring at the Mexican travel poster hanging over the file cabinet as he sipped the hot coffee. At first, his thoughts carried him into a fantasy of living the high life on a leisurely Mexican vacation, of relaxing with Beth at a luxurious seaside resort, and traveling around the country to see the colorful sights. What a pleasure it would be to immerse himself in Mexico's history and escape into the past. No pressures, no worries. But then his eyes focused again on the poster, which showed an arena full of people watching a bullfight, and his fantasy of comfort and relaxation suddenly turned into a frightening image of a bloody bullfight in which he was the bull, and it was his blood that was being shed. He took a deep breath and pulled himself together. "I'm not losing this company," he thought. "I won't let it happen—I put too much into it." He took another sip of his coffee, strode back to his desk, and resumed making notes for his meeting with Rick.

Rick arrived punctually at nine, carrying a box of donuts. "Nothing like a blatant attempt to bribe the troops," he said jokingly, setting the box on the conference table in John's office.

"Some storm, huh? The eye is passing over us right now—the sky is clear and the wind has stopped, but I guess it'll start up again within an hour."

"My yard is knee-deep in palm fronds," said John. "I wish the trailing edge of the storm would blow away the mess so I don't have to do it. Fat chance."

"That's life in the tropics," said Rick. "Are you ready to start?"

"I suppose so. You've been talking about how this company has outgrown some of the procedures we've been using, and I've been thinking that maybe it's also outgrown some of the people. I'm wondering if I should make some personnel changes."

"You're obviously thinking about someone in particular. Who is it?"

"You saw how negative and confrontational Pete was in yesterday's meeting. He's always like that. If he's not going to be happy working here as we grow, maybe it would be better if he left now."

"What about his work? Is he effective? Is he aware that you're not happy with his attitude? Have you formally reprimanded him and documented it with a letter in his personnel folder?"

"No, but we need team players, don't we? If he's not going to go along with what we're doing and participate enthusiastically in this company's growth, wouldn't it be better for everyone else if he just found himself another small company?"

"You should be the judge of that. I don't know your employees well enough to tell you who should be working here and who shouldn't be, but I will say that I haven't seen any obvious candidates for firing. You know, if you look at the characteristics of all truly effective managers, you'll find some common threads. One is that they replace people less frequently than lousy managers. A failure of someone to perform is also the failure of the manager who wasn't been able to properly train and motivate employees. I've seen many 'revolving door' companies where one employee after another has been fired.

These companies are run by managers who always blame someone else for the things that go wrong. They can always tell you exactly how the people they fired had let them down. And in no time at all they'll have another scapegoat and be ready to fire him or her at a moment's notice.''

"Well, I really think that Pete might be happier at a smaller company.''

"Is he really a problem, or are you concerned that he might become a problem? Could it possibly be that it bothers you that he doesn't accept your views without question, and that makes you uncomfortable?''

John couldn't deny that Pete's attitude bothered him. When he started Walpold Enterprises, he became accustomed to everyone treating him with deference. But Pete was always questioning decisions. "I suppose there's some truth in what you're saying,'' John reluctantly admitted.

"Right now, I'd recommend that you give Pete a chance. Don't forget, you hired him in the first place because you thought he was the best one for the job. Both you and Pete will have to accept changes in the company to operate effectively as the company grows. But let's focus on Pete. What function did you hire him to perform?''

"Tech support—to take customers' calls, help them figure out the source of their problem, and get them up and running. Basically, to keep the customers happy.''

"And is there a system in place to support his efforts?''

"A system? You mean a written procedure for taking phone calls and sending people parts? Why in hell would we need anything written down for that?''

"Didn't I hear last week about parts not being shipped when they were promised? And—''

"Yeah, but that was just because Joan had to go and see her lawyer, and she forgot to take care of a few details when she got back. Normally a screw-up like that doesn't occur.''

"Fine,'' responded Rick. "Normally it doesn't occur. The fact that it did just illustrates a point I made at yesterday's meeting: Some of your systems work only because certain people make them work. And the failure certainly wasn't a result of Pete's attitude. If every procedure is properly designed and administered, events like that won't occur. Don't do anything hasty about Pete, and in the meantime we'll give Tech Support a thorough review. Okay?"

"Okay," John conceded. "Do you want to start with that now?"

"No, I think we should begin by focusing on the procedures you've been using to control the flow of funds."

"You mean Marie?"

"Yes, Marie. What was her job description when you hired her?"

"She had her own bookkeeping service back then, and she started out working for us on a part-time basis. Pretty soon the work increased, so we talked her in to coming on full-time."

"So what was her job description?"

"Bookkeeping stuff, like I said," John answered curtly. "Paying the bills, doing the payroll, keeping the bank accounts reconciled, putting together the information the accountant needs—stuff like that."

"Do you ever ask her anything other than what the bank balance is?"

"No. What else could she tell me?"

"Large companies have a chief financial officer with a staff of people who prepare financial statements and other management reports. Small companies have a bookkeeper who just pays bills. When does a company graduate to a level where a bill payer isn't enough? The reason many small companies only have a bill payer is that they don't think they can afford any more than that, a perception that is usually wrong. The information that the 'bill payer' can provide can be very useful, and it isn't expensive, now that computers and good software are so cheap."

"I bought computers for practically everyone, including Marie, but she hasn't done much with it, even though Joan's brother-in-law wrote a program to help her keep track of billing," said John.

"Let's start by discussing her job function with her, and we'll see where things go from there."

"Oh, one other thing," said John as Rick stood up. "Dan's idea about a new product concerns me. I think we ought to think seriously about developing it."

"In the midst of everything else going on, you want to introduce a new product that's radically different from all your current products? Care to elaborate?"

"Well, I mentioned that Dan owns one third of Walpold Enterprises. If he decides that siding with Herb is more logical than voting with me, I'll lose control."

"Aha. So you're worried that Dan liked what Leonard said to him at the meeting yesterday, and you think you'll preempt Leonard with your own show of support?"

"I just know that with the way things are now, we can't afford to simply dismiss Dan's idea outright. If we develop an analysis of his product just like we did for our first products, it might convince him that this is not the time to proceed, or it might convince us that it's a good idea. Who knows?"

"Suppose the analysis shows that it's logical to proceed, but you don't have sufficient funding right now, and then Herb agrees to fund it as a separate business. Dan would have his own company and would be free to tinker to his heart's content, and you would have lost your voting ally."

This thought hit John in the pit of his stomach. He reached into his pocket for a Tums and popped one into his mouth. If he ignored Dan's new idea, he would surely lose Dan's support. But if he proceeded, and it turned out he couldn't fund the new development, he would lose Dan's support anyway. "Let's start the analysis and see what it looks like. We can decide what to do when we have more facts. Step One is to convince Dan that we aren't going to ignore him. I'll schedule a meeting with him to discuss it. Do you want to be involved?"

"Sure, just let me know when you want to meet."

"Okay. Now, shall I call Marie?"

"Nope. I think it would be better if we went to her office first to start things off. And how about asking Jerry to have lunch with us? I think he's going to need some stroking."

"Good idea. I'll give Jerry a call and catch up with you in a few minutes."

After Rick left, John called Jerry and invited him to join them for lunch. John noticed that Jerry's responses sounded a little strained. Then, on his way to Marie's office, he decided to stop by Dan's office to set up a meeting to discuss the 'miraculous computer pager.' Dan wasn't there, and it didn't appear that he was in yet, since the light in his office was off and so was his computer. He turned on the light and went in to leave him a note. As he approached Dan's desk, he saw that there was already a note on it from someone else:

Dan—

Just as Phyl & I expected, Herb is very interested in your computer pager. He wants to meet with you and discuss the funding requirements at your earliest convenience. When can we all get together?

—Leonard

"Swell," thought John, "the end-run has already begun." He walked out of Dan's office, deep in thought, and headed toward Marie's.

*i*n the meantime, Rick had gone to Marie's office. Her office was small, just barely big enough for her desk and chair, a table for her computer, a large gray filing cabinet, and two chairs for visitors. On her desk, Rick noticed, were several photographs of kids—her own?—but none of an adult male, and Rick wondered if she was divorced. Or maybe the kids were nieces and nephews. Her desk was very orderly, with all the papers organized in neat stacks, and on her table were several file folders in a vertical rack. Marie had a checkbook and bank statement open in front of her, and, with a pencil in her right hand and a calculator at her left hand, was attempting to reconcile them. As usual, her hair was pulled back in a ponytail. She looked up as Rick came in.

"How's it going?" he asked.

Marie removed her glasses and let them hang from the metal chain around her neck. "Have you solved all the world's problems yet?" she countered. Before he could say anything, she told him, "I'm reconciling this bank statement. With as many checks as I write, it's not that simple."

"John tells me that Joan's brother-in-law put together a computer program to help. Do you ever use it?"

"Ben knows an awful lot about computers, I suppose, but he obviously doesn't know what 'user-friendly' means. The program he gave me is supposed to help us keep track of the checks and also how much we're spending on different things, and I guess it would; but after I match the invoices with the packing slips and write the checks, I don't have time to enter the data into the computer. Even though I'm several months behind right now, it's hard to justify taking the time to enter the old data. And Ben's program doesn't make it easy. Based on several computer magazine reviews I read, I bought this new software program," she said, pointing to an unopened package near the computer. "I'm sure it's better, but I just haven't had time to install it and familiarize myself with how it works."

"Why don't you give me a quick demo of what Ben's software does?" Just then John came in. Rick looked up and said, "Marie was just about to show me the software that Ben put on her computer to track the checks."

"It's a joke," said Marie as she swiveled her chair around to face her computer. The menu on the screen contained several items, one of which was CHECK PROCESSING. Marie selected this option, and the program quickly loaded and displayed a new menu with the items ENTER CHECKS, EDIT CHECKS, RUN REPORTS, and

BACKUP DATA. Marie selected the first item; the screen cleared and a data-entry screen appeared, showing four rows titled DATE, PAYEE, AMOUNT, MEMO. Along the bottom of the screen was a list of the computer-function keys and the operation that could be selected by each.

"Looks pretty straightforward," said Rick. "What's wrong with it? If you could make improvements, what would you change or add?"

"The main improvement is to leave it turned off," she said contemptuously. "As for changes—I wouldn't know where to start. Writing the checks is important, but it's only a small piece of my job. Ben may be a computer expert, but he doesn't know shit about bookkeeping. He assumes that it's a batch processing job, so once the batch is entered, it has to be posted before the results show up on the bank balance. According to the articles I read, the new program I bought continually shows you the balance, and entries can be edited and changed any time you want. It also speeds up data entry by prompting you with previously made entries, another feature that Ben's program doesn't have. I could go on and on."

"You mean the money I spent on Ben was wasted?" said John.

"As far as I'm concerned, it was," she answered.

"There's a big difference between defining and writing a program," Rick agreed. "Before Ben installed this program, did he sit down with you and go over everything you do in this job?"

"No. I think he viewed giving John more data about our expenses to be the real purpose of his program. This other software will provide all the data anyone could need, and it's much easier to use. I just need to install it and get it up and running. But John, you've never asked me for any information about expenses or P&L or anything like that."

Before John could respond, Rick said, "Why don't you give us a short description of how you process orders and write the checks?"

"Okay. I usually write checks once a week." Pointing to the file folders neatly stacked on her table, she said, "The folder on the left contains purchase orders." She pulled it over to her and opened it up. "Each purchase order has to be approved by John and, if it's not, I don't put it in this folder. In fact, when Rita brings me a copy of a purchase order that isn't signed, I just throw it away. Sometimes she says that she already placed the order anyway because Jerry told her he had to have it and that John would sign it later, but I still won't write a check for it." She turned to John again. "You sent out a memo months ago that said I shouldn't pay for anything that you haven't approved, and I work for you, not Rita. So this folder has the signed purchase orders waiting to be paid. The next folder has packing slips that I haven't matched with purchase orders yet. And the third folder is the approved purchase orders with packing slips, ready for checks to be written. There is more to paying bills than writing and mailing checks."

"Do you keep a list of payables?" asked Rick.

"I try to figure it out each month because Cal Reilly says he needs it. It takes a while to come up with it, and since it comes from the folders I just showed you, I don't know how accurate it really is. I think that part of the problem with our vendors is that the paperwork gets lost, and I can't pay anything until I have all the pieces. Last week, Rita told me that Consolidated was pressing us for payment, but according to my records, we were current with them. If Sean loses the packing slip, there's no way I'll ever know if something has arrived, so it doesn't get paid for."

"Who's Sean?" asked Rick.

"You haven't met Sean Davis yet?" she asked.

"He's my nephew," said John.

"I suppose he's a nice boy," Marie continued hesitantly, "but I'm not sure he takes his job seriously. He works in Receiving for Jerry, but I think he feels that his only boss is his Uncle John—when he's actually working, that is. He's also taking a few classes at the community college. Anyway, if he doesn't bring me a packing slip, I can't close out the purchase order and send a check."

It was clear to Rick why Marie didn't feel like wasting time entering checks into the computer. Checks weren't late because she was inefficient but because the purchasing system had broken down. This would be very easy to remedy and wouldn't require much of a change on Marie's part. She was correct in her assessment that Ben's software would only be a distraction. If John had given her any encouragement at all, she probably would have already solved her problem by installing the new program. John's only support had been the gift of what she rightly considered worthless software. Coupled with his protection of Sean, who Marie perceived as the weak link in the system, it made her job very difficult. Rather than try to explain to John why she wanted to abandon Ben's program in favor of a different program, she chose to ignore the issue and just do the best she could manually.

"John," said Rick, "Ben evidently didn't taken into consideration everything Marie does. His program is organized around providing information for management and gives short shrift to helping Marie with her day-to-day responsibilities. This is clearly a case of software attacking the wrong problem."

John felt like an outsider during this interchange. Now that he heard Marie's complaints, Ben's software seemed very inadequate. He was embarrassed that he hadn't realized it sooner—but then, he'd never paid any attention to it before. "No wonder I've lost the respect of my key people," he thought. "I've become so detached from the day-to-day operation that I must seem incompetent to them." He turned to Marie and said apologetically, "I'm sorry I haven't given you the support you need. From now on, things will be different, I promise you. For starters, I want you to get rid of Ben's program and install the new one and then make it a priority to enter a few months' data into it."

"Yes," said Rick. "We can really use the information that will generate. As soon as all the data is entered, we should get a report prepared showing the distribution of the expenses and another on aged payables."

"What would you have to let slide in order to do that?" asked John.

"What about the lost packing slips?" she said, realizing that automating the books wouldn't solve the whole problem.

"Don't worry about that," said John quickly. "Just get the software installed, and I'll guarantee the packing slips don't get lost."

"Actually," Rick interjected, "we need to spend some time with Rita to work the bugs out of the entire purchase-order system, and then—"

"Wait a minute," Marie interrupted. "I was involved in the development of the purchase-order system we're using now, and I don't want changes being made in it without my input. I don't want to end up with another system that doesn't take everything into consideration."

"Of course," said John. "You're right. I'll set something up. In the meantime, how long will it take you to get your software going?"

"Are you sure this is the right time to start?"

"Absolutely," John said. "How long will it take?"

Marie tried to think of all the different tasks she had to do that week.

"Let me put it another way," he added. "When can you have it up and running without sacrificing something else?"

"Today is Wednesday. I should be able to get a couple of months entered by the end of the week. That's assuming that I don't have to stop in the middle to do something else."

"Like working on the purchase-order system?" asked Rick with a smile.

"I don't want to work on it—I just want to review whatever's being considered so that nothing gets overlooked. That won't take long. I can do that *and* get the data entered unless you also want me to compile a current list of payables, which the software will do for us anyway once it's running."

"No, you won't have to do anything else," said John. "But maybe you should hire someone part-time to help get the data entered."

"That won't be necessary. I can handle it. But what about Leonard?"

"What do you mean?" asked John.

"When he was in here, he acted like he's in charge or will be shortly. And he was very impatient with me, as though he was just tolerating me until he could replace me."

What Leonard was doing, John realized, was trying to bring his company to a halt. What better way to force a change than to predict doom and then guarantee that the worst happens by derailing the company's key functions. The company was like a ticking bomb that he was frantically trying to defuse, while Leonard was running around setting small brush fires.

"Forget about Leonard," said John. "Leonard isn't in charge now and never will be," he stated with finality.

Marie considered what John said for a moment and then grabbed the package, slit the shrink wrap with a letter opener, and spread the manuals and disks out in front of her. "Okay, you guys, beat it so I can finish the bank reconciliation and get started with this thing."

"We're outta here," said John as he and Rick headed toward the door. Before they left, she was already deeply engrossed in her task.

*W*hen they were in the hallway, John said to Rick, "It seems pretty clear that the purchase-order system has broken down. We should meet with Rita after lunch and try to figure it out."

Just then, they saw Leonard, Dan, and Pete together at the end of the hallway. Leonard was talking animatedly, with Dan and Pete listening intently. "Why don't you see what's going on down there," said John. "I'll wait for you in my office, and we'll go to lunch with Jerry." With that, John hurried off to his office.

When the group saw Rick approach, they quickly lowered their voices, and Dan and Pete scurried away together. Leonard approached Rick, and after looking around to see that no one else was near, said "I've been meaning to have a talk with you. Got a second?"

"I'm on my way to have lunch with John and Jerry but sure, what's on your mind?"

"I just thought we ought to have a meeting of the minds, consultant to consultant. It's obvious that this company's headed down the tubes if drastic steps aren't taken to save it. Herb has the resources to hold it together while I patch things up. And I'm sure I'll be needing some assistance, if you're interested."

"I'll bet," thought Rick. He had qualms about joining forces with Leonard, but he'd been in business too long to know that bridges should never be burned. Control of a company often shifts, and he didn't want to end up on the losing side. However, John might still be able to keep control of the company if the cash crunch could be overcome. At this point, it was too close to call. "What kind of assistance are you considering?"

"You name it. We'll probably need a CFO at least part-time, possibly full-time, and if you're interested, we could establish a long-term relationship. With me as CEO and you as CFO, we could do great things with this company."

"What about Phyl? If you end up as CEO, couldn't she handle the CFO functions?"

"She could, but I have a feeling she'll be tied up with something else."

"He's trying to buy me off!" thought Rick. He wondered what Leonard wanted in return. "Isn't it a little premature to be making plans? I thought John and Dan had control."

"Yeah, but that could change real fast. Herb doesn't need much more incentive to make his move—and your support might do it. Let me arrange a meeting for the two of you, so you can give him the lowdown on what's happening here."

Rick knew from Leonard's suggestion that he was worried about convincing Herb and needed some extra ammo. "If I provide it," he thought, "I might end up with a lucrative consulting contract working for this twit. If I don't provide it and he wins anyway, I lose it all." He told Leonard, "I'm really not prepared for a meeting yet. Why not wait a few days until we both know more?"

Instead of answering, Leonard asked, "What do you think of Dan's computer pager idea?"

"I'm probably the wrong person to ask. Among my many commercial misjudgments, I thought gas-powered leaf blowers for suburban homeowners would flop in the marketplace, but several companies have made a fortune with them."

"I think Dan's pager has great commercial potential. Everybody has a computer these days, and lots of people already have memory resident programs running in the background that pop up to remind them of meetings. The pager would just be an extension of that."

"Maybe you're right," said Rick. "But do you really think this company can afford to launch a new product that's so different from their existing product line at a time when cash is so scarce?"

"Of course not. But Phyl and I are thinking about putting together a business plan for it as a stand-alone venture. I'm pretty sure I could convince Herb to provide the initial funding. What would you think about helping and possibly getting a chunk of equity in a new company that we would form to develop and market it?"

Rick wondered why Leonard wanted his support so badly. If it turned out that the pager became the next hot item in the computer marketplace, it could make millions for its developers. He told Leonard, "After I take care of a few things, I might be free to consider other opportunities. Would you mind if I put off my decision for a few days?"

"Well, let's not wait too long. Time is money. And if Herb decides to move without your input, naturally I'll be less inclined to consider your involvement in the future. Get my drift?'' Without waiting for an answer, he turned and left.

*m*arie decided to get her lunch from the refrigerator in the break room and eat it in her office while she was working on the installation of the new software. She found Rita in the break room emptying her coffee cup and washing it out. Rita had a worried look on her face.

"What's the matter, Rita? You and Pete having problems?'' asked Marie.

"No, I'm just concerned about what's going on around here. John is acting like everything will be okay if we just make a few changes, but I'm scared of what Leonard's been doing.''

"Yeah, I've seen his type before, and he scares me too,'' said Marie. "If he convinces Herb that things are too screwed up, I'm betting Herb will force John out.''

"I hate to see anything happen to John,'' said Rita. "When he hired me, I didn't have that much experience, but he gave me a chance. I'm afraid if he's not around, his successor might decide to replace me with someone with a lot more experience.''

"Purchasing isn't a problem—I can't imagine why anyone would attack you. But what about me? Usually the first act of a new general manager is replacing the controller. If John goes, I'll be the most vulnerable, and I just bought a new house. And it would take me months to build a new stable of clients. Of course, the way things have been going, we're all pretty vulnerable—we're not exactly flush with cash, you know.''

"I know, but we've always managed to scrape by,'' said Rita.

"Hope springs eternal,'' Marie said, shaking her head.

Just then, Pete stuck his head in the door. "Oh there you are,'' he said to Rita. "Ready to get some chow? Want to join us Marie?''

"I was planning to work through lunch but what the hell—it'll wait. Sure, where are you headed?''

*a*s Rick walked to John's office, he wondered what was going on. Why would Pete have been involved in the discussion with Leonard and Dan if he wasn't also being courted? And Rick could think of no reason to involve Pete, other than to further disrupt the existing organization. How could anyone withstand such an attack? John's chances for survival seemed to be getting dimmer and dimmer.

When Rick reached John's office, he found Jerry already standing outside, waiting for John to get off the phone. In spite of the air conditioning, Jerry was perspiring. He held a damp white handkerchief in his hand and periodically used it to wipe the sweat from his forehead and balding head. "He'll probably be a few minutes." said Jerry. "He just started talking to Mike Smith."

"The company's attorney?"

"Yeah, he's an old college buddy of John's. They're really good friends, and I doubt they're talking business, so if you want to stick your head in and tell him we're here, he probably won't mind."

"That's okay. I wanted to talk to you about something anyway. Tell me about Sean."

Jerry frowned. "Sean Davis, John's nephew. He works in Receiving, or at least that's where he spends most of his time."

"Does he report to you?"

"Supposedly, but only because his Uncle John had me hire him. He's a nice kid most of the time, and he's had a lot of problems, but he would never get away with what he does if he weren't John's nephew."

"Like what?"

"Well, his hours, for one thing. He should be here from seven-thirty to four-thirty, but he usually strolls in around eight-thirty, saying he had an errand to run or was up late studying—he always has an excuse."

"What about when he's here?"

"Haven't you seen him riding the parts cart around the floor? If I say anything to him, he tells me to lighten up. Last week I needed him to take a box of spares to the airport, but I couldn't find him. I ended up doing it myself. That's about the way it works. For the time it takes to find him and get him to do something, it's easier to just do it myself."

"Have you discussed this with John?"

"Every time I bring it up, he tells me to go easy on the kid because he's had a hard time. John's sister went through a real messy divorce a few years ago, and Sean turned into a real discipline problem and almost flunked out of high school. John has sort of taken him under his wing. He encouraged him to finish high school and start taking courses at the community college, and he gave him a job here. He's more trouble than he's worth, in my opinion, but getting John to focus on something like that at the moment is impossible."

Just then, John finished his telephone conversation with Mike and got up to join them. "You should have told me you were waiting. Mike and I were just talking about his latest girlfriend. Incidentally, Dan can meet with us late this afternoon, Rick." He grabbed his coat and put it on as they walked to the front door. Passing Wendy, he said to her, "We'll be at lunch. If anybody's looking for me, I'll be back around one." She popped her gum and nodded in response.

Rick offered to drive, so they walked to his Jeep Cherokee in the parking lot. The eye of the hurricane had passed, and the high winds were beginning to pick up again. There were some palm fronds and tree branches down in the lot, but the local radio station reported that the roads were still clean. As they climbed into Rick's Jeep, John said, "Nice car. I wouldn't mind having one of these. My family makes fun of my van, but I don't know what I'd do without the carrying space."

During the drive, John asked Rick if he was familiar with the software that Marie had bought, and Jerry said, "I've got a friend that uses it. He says it's great. Why don't I just get a copy of it from him? She could take the one she bought back to the store and get a refund, couldn't she?"

"That would be great," said John. "Anything we can do to save a buck."

"Actually," said Rick, not bothering to mention that Marie had already opened the package and probably had it installed by now, "that might not be a good idea. You should own and register your own copy."

"Hey now," John protested, "you're not one of those software piracy fanatics, are you?"

"I suppose I am. It's unethical and illegal to use someone else's copy of a software product. But more importantly, when you buy your own copy, in addition to the disks you get documentation, support, and, usually, price breaks on upgrades. Most publishers provide some type of phone support if problems arise, which you won't have access to if you aren't a registered user. And even though most software has extensive built-in 'Help' features, you'll want to have the reference manuals for training purposes. There'll always be new people coming into the company, especially as it grows, and they'll need to be trained."

They hurried through the pouring rain when they arrived at the restaurant and settled themselves into a booth. After they ordered, John said, "Jerry, while we were talking to Marie this morning, we discovered that she was withholding payment to some of the vendors because of missing paperwork. It seems there's a glitch in our procedure for processing purchase orders."

"The procedure is fine. Like I said yesterday, it's similar to the one we used at Avcom."

"Marie said something about some missing packing slips," said Rick.

"Well, the procedure depends on everybody doing his part. When a box arrives, if the packing slip is misplaced, the system breaks down. Not much I can do about that."

John answered sharply, "You have control over everything related to production. I've told you that before, haven't I?"

Jerry kept his mouth shut. He knew that if he said anything just then, his temper would get him into trouble. After a few seconds of silence, Rick calmly said, "Jerry is in the uncomfortable position of having the boss's nephew working for him. What sort of control does he actually have, John?"

"Hmm," said John, as he scratched random lines into the place mat with his fork, "I just figured anybody could handle Receiving. It never occurred to me that Sean would screw it up. It'll make my sister unhappy, but I guess I'd better get rid of him before he does any more harm."

"Not necessarily," said Rick. "Maybe if you tell Sean that Jerry is his boss and will fire him if he doesn't shape up, he might get it together. But that means you can't intercede on his behalf. Having responsibility without authority is a frustrating position to be in. If Jerry is responsible for Receiving, it's important that he have the authority to control it. If you're willing to fire Sean, then you've got nothing to lose by giving Jerry a shot at him first."

"That's true. Okay, I'll do it. I'll tell him as soon as I get back this afternoon."

"So that means I can treat him just like everyone else? He has to work regular hours and quit goofing off?"

"Yeah, and if he doesn't, you can fire him, and he'll stay fired. Since he's still in school, though, he probably can't work a regular shift every weekday, so why not set up a realistic schedule with him, Jerry. And tell him to report to you whenever he leaves and returns. Also, you need to explain to him that the system breaks down when he makes a mistake. But let's not penalize him for his past sins, okay? Treat him like today is his first day of employment and see how he does. Tell him that in thirty days his performance will be reviewed, and a decision will be made whether to keep him or replace him with someone else. And I'll make it clear that I support you, so there'll be no reason for him to believe he can run to me to save him."

Just then, the waitress brought their lunch. They stopped talking only long enough to take the first bites of their food and then continued.

John turned to Jerry and casually asked, "By the way Jerry, did you mention anything to Leonard about the purchase order for the workbenches that I was holding?"

"You mean the workbenches Dan wanted? No, after I got your E-mail message, I sent a message back to you and forgot about it. Why?"

"Oh, I was just curious." John concluded that if Jerry didn't tell Leonard, he must have heard about it from Dan, but why would Dan have mentioned it?

"Speaking of Leonard," said Jerry, "this morning he and Phyl were asking me about the expertise of the assemblers. Phyl wanted to know if they had been trained only to build the current products or if they were capable of building a variety of products. Why would she ask me a question like that? Are they planning on funneling other products through our assembly line?"

Rick looked at John and said nothing. "Who knows what they're thinking," John responded, shaking his head. "What did you tell them?"

"I explained that they are all very experienced assemblers and could probably do anything but that they're already fully utilized. What's going on?"

"What's going on," thought Rick, "is that Phyl is planning to steal assemblers to jump-start production of Dan's pager."

"Leonard and Phyl seem to have their own agenda," said John, "and they haven't shared it with me. I think Leonard is trying to stir everyone up, so don't let him upset you. Just worry about production, and let me worry about those two kids. If they ask you anything that requires too much of your time, let me know. Otherwise, just give them the information they want, and maybe they'll stay out of your hair. Okay?"

"I guess so," said Jerry.

They started talking about baseball, and there was no more talk of business for the rest of the meal.

*b*ack in John's office after lunch, John said to Rick, "So what were my partner and my young Tech Support manager talking about with Leonard at the end of the hallway before lunch?"

"I don't know. They scattered when they saw me, except for Leonard, and he didn't tell me much. Something's cooking between him and Dan, but I'm not sure how far along it is."

"That's what I figured—that Leonard is working behind my back to lure Dan away. I saw a note that Leonard had written to Dan about backing his new invention. And when I asked Dan to meet with us to discuss his pager, he tried to get out of it but finally agreed. I wonder if I should tell him that I know what's going on."

Rick thought for a moment and then said, "There's probably nothing to be gained by that. Better to play it cool. After all, you know what they say—knowledge is power."

"Yeah, let's just play it by ear and see how much Dan tells us. Now, let's go work on the purchase-order system. We seem to be making progress. We got Marie set in the right direction this morning, and we made Jerry happy at lunch."

"Actually, at the risk of bursting your bubble, I wouldn't say Jerry's fine. To be perfectly honest, I get the impression that he's just tolerating you."

"You're kidding! How could that be?"

"Look at things from *his* standpoint. In his eyes, you've shown very little interest in his part of the operation—"

"I was leaving him alone, letting him do his job. That's not lack of interest."

"Possibly not, but like I said, look at it from his point of view. To him, it looks like you're not involved, and he interprets that as lack of interest. At a time like this, you need everyone's support. My concern is that others might have the same opinion but are being less vocal about it than Jerry and Pete have been. Even Marie seemed a little edgy to me."

John got angry. "These people wouldn't have their jobs if it weren't for me. It's because of my sacrifices that—"

"John," Rick interrupted, "you're familiar with the 'What have you done for me lately' syndrome? Sure you got the place started, but it's unrealistic to expect the people who work for you to be grateful to you for that forever. I think you've got two problems: The company's running amok, and you've lost the confidence of your staff."

John thought about what Rick was saying and realized that it would take more than a few minor adjustments to turn his company around. He'd let things get so bad that it was no wonder his employees were dissatisfied with him.

Rick looked at John as he sat across from him and watched him deflate. "John, there are things you can do to improve your relationships with your employees. Listening to what they have to say, considering their opinions, convincing them that you're concerned about their problems, really paying attention to them rather than just occasionally waltzing in to see what's happening—once you make the effort, you'll see an immediate improvement. You just need to reconnect with your staff."

John pondered this idea. "Why don't you go get started with Rita, and I'll catch up with you in a few minutes," he finally said.

After Rick left, John continued to sit there, thinking about what Rick had said. Maybe in his quest to avoid being a micromanager, he had gone too far in the other direction. He wasn't detached—or was he? It could certainly be interpreted as detachment, he decided. But how can you not be detached without appearing to be a micromanager? Do you meddle part of the time to let everyone know you're involved, then leave them alone so they can actually get something done? Well, there must be a way, he finally concluded, and he'd have to figure it out. He took a deep breath, stood up, stretched, and headed for Rita's office.

*W*hen Rick got to Rita's office, Pete was there talking to her, standing next to her desk and bending over so that his face was directly in front of hers, blocking her view. He was speaking in a tone too low for Rick to hear, but when he heard Rita ask, "How much stock?" he decided he'd better announce his entrance.

When he knocked, both of them looked up with a startled expression. "Sorry to interrupt," he said.

"I was just leaving anyway," said Pete, straightening up and heading for the door. "See you at five," he said to Rita. She smiled and waved at him as he walked out. Her office was larger than Marie's and included a bookcase filled with product catalogues. There were only a few stacks of papers on her desk, all neatly organized. Next to her desk was a table that had on it a computer and several healthy-looking plants. On the wall were several framed prints of landscapes that Rick recognized as Santa Fe and the surrounding area.

Rita wore a fashionable black suit, a bright pink silk blouse, and large gold hoop earrings. Not a hair on her head was out of place, and her makeup was flawless. Her face was still slightly flushed from embarrassment at having been interrupted during what must have been a rather private conversation with Pete. She tilted her head slightly and said, "Please sit down."

Rick was curious about what she and Pete had been discussing but knew it would be better at this point not to mention what he'd heard. "This morning when John and I were talking to Marie, we discovered that Sean's been causing some of the vendor problems by misplacing packing slips. When he does that, Marie doesn't know the parts have arrived, so she doesn't pay for them. That's a discipline problem, and we're working on a solution to it, but I thought it might be a good idea for us to discuss the rest of the purchasing system. Maybe we'll find other things we can fix."

Rita smiled and said, "Pete thinks the whole problem is not having the right software. If we had the software he told me about, I could enter the purchase order on my computer, and Sean could input the information from the packing slip on one of Production's computers, and Marie could use her computer to see when purchase orders are ready to be paid. The computers are already tied together, you know."

"That's true, some companies do have systems like that. Some even have it tied in with their sales department so that whenever an order is taken, if it causes any component to fall below a predefined stocking level, purchase orders are automatically generated to replenish the inventory. A system like that might make sense for Walpold Enterprises sometime in the future, but right now we need to determine where the existing manual system is failing."

"Aren't we looking for long-term solutions for everything? That's what you said at the meeting yesterday."

"I also said that automating a manual system that doesn't work won't cure anything—it would just make a bad system work faster. Suppose for a minute that a system like the one you described were already installed. What would happen if Sean failed to enter the information from the packing slip? You would be left with purchase orders that couldn't be closed out, which is exactly where you are today. The first step, then, should be to examine the manual system to make sure it's designed properly; then we can determine what additional training will be required and where the discipline needs further strengthening." Just then John walked in. "Did I miss anything?" he asked brightly.

"Rick says we need to go over our purchasing procedure, but I don't see why that's necessary. You've already discovered that the problem isn't with the procedure; it's with Sean."

"Actually," said Rick, "what we really have to do is step back and get an overview of how the procedure works. A purchasing system is more than the details about how each cog does its part. As I mentioned yesterday, the system includes design, training, and discipline. If any of these three are inadequate, or if one person or group of people makes it work, the system will eventually break down."

"But people are what make the company run. It sounds like you're trying to make everyone expendable. If I'm the one that makes the purchase-order system work, then my job is more secure, and I'm happier—and you said that happy employees are more productive, so that should be good for the company."

John finally jumped into the conversation. "Rita, you'll be much more valuable to the company if the purchase-order system you run can operate effectively under any conditions. And it would give you more flexibility, too. Wouldn't you like that?"

"Okay, okay. Where do we start?"

"By first examining what we've got," Rick said. "First, do you have any documentation describing how the procedure works?"

"No, nothing other than some notes Jerry and I made when we worked it out; it never occurred to us to write it down. It's pretty simple."

"Well, it needs to be formalized so new employees can have a good starting place. If it's only transmitted verbally, errors or omissions are likely to occur. So describe the process, and I'll take notes." Rick opened the small notebook he always carried with him and took out a pen.

Rita spoke without hesitating. "Jerry tells me what he needs. I call a vendor and get a price, and then I fill out a purchase order with the information, take it to John for his signature, call and order it, make two copies of the purchase order, deliver one to Sean and one to Marie, and that's it. Simple."

Rick looked down at his notebook, trying to decide whether he should write anything yet, and then looked up at Rita. "A little *too* simple. Aren't you leaving out a few details?"

"Yeah," said John, "like what happens when Jerry or anyone else needs something real bad, and I'm not around to sign the purchase order?"

"Or why do unsigned purchase orders keep ending up on Marie's desk?" added Rick. "And what happens when a vendor agrees to supply a part, and then later they discover that they don't have enough to fill your order?"

"Wait!" said Rita. "I was just giving you the general idea of how it works. You're talking about all the exceptions that happen."

"But for a system to work, it has to take into account the exceptions," said Rick. "Let's start over again at the beginning. When somebody here needs something, how do they tell you?"

"By phone calls, on slips of paper, or verbally if they bump into me in the break room. Pretty professional, huh?" said Rita sarcastically.

"Why don't we see if Jerry and Marie are free to join us," said John. "Marie said this morning that she'd like to be involved in any discussion of the purchase-order procedure."

Rita called Jerry and Marie, who agreed to come right over. As they were waiting, Rick asked her nonchalantly, "So how long have you been dating Pete?"

"Since shortly after he took the job here—a couple of years, I guess."

"How has it been working out, being together both professionally and socially?" Rick continued.

"So far it's been great. And having a steady sure beats the bar scene. I suppose I'd like a little time to myself occasionally, though. Being together so much can be pretty intense. You can never tell, though. Things have a way of changing when you least expect it."

John wondered which things were changing—her work situation or her relationship. Just then Jerry and Sean walked in.

After greetings were exchanged, Jerry noticed that there weren't enough chairs and sent Sean to fetch a few more. Jerry was taking advantage of his new position of authority over John's nephew and enjoying it. He turned to John and said, "If this is about the purchase-order system, I want Sean involved. It'll give him a better idea of his role."

"Good idea," said John.

Marie came in as Sean was leaving to get the chairs. "Are you reviewing the new procedure, or are you still hashing it out? I've got a lot to do, you know," she said curtly.

"Patience, my dear," said Rita. "I don't think this will take too long, and then you won't have to worry about reviewing it. Just have a seat. Sean will be right back with chairs for the others."

John was surprised at Rita's assertiveness, especially over Marie, who was older and usually more aggressive—or so he thought. It was clear that Rita intended to protect her turf and remain in charge of Purchasing. "I guess I don't know these people so well after all," he thought.

Sean dutifully returned with four chairs, and he and the three other standees sat down.

John started the discussion. "We've been going over all the steps in our purchasing system so we'll have a consistent procedure for future reference and to find out where the glitches are and fix them. Rick, why don't you take it from here."

"The simplest way to proceed, I think, is to just begin writing it down," said Rick, "and review it as we go."

"Okay," said Rita, picking up a pen and pulling a pad of paper from a desk drawer, "I'll do the writing. How do we start?"

After a short pause to see if anyone else would say anything, Rick said, "Suppose we require anyone who wants something ordered to fill out a purchase-order form, sign and date it, and drop it into a basket in your office. That will be Step One."

"Let everybody fill out purchase-order forms?" asked Marie.

"Why not? It can't go anywhere until Rita processes it, and it would formalize the request, complete with the date. Then Step Two would be to have the purchasing agent gather additional information, assign the purchase-order number, enter the pertinent information into a purchase-order log, and submit the purchase order for approval."

"Additional information?" asked Rita, writing as quickly as she could and trying to get every word down.

"Yes, especially price and availability from the vendor. With all of this information in the purchase-order log, it will make it easy for everyone to check on the status of an order and to resolve any questions that come up."

Rita said, "I already have a purchase-order log book, but I just use it to figure out what the next purchase-order number is. What are you saying it should also contain?"

"Date submitted, requester's name, date approved, date ordered, vendor's name, vendor's expected delivery date, and date received."

"That makes sense. Now everyone will know when an order gets held up because of the backlog in John's office," said Rita, looking at John. "I'm tired of people complaining that I haven't placed an order, only to find out that the purchase order is stuck under a mile-high stack of papers on your desk."

"*Mea culpa*," said John, holding up his hands. "Guilty as charged."

"I've never been at a place where every single purchase has to be approved by the president," said Jerry. "If I could approve the purchase orders for my department, that problem would be solved."

"Fat chance," whispered Marie, but everyone heard it.

"Jerry's right," Rick added. "He should take over approval of production-related items up to a predetermined dollar limit. That would certainly speed things along. What do you think, John?"

"Well, I don't like the idea of losing authority over spending," he responded almost reflexively. "I've heard about owners that let themselves get spent into oblivion. The procedure we've been using prevents that from happening."

"That's true, but it also bogs down the system," said Jerry. "When the volume of orders was lower, you managed to keep them moving through the pipeline. These days, you're holding things up, and I doubt that you even know why a lot of the orders are placed."

"Well, of course not, but I hate to just give everyone *carte blanche* to order whatever they want."

"You're doing about three million dollars in sales right now," said Rick, "which translates to purchases of about a hundred and twenty-five thousand dollars per month. Let's say you get to ten million—that will be over four hundred thousand dollars in purchases per month. Do you really think you can be effective if you have to spend time approving all those purchases?"

"All right, all right," John admitted reluctantly, "I get the picture. But how do I keep everyone from spending me into the poorhouse?"

"It's simple. There'll be a monthly report showing all purchases, which you could review anytime you want and ask Rita or Jerry about anything that doesn't make sense to you. You'll still be able to control things, but you won't be bogging down the system. If inventory gets out of line, you'll know it."

John thought a moment and then said, "Okay, let's do it."

"You're going to agree that easily?" asked Jerry incredulously.

"Sure, why not?"

"No reason, I guess." He shook his head in disbelief.

"What's Step Three?" asked Marie, anxious to get on with it.

"Make two copies of the purchase order," said Rita. "Deliver one copy to Receiving, one copy to Bookkeeping, and file the original."

"File it where?" asked Rick.

"In Purchasing's file cabinet, of course," she said, realizing that Rick intended for every detail to be spelled out. "And after that I'm done, right?" she asked, putting her pen down and sitting back in her chair.

"What about expediting the shipments?" asked John. "Don't you call a vendor when a shipment is late to find out why?"

"Only if somebody complains to me that something hasn't arrived. I've never had a way to figure out what's late."

"But you will now," said Jerry, smiling. He hated having to expedite his critical purchase orders, and now it was becoming clear he shouldn't have to. "It'll be obvious from the purchase-order log which orders are late, and since you already have the relationships with the vendors, it's more logical for you to call them to expedite the orders than for me to do it. That's the way it worked at Avcom."

Rita picked her pen back up. "Okay," she said as she began to write. "Step Four: The head of Purchasing reviews the purchase-order log weekly and expedites the orders." She looked up and asked, "Now what?"

Rick continued, "That takes us to Step Five: The Receiving department compares the items received with those listed on the packing slip and with those listed on the purchase order. Receipts of said items are noted on the purchase order."

"And what if some of the items on the purchase order didn't arrive?" asked Sean, starting to understand what they were talking about and his role in it.

"Then you record only the items that did arrive," said Jerry, "and file the purchase order and packing slip away until the remainder of the order arrives."

"Right," said Rick, "and then Step Six: When all items on a purchase order have been received, Receiving updates the purchase-order log and delivers the purchase order with the attached packing slips to Bookkeeping." He turned to Rita and asked, "So why do you give Marie a copy of the purchase order before the parts arrive? She isn't going to pay for anything until then."

"Hmm, I guess she doesn't need it, but Jerry said that's the way they did it at Avcom, and he told me to do it that way."

"That's true," said Jerry.

"Well, I can think of one reason to do it," said Rick, "even though she won't be paying for it yet. When you order something, you're also making a tacit commitment that the company will pay for it—in effect, you're tying up company money. Do you know how much money is tied up in orders right now?"

"No," said Rita, "but why does that matter? We need the parts, and John already approved the purchases."

"Because for cash planning purposes," answered Marie, "we need to know what's been ordered. One of the features of the new bookkeeping software I just installed is purchase-order tracking, which will always keep us up-to-date on the dollar value of items on order. That's why I need that extra copy!"

"Good," said Rick. "Now, what did we forget?"

"Changes," said Rita. "At least one of the items on a purchase order always gets deleted because a vendor won't have it in time, and I have to order it somewhere else."

"Right—exceptions," said Rick. "You need a rubber UPDATED stamp and a red ink pad so you can make changes to already released purchase orders. When you note any additions or deletions, make copies for Receiving and Bookkeeping and stamp them UPDATED. Then the changes won't bog things down. Anything else?"

"Yeah," said Jerry, "what happens if Rita isn't here? Does everything grind to a halt?"

"Good point," said Rick. "Notice that our procedure doesn't refer to names, only functions. As long as everyone has someone designated to fill in during his or her absence, the process should continue without a hitch."

Everyone looked around with a satisfied look. "Why don't I write this up and make copies for everyone," said Rita, taking control of her domain. "Then we can all review it and see how it sounds after we've had a chance to think about it."

"Okay, but how does writing this down solve the problem of lost packing slips?" asked Jerry, who knew the answer but wanted to have it spelled out.

"Ah, discipline—the final piece of the puzzle," said Rick. "How do you ensure that everyone faithfully does his or her job? Frequent interaction and encouragement helps, but there's nothing like a variance report to keep people on their toes. In this case, Rita can create a variance report that lists outstanding purchase orders and have it distributed weekly for everyone's review. Jerry, since you're in charge of Receiving, it will be up to you to check the report periodically to make sure that items that have been received are not still on the report. Now that Sean knows that Jerry will review this report and that his job depends on the report being error-free, he'll have an incentive to be conscientious."

"Right, Sean?" added John.

"No problem," said Sean. "It never seemed like a big deal before. But what if the packing slip is wrong? Should I make the delivery-truck drivers wait until I check it out?"

"Lots of luck," said John, recalling the days when he met the UPS truck and received the day's shipment. "I doubt that you'll get UPS to change their operating procedures and let you open all the packages before you sign for them."

"If you find a discrepancy with a packing slip," said Rick, "just write a note and give it to Rita, and let her deal with the vendor."

"I'll have this procedure written up by tomorrow." said Rita. "I'll leave a draft on everybody's desk. If anyone thinks of anything else, let me know. Now get out of here and let me get to work," she said as she swiveled her chair around to face her computer.

*t*he meeting was over just a few minutes before John and Rick were supposed to be back in John's office to meet with Dan about the computer pager. When they got there, they found Dan already sitting at the conference table, looking through a stack of papers. As they entered the room, he avoided making eye contact with either of them. "Ready to start?" asked John amiably, sitting down across from Dan. Rick took a chair next to John.

"I guess," said Dan. He still needed a haircut, and the pocket of his wrinkled short-sleeved shirt was still stuffed with several notes and pencils. He pushed his hair out of his eyes and said, "Why are you suddenly so interested in this project, Rick? Monday you acted like there were a million reasons not to proceed."

"If that's the way I came across, I apologize. I just rattled off the first questions that came to my mind. I'll admit that I may seem a little negative at times, but my intention is to be thorough," said Rick.

"Why don't we start over," said John. "Let's treat this like any new project. You wouldn't expect to start a new project without looking at all the details, would you? Dan has already demonstrated that the concept works, and he can probably estimate the product cost pretty well. So what do you think are the most important marketing issues, Rick?"

"I'd say we need to define the target market and determine what the distribution channel or channels should be so we can estimate the pricing and the various marketing costs. Then we can estimate the cost of any additional equipment that will be required for production and the minimum amount of stock that will be necessary for the first production build. Then—"

"Wait a minute," Dan interrupted. "We didn't have to go through all that crap to get this place started, and we're a multimillion-dollar outfit."

"But when you started, weren't you planning to build and sell a product in a marketplace that you were already familiar with?" asked Rick.

"Well yes, but . . ."

"Come on Dan, let's face it," said John. "We lucked out the first time. We knew our target market because we were already selling other products to them at R.S.S. We knew what trade journals they read because we read the very same ones, so we knew where to advertise. We knew how to sell our product because we knew what features our customers would demand. Now we're talking about a totally different type of product. Where will we advertise, and how much will that cost? Who is really more likely to buy it—our current customers or a completely different set of people? If we make the wrong choices, it could suck money out of areas that need it more. I just don't see how we can make any funding decisions without getting down to the nitty-gritty."

"Maybe funding won't be a problem. Suppose I've already convinced someone to fund it. Then what?" said Dan assertively.

"You've already talked to someone about funding without discussing it with me?" said John angrily.

"I didn't say I had, I said *suppose* I had. You complain every day about our cash problems, so how could you possibly be interested in an idea that will take more cash? We had a really great idea when we started this company. Now things are so screwed up here that it *would* be stupid to introduce a new product line. You'd just screw it up too."

"Do you really think Herb is going to fund your untested idea? He's just leading you on to get control of your stock," said John, getting even hotter.

"Who said anything about Herb?" responded Dan, remaining remarkably calm.

"You know damn well what I'm talking about," shot back John. "If you would start acting like a partner and quit acting like a damn *prima donna*, you might realize that there's more to running a company than tinkering around like a mad scientist all day and night."

"Screw you," said Dan. He glared at John as he stood up, grabbed his papers, and stormed out of the room.

The silence was deafening. Rick hesitated to say anything, for it seemed more prudent to let John cool down on his own. When the color in his face was more normal, John finally said, "Well, I did a masterful job of handling that situation, didn't I?" He stood up, walked back to his desk, and flopped into his chair. He leaned back and propped his feet on the desk, looking up toward the ceiling. "I've done enough damage—let's call it a day," he said, in effect dismissing Rick.

Rick hated to end the day on such a negative note, but perhaps it was better not to intrude in what was really a fight between two good friends. "See you first thing tomorrow," he said as he got up and walked out.

*i*t was still rainy and windy when John reached his driveway, and he had to stop, get out of his van, and move a bicycle blocking the garage. Then he got back into his van, soaking wet, and pressed the automatic door opener. The garage door opened about two feet and stopped, apparently blocked by something. He grabbed the opener that was clipped to the sun visor, got out of his van again, pointed the device at the garage door, and pressed the button to close it. When the door was fully closed, he walked up to it, pressed the button to open it, and at the same time pulled up on it, hoping to overcome whatever was inhibiting its movement. He felt a bump when the door was open about two feet as a stick that had been wedged in the running track broke free, and the door continued to open. He got back in his van, put it in gear, and started inching forward into the garage. But the plastic laundry basket full of towels in front of the washing machine was blocking his path. He gave up. He left the van where it was, turned it off, and got out, slamming the door behind him.

He was in a foul mood as he entered the house. Barney, who had been waiting at the door since he heard John's van drive up, began to jump up on him excitedly. John stooped down to scratch the dog's head, and said, "You're not planning to pee on my foot, are you, Barney? Everybody else did today." The dog, not acknowledging anything but the attention, stopped jumping and contentedly sat still while John continued to scratch his head. "How would you like to be head of R&D? We might have an opening," he said to Barney. "I think given a choice between competence and loyalty, I'd rather have loyalty this time around." He stood up and walked into the kitchen, where he found his fourteen-year-old son Zach standing in front of the open refrigerator. "Zachary, how many times have I told you not to leave your damn bike in the driveway! I had to move it again to get into the garage. And close the damn refrigerator door, you're letting all the cold air out!"

"Sorry, Dad. And by the way, we learned at school that when you leave a refrigerator door open you don't let the cold air out, you let the warm air in. Anyway, I don't have X-ray vision, so how am I supposed to know what's in here if the door's closed?"

Beth, hearing them argue, entered the kitchen. "Zach, we'll be eating in thirty minutes. Go find Andy—I think he's over at Brad's."

"Why don't you just call Brad's house if you already know where he is?"

"Go, Zach, before you get stuck with cleaning up the kitchen tonight." Zach gave up and wandered out of the kitchen.

"You're sopping wet!" she said.

"It'll dry," said John, already mixing himself an extra-large drink. He took a swig before making one for Beth. "Rick and I tried to have a meeting with Dan about his pager, but Dan and I ended up in a shouting match. He told me to get screwed and then stormed out of my office. I'm pretty sure Herb's already told him he'll fund his new project, possibly somewhere else."

"Somewhere else? Like where?"

"I don't know. Maybe he told him he could start another company. Dan won't give me the time of day right now. I can't believe things have deteriorated like this."

"Can he do that? I thought you both had employment agreements that kept you trapped with each other until the end of time."

"Hmm. I'd forgotten about that. Back when Mike suggested we draft them, I never imagined I'd actually care what they said. Maybe I'll give him a call tonight and see if he's free for lunch tomorrow."

"Do you want me to call Liz and see if I can get a sense of what's happening?" she asked, referring to Dan's wife. They occasionally socialized together but had never grown very close because they didn't have much in common. Things might have been different if Dan and Liz had had kids.

"No, don't—not right now. Let's see what happens in the next couple of days."

Beth opened the oven door and removed the meatloaf.

"The problem with Dan is just the worst of many catastrophes lately," John continued. "Rick is convinced that everyone has lost confidence in my ability to run things. And the more I've thought about it, the more examples I came up with that supported what he was saying. I guess I just haven't been paying close enough attention to them or to my own end of the business."

"How were you supposed to be giving them all that attention when you were out of town all the time?"

"I don't know. Maybe pat them on the head more often when I was here, show more interest in their ideas, stop to answer them when they asked me something as I rushed out the door to catch a plane . . . I don't know."

Just then Andy and Zach entered the kitchen and to John's relief, broke the mood.

"Let's eat," he said, heading for the table.

T

H

u

R

S

D

A

y

August 3, 1995

*t*he sky was still overcast from yesterday's hurricane, but the wind had already died down. As John pulled into the parking lot at 6:45 on Thursday morning, he avoided fallen branches and several boxes that had blown onto the lot from behind a nearby grocery store. He was surprised to see Joan's car already there. "Maybe she couldn't sleep either," he thought. As he entered the building, he detected the pleasant aroma of freshly brewed coffee, but he didn't see Joan. He hung his coat behind the door in his office and headed for the break room.

He found Joan standing in front of the open refrigerator, the contents of which were piled on a nearby table. Seeing John enter, she said, "No one ever cleans this damn thing. There were dried-out sandwiches in there that are God knows how old. Some of this stuff is so moldy you can't even tell what it is." She stood with her hands on her hips, surveying the now empty refrigerator.

"You got here at this hour to clean the refrigerator?" he asked.

Joan looked even more haggard than usual. She was neatly dressed and her hair was in place, but her makeup didn't hide the dark circles under her eyes. "I couldn't sleep, so I decided to come in here rather than toss and turn in bed."

"I'll help you with this mess, and then let's get some coffee and go sit in my office and talk." They figured out what to throw away, and after they refilled the refrigerator with what was left, they headed back to his office. As they sat down, he asked, "Did something happen to aggravate your insomnia, or have you just reached that age where you don't sleep much anymore? I thought that only happened to old people."

"I'm not much older than you, you know, and you don't seem to be doing any better than I am. But you're right, something did happen. Bill invited the kids to go on a cruise to the Bahamas. Can you imagine—Jennifer and Paul together with Bill and his girl friend on a cruise ship? Paul's just hit puberty, and for him to be exposed to his Dad slobbering all over Tracy, who's almost young enough to be his daughter—well, it's obscene. And Jennifer loves the kind of clothes that Tracy wears, and Tracy will probably be super-friendly to her, and then they'll start laughing and giggling about secret girl stuff—and I don't want my daughter learning anything from that tart."

"Your kids have been spending a lot of time with Bill and Tracy, haven't they?"

"Yeah, they have. Things are bad enough for the kids with Bill moving out, so I haven't wanted to make things worse by putting them in the middle. But it's really getting out of hand. When the kids are with Bill, it's all fun and games—boating, camping, tennis, restaurants—and then they come home and hear me nagging them to do their homework and their chores, and I turn into the bad parent. Now if I forbid this cruise, they'll hate me, but if I don't . . . "

"Maybe it won't be so bad," said John, trying to help her accept the inevitable. "You really don't think Bill's going to do anything sleazy in front of his own kids, do you?"

"It's just not the right environment for impressionable teenagers. But what can I do?"

"It's simple. If you can't persuade Bill to withdraw the invitation, then you'll just have to put your foot down and let the chips fall where they may. The kids are going to think you're the bad guy, but they'll come around, and eventually they'll even appreciate all the effort you've put into raising them. If you give in now, Bill will know he can keep on massaging your guilt over depriving the kids of whatever glittering promises he dangles in front of them, and you'll always end up as the loser. Your first priority is to do what you think is right for the kids, and they'll never learn the proper values if you don't teach them."

John's argument reassured Joan. "I guess you're right," she said. "I'll talk to Bill, and if he refuses to be rational about it, I'll simply tell them they can't go."

Just then they heard the outside door open, and a few moments later, Rick walked into John's office. When Joan saw

Rick, she stood up, sighed, and said, "On with the day. Next time, I'll stick with guppies," as she walked out past him, waving a hello.

Rick sat down and asked John, "If you had to guess, what would you say Herb is planning to do?"

John leaned back in his chair and propped his feet on his desk. "I think he's trying to win Dan's allegiance so that Dan will vote with them, and then he'll remove me as president and install Leonard in my place."

"Does he have a reputation for doing that kind of thing?"

"I've heard that he's been involved in the takeover of several companies, if that's what you mean."

"And what do you suppose his main reason is for doing it?"

"He's turned into a jerk, I guess," said John offhandedly. "What are you driving at, Rick?"

"Maybe he's just trying to protect his interests and doesn't see any other option. What would you do if you had invested big bucks in a company and you felt the president had lost control? You'd probably do just what he's doing—send someone in to assess the situation, and if it turned out to be necessary, you'd replace the president. And that's exactly what he's going to do unless you can convince him you're on top of things. But it's my bet that he'd rather stick with you than change horses, especially when the new horse has had so little line-management experience."

"Maybe he's already lost confidence in me. I'm sure he's getting glowing reports about me from Leonard."

"Well, the way it looks to me, you've got a problem with Dan and a potential problem with Herb. But unless Herb has already formed an opinion, the game isn't over yet."

"Maybe you're right. Maybe I just need to convince him I'm not as screwed up as Leonard says." He paused as a thought popped into his head. "If I could only figure out a way for him to see Leonard's true colors."

"In the meantime, let's meet with Pete and see what's happening with Tech Support."

They left John's office and headed down the hall. As they approached Pete's office, they could hear Pete say, ". . . it'll be a lot better than this, I'll tell you that." When they reached the doorway, they could see that Pete was talking to someone on the phone. The clothes he was wearing seemed a little dressier than usual, and John wondered why. Pete turned and saw them, and he said into the phone, "Gotta go. I'll see you at lunch." As he hung up the phone, he tried to hide his annoyance at having been interrupted. "Good morning," he said. "What can I do for you?"

Pete's office was furnished much like all the other offices, with a secondhand desk and swivel chair, a table with a computer, and two additional chairs. His desk was almost completely devoid of any clutter, and the few papers that were visible were neatly arranged; the only personal touch was a small framed picture of Rita.

"We're in the process of putting together a set of management statistics to track things," said John, "and we wanted to know how much and what type of data you have available."

"Ben wrote a database program for compiling customer-call data," answered Pete, "but I haven't had time to keep it up-to-date. If I had a few uninterrupted hours, I could put something together. Should I ignore the tech-support calls for now and do it?"

"First let's see what you have. How current is the data?"

"In Ben's program? I haven't entered any data in several weeks. No one seemed to be interested in it, and I have more important things to do."

"Well, maybe we can get some part-time help to enter the data and keep it up-to-date," said John.

Pete reluctantly agreed to show them the data file on his computer. He tapped some keys, and in a few seconds a menu similar to the one they had seen on Marie's computer appeared: ENTER DATA, EDIT DATA, RUN REPORTS. Pete selected ENTER DATA, and the menu screen was replaced by a page divided into different categories: DATE, CUSTOMER, CONTACT, PROBLEM, ACTION.

Rick asked, "How does this program handle multiple calls for the same problem?"

"With a separate record for each call. Ben's never really been involved in a tech-support department, so he didn't realize it was important to link the files in that data field automatically."

John asked, "The PROBLEM field seems to be a description field. Is there any way to sort the problems by type?"

"Nope. DATE and CUSTOMER is about it. But nobody seems to care, so I never bothered to have Ben change it. Besides, I keep my own records manually." Pete opened his top drawer and pulled out a loose-leaf notebook. He opened the notebook, and Rick could see that each page represented a customer call. The first page concerned a problem that had required three calls to complete. Each call was recorded in meticulous detail. At the top of the page was a place to enter a two-digit code; the first number had been scratched out and replaced by a different one."

"What's the code at the top?" asked Rick.

"That's where I keep track of what caused the problem. At first it seemed to be a bad board, so I called it '01.' It wasn't until the third call that I figured out that the turkey hadn't even looked at the manual and had the board setup all screwed up, so I changed it to '09'—cockpit error. That happens a lot."

"Which happens a lot—changing the rating or setup problems?" asked John.

"Setup problems. If people would read the manual, it would eliminate half the calls."

"Have you ever told this to anyone?"

"I mentioned it to Dan once, but he said the users are just jerks and never read the manual, so there's nothing you can do about it. He wrote most of the documentation, and he doesn't seem to think it needs changing."

"What about the calls themselves—do you take them all?" Rick asked.

"All the ones that get transferred to me. There's not much I can do about the rest of them, is there?"

"I think your method of collecting the data manually is a good start," said Rick, "and it wouldn't take much to turn it into a comprehensive system. If you set up your own database to keep track of the calls using the format you have defined, you'd be able to provide quantitative data about the calls and possibly influence the direction of things. What do you think?"

Just as Pete was about to answer, Leonard walked in and said, "Pete, let's plan to—" He interrupted himself when he saw Rick and John. "Oh, I didn't realize you were busy."

"It never stopped you before," John shot back.

"We're discussing customer call trends, but we're almost finished," said Rick.

Leonard didn't want to wait. He said curtly, "Pete, give me a call when you're free," and turned and left before Pete could say anything.

Pete was obviously uncomfortable with the exchange, and John decided to push a little to see if he might get a sense as to how far along Leonard was in his planning. Was Pete already involved in the plot to start another company, or was he just being courted? "What was that all about?" he asked Pete.

"Nothing," said Pete rather sheepishly. "Now where were we?"

"We were talking about a method to accumulate the call data more efficiently," said Rick. "There are several database programs that would handle the data, and you could set them up yourself to suit your needs. What do you think?"

"A database program? Then I'd still have to enter all this data from each report. I don't have a secretary, or didn't you notice? Besides, there's a lot of important information on these sheets—why duplicate the work by typing what's already written here into the computer? If what you're after is identifying trends and amassing statistics about types of problems, why don't I just take the pertinent data from these reports—such as call date, problem type, and customer—and enter it into a simple spreadsheet? It would be simple to enter the data and keep it current and wouldn't require duplicating my manual system with a database program that would require constant tending."

"That's a great idea," said John. "How long would it take to put something together that would give us some statistics?"

"I'll lay out the spreadsheet later today and see how much data I can enter. I can probably have at least a month's worth loaded by tomorrow, if I don't have too many distractions. Of course, if Dan discounts the data from the reports like he normally does, what good are they? And that only takes care of the customer calls I get. What about the rest of them? How will I ever be certain that I'm getting information about all the calls?"

"I'll explain the benefits to Dan," said John. "It's too logical to be ignored. As for getting all the calls, that'll be simple. Make a form that everyone can keep on their desk to record the pertinent information whenever they take a tech call. We'll simply shoot anybody that forgets to fill it out. There's nothing like a public execution to raise everyone's level of awareness."
Pete looked like he wasn't sure if John was joking.

As they were leaving Pete's office, John said to Rick, "I'm meeting Mike for lunch at about noon. Want to join us?"

"Shouldn't we talk to Dan about the setup problems?" he asked.

"After yesterday's blowup, I doubt he'll be very receptive," said John.

"Maybe I could soften him up—give my psychology skills a workout."

John thought for a moment and said, "Sure. Why not? See you later." They parted in the hallway; John headed for his office, and Rick went in search of Dan.

*r*ick found Dan working intently in the lab. "Hi, Dan. I was wondering if you might have a few minutes to help me with something."

Without looking up, Dan said "I'm in no mood to discuss the pager, if that's what you want. Besides," he said curtly, "I promised one of our customers I'd have a customized board finished this morning so I can ship it out this afternoon. Check with me later in the afternoon, okay?"

"No problem. See you after lunch." Rick was afraid that Dan might be the kind of person who, if confronted, would take a hard-line position before he had all the facts and then refuse to listen to reason. He walked away wondering how to deal with him and decided in the meantime to see how Marie was doing with her new software.

Rick walked into Marie's office and found her busy at the computer. When she heard him enter, she looked up and said, "After you get a few checks entered, this gets easier and easier. I'll have the first month's bank statements reconciled pretty soon. And I noticed in the manual how the program keeps track of outstanding payables and can also print invoices."

"Yes, so you'll be able to accumulate data for Rita's purchasing system and print invoices for Joan, too. But don't worry about that yet. The first step is to get the bank transactions entered."

Marie found Rick's manner patronizing, but she had something more important to complain about. "Leonard came in this morning and asked me what I was doing, with the implication that whatever it was, I must be doing it wrong. And when I started to explain it to him, he cut me off, told me to have fun, and walked out. He acts like it's a foregone conclusion that he'll replace John. I hate that superior attitude of his."

"Marie, there's nothing we can do about him right now except ignore him."

"Easy for you to say," she responded. "You didn't dissolve your client base when you started working here."

Rick left her to her work and walked down the hall, preoccupied with the thought that he had to do something about Dan. It was almost noon. Maybe he could surprise him and take him to lunch. He wandered back to the lab and found Dan still seated at the bench, still engrossed in his work. "Got time for a sandwich?"

Caught off guard, Dan didn't have a ready answer. "I suppose so. Just let me drop this board off with Sean so he can ship it out." He stood up, oblivious to the fact that his shirttail had become untucked, and headed toward the shipping area, with Rick following. When they got to the shipping-and-receiving area, Sean was nowhere to be found. "Typical. If he weren't John's nephew, he'd have been fired ages ago. This company's gotten so screwed up, it's almost beyond saving." Just then, Sean came out of Jerry's office.

"I was just going over the shipping schedule with Jerry. What do you need?" he asked Dan.

Dan, shocked at this display of newfound efficiency, handed the board to Sean and told him where to ship it. "Send it FedEx, and I need to call the customer to give them the shipper number, so drop the receipt off on my desk," he said curtly, and walked away.

"No problem," said Sean to Dan's back.

Rick followed Dan out the door and into the parking lot, where Dan said, "Let's take my car." Rick had to wait until Dan made room for him in the front seat of his beat-up Chevy station wagon by tossing several piles of magazines and boxes of electrical parts into the back. Without asking Rick where he wanted to eat, Dan drove right to Harold's. During the drive, Rick tried to make small talk, but Dan responded to all Rick's questions with short answers.

When they got to the diner, they took a table by the window. Rick reached for a menu, but Dan told him to forget the menu and just order one of the specials, which were rattled off by the waitress who appeared an instant later. After they ordered, Dan continued to respond to Rick's comments with monosyllabic answers, until Rick asked him how he and John started Walpold Enterprises.

"One night at R.S.S. after we had been working real late, we came here for breakfast about four a.m. We were talking about the video processing, and it occurred to both of us simultaneously that there was a much more elegant way to handle it. We worked through the details of how it could be implemented and then talked about what to do with this new approach."

"So working in the middle of the night isn't something new?"

"Hardly. Engineering involves a lot more trial and error than people realize. You work on a solution, implement it, and then discover more about the problem. And you lose track of time when you're hot on the trail of a problem—suddenly it's the middle of the night. It was more fun when John and I were working together though," he added. He went on to explain the negative reaction they encountered when they offered their idea to R.S.S. management and how they got Walpold Enterprises started with the help of Herb Chandler.

"What is your title?" asked Rick.

"I guess Vice President in charge of Research and Development, and I'm a director of the company. We have hokey annual meetings every year and a board of directors meeting every quarter. It seems like a waste of time, but Cal Reilly says we have to do it or the I.R.S. will crack down on us. It's stupid."

"Cal is right though, Dan. Since you're incorporated, you get certain privileges related to taxes, and it's important to follow the rules so you don't lose the advantages. Do you realize that as an officer and director you have a fiduciary responsibility to the owners?"

"What does that mean?"

"It means that you're responsible for protecting the interests of the stockholders, and if a decision is made that isn't in the best interest of the stockholders, all the officers are potentially liable."

"There aren't any stockholders except John, Herb, and me. Big deal."

"It might not seem like a big deal now, but it could be in the future. Just don't forget that as an officer, you can be held accountable for your actions and for the actions of the other officers."

"You mean that if John makes a stupid decision, I'm responsible for it too?"

"You and all the other officers. In simple terms, as an officer, you're more than just an employee—you act on behalf of the stockholders."

Dan eyed Rick suspiciously. "Why are telling me all this?"

"I'm trying to get you to look at things from a different perspective. As an officer, you owe it to yourself to cover all bases when you make a decision. If there is even the remotest possibility that you might be wrong, you need to have a contingency plan."

"Yeah, yeah, but you must have something specific in mind." He stopped as the waitress arrived with their food. She asked if they needed anything and then left. Dan grabbed a roll from the basket she had brought, poked it into the gravy on his plate, and started eating.

Rick wanted to talk about Leonard and the whole problem of the pager, but he decided to attack a less inflammatory issue first. "All right, I'll be more specific. What's the chance that the documentation for installing the board isn't perfect?"

"Nothing's perfect. But it's good enough."

"What if it isn't?"

"It is, trust me," he said, shoveling a forkful of mashed potatoes into his mouth.

"But what if it isn't? Isn't there a chance that it could be improved to reduce the customer's installation time and the problems that crop up?"

"No, the directions are clear and complete. The problem is that they don't read them."

"I reviewed the documentation over the weekend, and it seems to be comprehensive. But Pete thinks that the documentation is the cause of quite a few customer calls."

"That's baloney. He doesn't have any facts to support that. Those customers are whiners that want you to jump through hoops for them."

"Actually, he does have data to support it in the form of several months of customer-call reports. He's categorized the problems by cause and found a significant percentage resulting from customers not performing the setup properly."

"So what. There's nothing you can do about that. You can't make people read the manual." By this time, he had finished eating everything on his plate except for a few drops of gravy, which he sopped up with another roll.

"Now just for a minute, look at the problem from the perspective of an officer. If the problem really does exist, is there anything that could be done to improve the situation and reduce unnecessary work by Pete? If there is, it will reduce the number of calls, which means happier customers."

Dan paused a moment, considering the situation. "Hmm. You might have a point. Well, suppose we added a separate sheet, gave it a bold heading like SETUP BASICS, and included a simplified list of the most common setup configurations? Come to think of it, I guess I've seen other products that have something similar. Is that what you mean?"

"Exactly. I know that the manual contains all the necessary information. But when it looks like extra information will help, it sure doesn't hurt to include it. And with Pete's call-tracking system, you'll be able to monitor the effectiveness of the change."

Rick was encouraged by Dan's attitude. He had dropped his usual hard-line view and considered an alternate idea. It wasn't much, but Rick felt he had made significant progress.

The waitress reappeared with two pieces of apple pie. Rick looked up, but before he could say anything, Dan said, "It's included," pulled one of the pieces toward himself, and began eating it.

"You know," said Rick, "if all my clients were running their companies as efficiently as this place, I'd be out of business."

"What do you mean?"

"The place is clean, the service is fast and courteous, the food is good and there's plenty of it, and it's cheap. The customers must like it, because it's been crowded the entire time we've been here."

"Yeah, it's a good place. I eat here all the time."

"But it's not the only restaurant around here, is it?"

"No. I just like it better than the others."

"Well, there's a lesson to be learned from that, don't you think?" Dan just shrugged and got up to pay the cashier.

As they drove back to the office, Dan was quiet, and when they arrived, he muttered that he had "stuff to do" and wandered off.

Rick dropped by Pete's office to tell him about the improvements that Dan promised to make in the setup instructions, but Pete wasn't there. And Rita wasn't in her office either. But on each of their desks was a newly created form with the heading CUSTOMER CALL INCIDENT and a layout that made it easy to record all the information in tracking support calls.

*a*t noon, John arrived at a rib joint and found Mike uncharacteristically already at a table waiting for him. "Boy, this is a first," said John, sitting down across from him. "What happened, did you get fired this morning?"

"I was visiting a client near here and finished up early. I could make a few phone calls if it would make you feel better, though," said Mike, reaching for his cellular phone.

"Don't bother. Hey, I forgot to ask you about the cruise last weekend."

"Are you kidding? We canceled. When we heard that the storm was heading this way, we realized that it would have been a disaster. We spent the weekend in a beachside bungalow at St. Pete instead—not the lavish surroundings of a cruise ship, but we didn't have to worry about getting seasick either. By the way, I talked with people about your buddy Leonard like you asked me to. He's described as very competent, unemotional, and at times vicious—a valuable ally or a formidable foe. I certainly wouldn't turn my back on him."

"Don't worry. Did you have a chance to review our employment agreements yet?" asked John.

"Yeah. In my typical masterful style, I have both you and Dan trapped for life—neither of you can escape, and anything you develop belongs to the company. Do you really think Dan is planning to leave?"

"Who the hell knows? But what if he sides with Herb, and they use their sixty-six percent to outvote me?"

"Then you're screwed. I suppose you could file a class-action suit if they do something that isn't in the best interest of the company since they'd be violating their fiduciary responsibility, but it would be a major mess. I'd be forced to resign as corporate attorney because of a conflict of interest. Herb would retain his own lawyer, probably someone who specializes in class-action suits. Representing you in the suit would be very expensive, and my partners aren't wild about *pro bono* work. Like I said, a major mess. On the plus side, it would cost Herb a lot too. What's the timing?"

"Do you mean when is Herb coming in with his hatchet? Leonard is moving fast, stirring everyone up, and I'm sure he's reporting to Herb daily. I expect to hear from Herb in the next day or two."

"And what shape are you in?" asked Mike.

"In my quest to avoid micromanaging, I've been too lax and let things get out of control. Lately, we've made a lot of progress getting things organized, and it's clear to me what we need to do. But if my managers were polled today, I'm pretty sure I'd get a resounding vote of no confidence—it'll take time to regain their faith in me."

"Anything you can do to buy some time?"

"Yeah, win the lottery," said John. "Oh yeah, one more thing—could you have one of your associates research computer fraud?"

"You mean accessing confidential files, like Phil was doing? Are you thinking about suing him?" asked Mike.

"I'm just interested in the latest rulings, that's all," said John noncommittally. "Now that we've got that out of the way," he said, picking up the menu, "I'm ordering a huge barbecue sandwich—I'm starved!"

They discussed the baseball playoff possibilities while they enjoyed their lunches. When they finished, John returned to the office rejuvenated and refreshed and with a look of resolve on his face. He went to the break room to get some coffee, and Rick walked in.

"So how was lunch with Mike?" asked Rick.

"Fine. He had some interesting comments on—" Before John could finish, several electronics assemblers entered the room, and he felt uncomfortable discussing confidential matters in front of them.

"Hi, Mr. Walpold," said a young woman John was sure he had never seen before.

"Hi," he responded. "Having a good day?" he asked neutrally. Before waiting for an answer, he headed for the door with his coffee, Rick following close behind.

Back in his office, he forgot that he had been interrupted midsentence and asked Rick about his lunch with Dan.

"We had a good chat, actually. I'm sure he's been talking to Leonard about his pager, but I gave him a few things to think about. And he admitted that the installation documentation might be improved with a separate sheet about the setup, since a significant number of new customers seem to have trouble with it."

"No kidding? Great."

"Yeah, and it might encourage him to acknowledge other problems and find ways to improve them too. I also talked to him about his fiduciary responsibility as an officer of the company."

"Huh?"

"I just mentioned to him that he has the obligation as an officer to do whatever is necessary to protect the interests of the stockholders, and apparently he'd never realized it before. It might be worthwhile for you to try talking to him again. He doesn't seem quite as confrontational as he was yesterday.''

"Actually, I've been avoiding him. But I guess it won't hurt to be the first to offer an olive branch. Now, back to the issues at hand—we haven't updated the sales forecast in quite a while, and without it, Jerry will never have the right parts on order. Let's go talk to Phil—I mean Scott.'' He suddenly remembered that Phil Jackson was history. He and Rick walked over to Scott's office.

*t*hey found Scott poring over several pieces of paper that he'd taped together on his desk to make a large chart.

"Working on the sales forecast?'' asked John.

"Yeah, it hasn't been updated since Phil left, and I decided it was time to get on it. What format do you think I should use?'' Scott had never held a management position before, and although he was familiar with the forecast Phil had prepared, he didn't really know everything involved in creating one.

John deferred to Rick for an answer. Rick asked Scott, "You can probably predict fairly closely what next week's sales will be, can't you?''

"Sure, I know several customers who've already called for quotes, and as soon as their purchase orders are approved, they'll be calling back to place the orders. But that's only one week.''

"Yes, but you can predict the following week's sales too, only with a slightly lower degree of certainty. The same thing for the week after that and so on, with constantly decreasing certainty. For six months from now, your prediction would be a wild guess, right?''

"For sure,'' said Scott, leaning back in his chair and taking the last sip from a can of Mountain Dew, emptying it. He deposited the can carefully in a box labeled ALUMINUM CANS under the table next to his desk, beside another labeled PAPER and a third labeled PLASTIC.

"You have an advantage since you have a tremendous amount of historical data. My advice is for you to load at least six months of weekly data into a spreadsheet. Calculate a trend line for each item, and use that to predict the weekly sales for the next three months. Then publish the forecast in biweekly increments for Jerry to use to drive his inventory purchases, with changes entered in to reflect shifting costs or any unexpected event that you think will affect the computed forecast. And every other week you should create a variance report that shows how the actual sales compared with what you predicted and update the future forecasts accordingly. That'll give you a constantly adjusted model and a means to deal with the differences that will always exist."

"That makes sense," said Scott. "So if we open a new market or change prices or if we find out that a competitor is about to slash prices, we'll be able to change the forecast to reflect the changing conditions. The only problem I see is that I'm not sure how good the prediction would be, even with all the adjustments."

"What's important is that you have a model for what will happen if all things remain equal. If you get wind of something that will affect your forecast, you have the option of countering with your own strategy. At your weekly operations meeting you can raise it as an issue, and you can decide jointly how to respond."

"What weekly operations meeting?"

John answered, "The one you'll be attending every Monday afternoon from now on. The information that you and Marie and everyone else will be generating will be crucial to the progress of this company."

"Right," said Rick. "Your ability to influence things goes up dramatically when you can report, 'My forecast for next month was x units, but due to an advertising blitz by a competitor, I predict that unless we respond, the forecasted amount will be reduced by fifteen percent.' It won't matter that you might be off a few percent either way. The important thing is that you have identified a potential threat and can attach a dollar value to its impact."

"Who's going to believe *my* prediction? Dan has his own ideas about the effects of a competitor's new product or of a change in pricing, and you probably do too, John. Why will everyone suddenly believe *me*?"

"Initially," said John, "maybe no one will. I trust Dan's judgment because he's established a track record over the years. You'll have to establish your own. If your estimates are accurate, we'll begin to rely on them. The important thing is to make logical assessments based on the data."

"A sales forecast needs to be dynamic," added Rick. "You have to adjust it constantly to keep up with the changing market. If all your competitors kept their products and prices the same over time, your job would be simple—but that's not how markets work."

"I guess I'd better start entering the data. I'll have something ready for you to review tomorrow, John. Okay?" Scott was beginning to feel a little more confident about processing the raw data, but he still had doubts about the reliability of the resulting forecast.

John agreed to review Scott's initial forecast whenever it was ready. As they were leaving Scott's office, they passed Wendy. "Is Pete back from lunch yet?" asked John.

"Beats me," she said, with a look that indicated she couldn't imagine why anyone would ask her such a question. She sauntered to her desk, sat down, and started working on her nails.

John said to Rick as they approached John's office, "Hey, we're on a roll. What should we attack next?"

"Well, we've already dealt with bookkeeping, order tracking, customer service, and sales forecasts. Let's go over receivables with Joan," he said as they entered John's office.

"Looking for me?" said Joan, looking up from where she was seated at John's desk. "I was just trying to get the mail organized. What's up?"

"Invoicing," said Rick as they both took seats in front of John's desk facing Joan. "How does your invoicing work?"

"It's pretty simple. I get a sales order from Scott, verify from Jerry that he has the parts, and type a packing slip. Then the packing slip goes to Sean. When he ships the order, he makes a copy of the packing slip marked up with any changes, and gives it to me. I type up the invoice and mail it to the customer. That's pretty much it."

"And you add the information to your file of outstanding invoices so you can keep track of who hasn't paid?"

"Yeah, and then I delete it from the list when we receive the check. Is there a better way?"

"As a matter of fact, there is," said Rick. "The program Marie started installing yesterday to manage the bank accounts also has the ability to print invoices and packing slips. With the data entered, it can print an aged receivables list to aid in your collection activities. Do you send out dunning notices?"

"Whenever we need to but not automatically."

"Well, most companies see a marked reduction in their aged receivables when they start sending out dunning notices a few days before the payments are due. Who would be the logical person to send out the notices?"

"Me, I guess."

"What about Wendy?"

"Wendy? Are you kidding?" said John.

"Sending out form letters to customers doesn't exactly require a Ph.D., and I've noticed that she doesn't seem to be overworked," said Rick. "We should set up a procedure for her and see how she does."

"I guess so, but on a trial basis. First, we have to have an aged receivables list from Marie. When do you think it'll be ready?"

"We need to let her finish processing the bank-account data first. She's already noticed that the purchase-order tracking function is in the software, and I'll bet that she takes care of it before we even ask her about it. In the meantime, Joan, you should make sure that your receivables list is up-to-date so that the data will be ready to enter. Okay?'' Joan agreed to get the data together and left John's office to talk to Wendy about the added responsibility.

*a*fter Joan left, John moved to his seat behind his desk. He noticed the latest issue of *Computer Weekly* that he had been reading earlier in the week. Pointing to an article on the cover, he said, "It looks like we're going to have to lower our prices. I wonder what effect that will have on everything?"

"As soon as we have the data everyone is working on, we can build a model and project the future performance. We should wait a few days though, until each department has had a chance to work through their numbers a couple of times. What we need to talk about now is quality assurance."

"Okay, what about it?"

"How do you have it set up?"

"Jerry uses Jackie, who used to be the lead assembler. She's been here forever, is very conscientious, and knows how everything is built."

"How does she know if a board is working correctly after it's completed?"

"We built several test fixtures. She plugs the board in, punches a button, and a test is performed. If there's a problem, a red light comes on."

"How comprehensive are the test fixtures?"

"Dan designed them, so I guess they're pretty good. What are you getting at, anyway?"

"You have a built-in conflict. The quality assurance manager should never report to the person responsible for shipping products out the door. The quality assurance manager has to have the authority to shut down production when a problem is identified, and if he or she reports to the head of production, it's the head of production who ends up making those decisions."

"You're right. Jerry could kill us by shipping a board that hasn't been completely tested."

"It's more than just the testing, though. Quality assurance is your last line of defense against shipping *anything* that will tarnish your reputation. Everything from the operational characteristics of the boards to the contents of the shipping container should be constantly and closely scrutinized, and a procedure must be in place that is scrupulously followed. Do you periodically ship one of your own packages to yourself to see what condition it's in when it arrives?"

"I never thought of that, but it sounds like a good idea."

"QA really consists of two parts: ensuring that products don't get into production prematurely, and ensuring that whatever is in production gets to the customer in a manner that protects the reputation of the company. Have you worked out an acceptance test procedure for each of your products?"

"You mean a formal document?"

"Yes, you need a document that describes in detail the procedure to be followed to verify the correct performance of each product—in every mode and in every configuration it could conceivably be used. This type of procedure generally has to be prepared by the development team, since they are usually the only ones with the knowledge to do it. It will be the ultimate test to guarantee that the product functions properly, and when it's complete it should be signed by all responsible parties.

"However, it often happens that after a product is released, a customer will use it in a way that hadn't been considered by the development team and which prevents it from working properly, and a change will have to be incorporated in the product. When this happens, and it always does, the procedure should be modified to include this new information, and when the product is modified, it must be retested to ensure that the modified board works properly. It's not uncommon that a seemingly innocuous change made to correct one problem will affect something else, creating a new problem that might remain unnoticed unless an exhaustive test is performed."

"I think that happened last week," said John. "Dan made a simple modification for one of our customers, and nobody realized that the change inhibited a peripheral function. Fortunately it was one of our good customers, and they had requested the modification—otherwise it could have been much worse. But Jerry ended up spending a lot of time figuring out what the problem was, and it took a few days to recover that time."

"When you ship anything without a comprehensive acceptance test procedure on file, you are leaving too much to chance. I doubt that product liability is much of an issue with your products, but in other industries, shipping products that haven't been extensively tested under a well-documented procedure can leave a company vulnerable to serious product-liability claims. Suppose you manufactured a car, and its brakes failed under some peculiar condition. If you can't show that you tested the brakes under that condition and that they operated properly in your test, you'd better hope that you have good liability insurance."

"But most small businesses don't have a separate quality-assurance department—who could afford it?"

"You're right. If a business is small enough, the key players can take care of it, and that's often the way it goes. If the volume of production is manageable, the head of production can personally check everything before it gets shipped. But when the volume exceeds what can be monitored by that person, products start slipping out without being checked. Everything is still okay until a customer reports a production problem, and then they have to scramble to recover. Every growing company eventually gets to the size where they need a separate quality-assurance department, the sole purpose of which is to ensure that only properly operating products are shipped."

"We had a group like that at R.S.S.," said John. "I was mostly involved with R&D, but I remember that sometimes they really slowed down our shipments. How can we prevent the same thing from happening here?"

"By building an escape hatch into the system but only allowing it to be used under extreme circumstances. When Dan makes a modification for a customer, is it rigorously tested before it's shipped, or does it bypass this step because it's similar to another product that's regularly tested?"

"Based on recent history, it's safe to say that it's easy to bypass the testing. Especially if the customer really squeals about needing it fast."

"When you're small," Rick continued, "it's relatively easy to overcome most production problems. But as you grow, the ramifications of shipping untested products can be very far-reaching. One way of viewing it is to consider all possible outcomes of shipping a product prematurely. If all goes well, then you've lost nothing. The customer got his product when he wanted it, and everything was okay. Suppose that shipping it on time increases the probability that everything won't be okay. Then you have two choices: You can ship it on time and run the risk of a problem occurring, or you can take the time to ensure that there are no problems. I've heard people at other companies ask, 'Why is there never enough time to do it right, but always plenty of time to do it over?' With a strong QA department, you avoid the ill will that results from shipping products before they're ready."

"This won't be so easy to change," said John. "Everyone is conditioned to jump through hoops for the customers—that's one of the reasons we got where we are. It sounds like we're going to have to become less responsive. Won't that mean we'll lose business to our smaller competitors who can react faster, the way we used to?"

"The business you lose to people who demand quick response will be more than compensated for by the business you save by operating professionally—shipping high-quality products that always work and that arrive on schedule."

"You mean our customers will be happier waiting a few extra days for a product that's guaranteed to work instead of quickly getting one that immediately malfunctions."

201

"That's one way of putting it, I guess. But I mentioned that QA should be involved in two areas, and so far we've only discussed the procedure for releasing new products and options. You also have to maintain testing of the products that are already in production, since every once in a while a product that was once properly assembled will suddenly not work. A change in a component from a vendor, a shortcut taken in the assembly process, inadequate screening of the components—there are many reasons for a sudden malfunction of a product that you thought was reliable. It's dangerous to assume that just because something *was* okay it will continue to be okay."

Rick saw that John wasn't quite convinced. "The QA system should be highly structured; so structured that it may seem unwieldy at times. But the benefits of having such a system will far outweigh any complaints people have about it. And if a situation arises where there's not enough time to go through the normal QA procedure and you want to bypass the system, that decision should be made only by you."

"I thought I was supposed to be figuring out ways to delegate more things. If I have to rule on every QA exception, I might as well move my desk out to the production floor."

"No, you'll only be involved in exceptional circumstances. Give QA the authority, and you'll find the weak links in the system."

"Weak links?"

"Are modified products being released to production before they've been adequately tested? Are the assembly people careless? Is the design faulty? Things like that. Tell me, how do you handle the change-control process?"

"Change-control process—you mean ECOs and document control? Those are things that Dan and I decided really bogged down R.S.S., and we decided to minimize it when we started Walpold Enterprises." He thought for a moment and then said, "Let's get some more coffee. I need a pick-me-up."

"Yeah, me too."

They headed toward the break room, each of them clutching his empty mug.

*m*arie, what's this item on the previous month's income statement?" Phyl was in Marie's office, going over some records with her.

"Oh, it's the expense for the agency that creates and prints our sales literature," said Marie curtly.

Phyl thanked her for the clarification and started to leave but stopped short of the door and turned back to face Marie. "I'm curious about something, Marie. You obviously aren't happy with the way John has been running things, and yet you treat me like I'm the enemy. I'm only trying to help, you know."

"Yeah, right," said Marie skeptically. "I get the feeling from your pal that as soon as you get rid of John, I'm number two on your hit list. Pardon me for not welcoming you with open arms, but it seems pretty clear that whatever you're doing here is not going to be to my advantage."

"You've got it all wrong, Marie," said Phyl in a conciliatory tone. "First, Leonard is not my pal; he's my colleague. Second, we have no plans to replace you as controller, in spite of the impression he's given you. In fact, we were going to wait until next week to discuss it with you, but I'll give you a preview right now. We'd like you to be involved with the new start-up company that Herb's going to fund to develop and market Dan's computer pager."

"Oh really? I already have a job. Why would I want another one?"

"For a piece of the action—stock in the new company. The initial work shouldn't be too demanding. I just need someone to pay the bills and keep the accounting data current. It would take very little of your time, in exchange for which you'd be an owner in the new company."

"*You* just need someone to pay the bills? *You're* going to run the new company?"

"Sure, why not? Dan will be doing the engineering, and I'll manage things."

"And what will Leonard be doing?"

"I think that's pretty obvious, isn't it? He sure won't have any time for the new company. Don't say anything to anyone yet. We'll discuss the details next week. Okay?"

"I suppose," said Marie, noncommittally.

*W*hen John and Rick returned to John's office with fresh coffee, they resumed their discussion of change control.

"You're too big not to have controlled documents," said Rick.

John shook his head. "Freeze the design and require engineering change orders for every change? Yuck."

"It's more than that. Test procedures need to be modified, assembly procedures reviewed, inventory examined for obsolescence. It may seem like an unnecessary complication, but without a rigorous change-control procedure you'll have problems that you're not even aware of, and when you *do* find out about them, they could be very serious."

"But we've always been a small, aggressive, hi-tech company. What you're describing sounds like one of the ponderous companies we've succeeded in stealing customers from. When we lose our edge, what's to keep another Walpold Enterprises from stealing our customers away, just like we stole customers from our larger competitors?"

"John, you're already losing customers. You basically have two choices: get the existing operation organized so you can be responsive and still make money or reduce the size of the operation down to the level where the quality of work is acceptable with the current operating procedures. Would you consider limiting the size of your operation by reducing the number of products or customers?"

"Of course not. That would make us more vulnerable. The more variety we have, the less likely we are to get clobbered by any one event. If we limit our business to a few customers, the effect of any one of them canceling an order would be much more serious. And the more products we have, the easier it is for our sales people to make their numbers and the less vulnerable we are to a competitor stealing our customers."

"Then it's simple," said Rick. "You need to alter the operation so it can handle the amount of business you now have."

"That's my only option? Either go back to the way things were two years ago or completely change the entire operation?"

"Let's look at it this way," said Rick. "What is happening to you is not unique. It happens to almost all growing companies. You simply have to swallow hard and accept the fact that things can't stay the same as they were when you started. To protect your investment and improve the probability of continued growth, you need to become more structured. It's as simple as that."

"Are you saying that I'm not suited to continue being president when we get bigger?"

"Do you really want to be? If you accept the fact that more structured techniques are required as you grow, you can decide if you want to be the one to implement them. A logical approach might be to hire a general manager with the management skills to do it. This would free you up to do whatever you want—tinker, start another division, take up golf. It's up to you. The key is to make the decision yourself, not have it made for you because you lose control."

John sat back in his chair and pondered what Rick was saying. Then he abruptly sat up and said, "Okay, I'm convinced—we need to be more structured. I'm going to discuss QA with Jerry. I'm sure he'll agree that Jackie is the right person to head up our new QA department. Assuming he does, I'll talk to Jackie about her new responsibilities and promote her to manager of QA, reporting to me. How does that sound?"

"Sounds good to me. We also need to talk to Jerry about production and inventory control. But," he said, glancing at his watch, "it's getting late, so let's tackle it tomorrow morning."

Rick left John's office, and as he was walking toward the outer door to leave, he heard raised voices coming from Rita's office: "—it's not fair to John," he heard Rita say.

"Who cares? You have to look out for yourself these days," said Pete, and then Rita's door slammed shut, and Rick could hear only muffled arguing.

FRiDAy

August 4, 1995

*a*s Rick was driving to Walpold Enterprises on Friday morning, he reflected on how much had been accomplished since he first met with John Walpold the previous Friday. In spite of all the progress they'd made, however, Rick was still concerned about the cash squeeze. He agreed with Leonard's assessment that the banks would have little interest in extending additional credit, leaving Herb as the most logical savior. But with the input that Herb was undoubtedly getting from Leonard, that was a remote possibility without John's removal from the company.

Rick was a pragmatist. Things being the way they were, he had to accept the fact that John had little chance of surviving unscathed. He sighed as he drove into the parking lot and decided to just do the best he could until Herb pulled the plug and to avoid alienating Leonard. He didn't want to ruin his own future consulting possibilities.

Rick found John in his office, and together they headed out to the production area to talk to Jerry. It was only 7:45, but they found the production team already hard at work. Jerry was sitting at a desk in the middle of the production floor, studying a report. "Good morning, Jerry," said John. "Got a minute?"

Jerry brushed the few remaining strands of hair across his shiny pate with one hand, looked up at John, and said, "Sure. We're missing some parts, but I'll figure it out later. I'm pretty sure where they went." He put down the report and stood up.

"That's what we wanted to talk to you about—inventory," said John. "According to Rick's analysis of the financial statements, the inventory level is above the industry standard. We were wondering what you thought about that."

"What are the numbers exactly?"

"Well," said Rick, "the inventory turn rate is more than a hundred and twenty days, as compared with the industry standard of only eighty-two days, which translates to a difference of over a hundred and seventy thousand dollars. Would you say you have over a hundred and seventy thousand dollars too much inventory?"

Jerry couldn't believe his ears. Were they making him the fall guy again? Jerry had seriously been considering quitting and finding a job where he could deal with people that understood production and inventory control; these clowns obviously didn't. They'd finally given him authority over his department, including Sean, but they still hadn't addressed the underlying problems with inventory. Just then, Dan walked by, looking even more disheveled than usual; he needed a shave, and his clothes looked like they had been slept in. "Hey Dan," said Jerry, "you wouldn't happen to know anything about the boards that were sitting on Sharon's bench when she left yesterday afternoon, would you? Twenty of them are missing."

Dan stopped and turned around. He looked up and rubbed his unshaven chin. After a few seconds he said, "Oh yeah, I needed them last night for a modification I was working on for E.D.T." He yawned, stretched, and started to walk away.

"A note might have been nice," said Jerry through clinched teeth. "Those were production boards we were planning to ship today."

"Yeah, yeah, get off my case—I've been here all night. Do you want me to call you at three a.m. and ask your permission to use your precious boards? I'm going home." With that, Dan turned and walked away.

John quickly said to Rick, "Why don't you two continue this discussion without me so I can talk to Dan. I'll be back as soon as I can."

J ohn caught up with Dan and started walking with him. "Been here all night again?"

"Yeah, Warren at E.D.T. called yesterday and said he was desperate for some boards, but they needed to be modified. Now Jerry's got his knickers in a knot because I did something to satisfy a customer. This place is really getting to me."

"Why don't we head over to Harold's and talk," John offered.

"Why not," Dan responded glumly. "I've had it for today."

They drove to Harold's in relative silence. When they arrived, Iona seated them at their regular booth in the back. "Iona Chevy station wagon," Dan said halfheartedly.

"That's remarkable," she responded, shaking her head. "You want coffee?"

"Yeah, just coffee," said John. She filled their cups and left. John decided that the time had come to confront Dan. "Do you regret leaving R.S.S. to start this company, Dan?"

"No, but I regret that things aren't like they were during the first year. We worked our asses off, but it was fun. Now everything is such a hassle." Dan absently poked at the paper placemat with his fork. "Every time I turn around, something goes wrong, and half the time I get blamed for it."

"Yeah, me too. It seems like after all we've done, we should be entitled to a little respect, but all I hear is, 'Why haven't you signed the purchase order that's been on your desk for three days?' "

"It sucks," said Dan. "Jerry should be thanking me for slaving away in the middle of the night, trying to keep our customers happy. What a jerk! And an idiot too. Do you think he really believes that draping his five remaining hairs over the top of his head keeps him from looking bald? Do you suppose he'll continue to do that as the number of hairs decreases until they're all gone?"

"Maybe he'll get a toupee. Or join the Hair Club for Men."

They both laughed. "That's the first time we've laughed together in a year," said Dan.

"You're right. But we haven't had much to be happy about. I knew things were screwed up but didn't know what to do to fix them. Rick's advice has helped a lot, and I'm beginning to think we're going to be okay."

"You mean you think we can get the company back to the way it used to be?"

"Well, not exactly. We have to change certain things so that we can handle the increased volume of business. We have to be more structured and organized. I've been much too lax a manager for the past couple of years, but I'm looking forward to getting it all under control again and turning the company around."

"Great, so you're going to be the next Lee Iacocca. What about me?"

Just then, Joan came into the diner and looked around until she spotted them. As she approached their booth, she said, " I thought I'd find you here. We've got problems." She slid into the booth next to John.

"Joan Richards, master of the understatement," said John. "What more could be going wrong?"

"Leonard and Phyl are telling everyone that next week Leonard will be in charge and that Phyl will be running Dan's new pager company. And everyone believes what they're saying. Especially Pete," she said, turning to Dan, "who says he's leaving with you, Dan. And Marie, who told me that Phyl offered her stock in the new company."

"Jeez! I never agreed to anything with those two. They've been trying to get me to talk to Herb, but I've been avoiding it. Pete overheard Leonard talking to me about funding a new company, and he told me later that he'd rather work for me if I was leaving than stay and work for fancy-pants, as he calls Leonard. I told him I didn't know what was going to happen yet. I really don't know what to do."

"What do you want to do?" asked John.

"I'd like things to be the way they were and continue doing the things the way I have been, developing leading-edge computer products. What's wrong with that?"

"You can't have it both ways, I guess. Don't forget, we made certain promises to Herb in exchange for the use of his money. So far he's made zip on his investment, and just as we're getting to the point where he might start realizing a return, we can't throw in the towel and say 'April Fool! This isn't fun anymore—we quit.' Are you really thinking about taking more of his money and starting another company?''

"Leonard and Phyl say that Herb is excited about the pager, and that he—''

"You want to run your own company? I can't believe it,'' said John, shaking his head.

"Not me. Phyl says she'll run it, and I can do the development. Maybe it would be like when we started this company.''

"I can't believe Herb would be willing to fund it. Isn't he the one that says he invests in people? His last investment with us isn't looking too great.''

"Well, maybe since Phyl will be running it he figures he'll have better protection or control. I don't know.''

"Dan, you're already tapped out. What protection would he have that you wouldn't lose interest and walk out?''

"Well, he'd have my Walpold stock as collateral. That's what bothers me. It sounded good at first, but it's starting to sound more and more like he's just trying to get control of my stock so he can replace you with the whiz kid. I don't know what to do. If I agree to take seed money to start another company, I'm out, you're out, Leonard's in, and who knows what'll happen to the company. If I refuse, Herb pulls the plug, and we both twirl down the drain.''

"Maybe there are other options,'' said John, drumming his fingers on the table, trying to sort out the possibilities.

"Like what? I'm not even sure I could legally take money to start another company. I've been thinking about what Rick said to me yesterday about my 'fiduciary responsibility,' and when it sank in, it really scared me. Apparently, if I do anything that isn't in the best interests of the company, the other stockholders— meaning you—can sue me. Did you know that?''

"I'm starting to understand a lot of things that we really should have understood at the beginning. According to the employment agreements we signed, neither of us can take anything we developed here to a new company. Did you know *that*?'' countered John.

"Boy, you guys are doing wonders to instill confidence in your loyal office manager," interjected Joan. "I'd better hurry up and submit the receipt for the coffee supplies for reimbursement while there's still money left in the till."

"What a couple of nitwits we've been," said Dan. "But wait a minute. Don't you think Herb knows all this? How could he be waving money in front of my face if he knows I can't legally leave and start another company?"

"I've been wondering the very same thing. The only thing I can figure is that he assumes we're too stupid to know what's happening. But if his subterfuge allows him to protect his investment, then I guess he figures that the end justifies the means."

"But wouldn't it leave him open to lawsuits too?" asked Dan.

"He must feel the situation is pretty desperate to risk exposing himself like that."

"Well, exactly how desperate is it?" asked Joan. "Is Herb really on the verge of pulling the plug?"

"Rick asked me the same thing yesterday," said John. "He thinks that Herb is just trying to protect his investment from what Leonard has convinced him is imminent failure."

"Somebody should step on that slimy little bastard," said Dan.

"Maybe somebody can. Remember the request for work-benches you tacked onto Jerry's purchase order last week?" John asked.

"Sure, what about it?" asked Dan, wondering what this could possibly have to do with Leonard.

"Well," John continued, "you didn't mention anything about it to Leonard, did you?"

"No, of course not. Why would I?"

"I didn't think so. I have an idea," said John, grinning. "And Joan, you're just the person that can help me pull this off."

*a*fter Dan and John left the production area, Jerry said to Rick, "That little confrontation with Dan that you just saw isn't unusual—in fact, it's a daily occurrence. I'm supposedly responsible for the inventory, but everybody and his brother-in-law wanders through here and helps themselves. Inventory control is a joke. The numbers you've been using for your calculations are pure fiction."

"Have you told that to John and Dan?"

"They're both engineers. They've never been involved with a production operation before, and they think it's just a matter of pouring in parts and turning the crank. They don't need me here—they just need someone to hold the assemblers' hands and make sure that they work eight hours a day. You want to know where a big chunk of the hundred and seventy thousand dollars' worth of inventory is? Come here and look at this."

Jerry led Rick around the corner and pointed to a shelf that contained dozens of completed boards, stacked haphazardly on top of each other. He picked one up and handed it to Rick. "These boards all work. But in one of Dan's all-night sessions of inspiration, he came up with an improvement in the graphics. Incorporating the change required a modification to the printed circuit board, and the engineering brain trust decided to rush through the new artwork, at a premium, and only ship the new configuration. Since the parts can all be salvaged, they viewed it as a trivial change to implement. So sure, we've got lots of parts. Unfortunately, they're already soldered to these boards. Taking them off requires considerably more time than putting them on, and who should I assign to the job? If you'll notice, all the assemblers are busy."

"Tell me how the change-control process worked in this situation. How was the decision made?"

"Without me, that's for sure. John called me into his office and told me they've already got the new boards on the way. Just like that."

Rick thought for a moment. John and Dan had hired Jerry to handle production, but they never gave him the authority that he needed to succeed. Jerry was probably right—John and Dan had only a cursory knowledge of production and its requirements. But they could probably be persuaded of the need for making changes. "Jerry, before we get bogged down in change control, tell me how you manage inventory control around here."

"I use a card-file system to keep track of the most expensive parts—you know, the eighty-twenty rule: eighty percent of the total cost results from twenty percent of the parts. With Dan wandering through in the middle of the night helping himself to whatever he wanted, I've had to order more than just for production. I try to keep a minimum number of the inexpensive parts on hand but, again, if I don't have extras of everything, I may run out before I can replenish the supply. Do I run out of key parts? You bet. Unless I know what parts are going to disappear and can order enough extras to compensate for those midnight raiding parties, I'll always run out."

"Doesn't the extra inventory worry you?" asked Rick.

"Look, my job is to keep the production line running. The longer it takes Rita to get parts, the more I need in reserve. You say the average inventory turn rate is eighty-two days? I'll bet the average company doesn't have purchase orders getting lost on the president's desk and vendors refusing to ship because of nonpayment."

Rick said, "I'm surprised you don't have one of Ben's programs. Everyone else seems to."

"Oh he brought one in, all right, but I had sense enough to ignore it. It didn't handle subassemblies and was difficult to use, but the method of ordering and expensing parts isn't our problem anyway—you can see that."

Jerry appeared to be much more capable than the casual observer would deduce from the problem-laden operation he was nominally in charge of. He was accustomed to running a production operation in a more mature company and was frustrated with having to deal with the lack of structure. It was clear to Rick that increasing Jerry's control would be a giant step toward solving the production problems, and it would probably keep him from quitting, too. However, increasing his control could only occur at the expense of the people who were enjoying the benefits of these lax procedures. It was time to address these issues with John, but Rick needed to give Jerry a glimmer of hope first.

"Jerry, there are half a dozen off-the-shelf inventory-control programs that would ease your problems, assuming that discipline can be enforced. Are you familiar with any of them?"

Jerry mentioned three that he had used in the past but said, "It won't matter which program I use. It'll take more than software to straighten this place out."

"You're right, and I'm going to discuss it with John. Why don't you pick the program you think would be best and prepare a short presentation explaining why you selected it. Could you have something by next week?"

"You're sure it'll help?"

"You've got nothing to lose. In the meantime, I'll discuss the discipline issue with John and Dan."

*r*ick thanked Jerry and then left to find John. John wasn't in his office, and Joan was no where to be found either. Rick asked Wendy where everybody was, but she just shrugged her shoulders and went back to her manicure. Rick wandered into the break room, but it was empty. He went to John's office, sat down, and waited. In a few minutes he heard the front door open and John and Joan speaking in hushed voices. When Joan saw Rick she waved hello and went back to work. John entered his office and greeted Rick.

"John, I just finished talking with Jerry, and I wanted to discuss some things with you."

"Sure, Rick. What's on your mind?"

"I think Jerry's very capable, but he's losing a battle that he should be winning. Let me ask you about the change that Dan incorporated recently that made quite a few boards obsolete. Did anyone consider the cost of the change before it was adopted?"

"That change was a major improvement. Dan stumbled onto a much better way of handling the retrace problem, reducing the flickering to an almost negligible level. It gave us a real advantage over our competition at a time when they were just announcing new products. It would have been stupid not to incorporate it immediately."

"But did you consider the cost?"

"What difference does the cost make when we can blow our competition out of the water?"

"Whenever a production change is required, the time factor should be considered. Certain changes should be immediate, regardless of the cost—changes that correct serious product-liability deficiencies, for example. But product enhancements can usually be phased in so that the cost is minimized. The point is, all these issues have to be considered before making the final decision. The change we're talking about was simply a product enhancement. How many sales would you have lost if you had delayed it one week until the existing stock had been used up?"

John threw up his hands. "Dan had already told some of our customers about the improvement before I heard about it. What could I do? Tell the customers to continue using the outmoded boards until we used up our stock?"

"Well, it shouldn't have gotten to that point. Two major modifications need to occur. First, as we started to discuss yesterday, you need to develop and implement a more structured change-control process, and it's becoming increasingly obvious to me that you can't postpone it. You need a change-control team composed of representatives from all the departments concerned, with one of them as its leader. Any proposed change should be analyzed by each member of the team, and the impact to each area should be quantified. The team leader will schedule the meetings and act as the moderator. Occasionally you'll have to rule on issues brought to you by the team when they are deadlocked, but those occasions will be rare. Usually the members will compromise and work together to do what's best for the company."

"I'll admit I've avoided implementing a change-control team—I just hate to tie everyone up for it. Isn't it good enough to just determine what the change will cost?"

"Is it? Let's look at each department and what it might be asked to contribute. Production is the most straightforward. They determine what the new change will cost in terms of the inventory that will be made obsolete, both raw stock and work in progress and the cost to rework already completed inventory. Quality Assurance determines the cost and the time it would take to update test methods. Whoever is responsible for documentation determines if changes will be required and, again, what will be the impact to the existing documentation? Should it be scrapped, modified, or phased in after the current supply runs out? Packaging might even need to be changed.

"Tech Support needs to evaluate the effect on already existing spares that are in the field and to determine if a Tech Bulletin should be issued to inform the people in the field. Sales and Marketing must be made aware of the change, because it may affect contracts that are currently being negotiated and possibly might justify a change to marketing literature and even advertising campaigns. All of these things need to be considered after R&D says, 'Here's a change all ready to be incorporated.'"

"That's similar to the process we used at R.S.S. I never imagined that we would end up having to operate the same way so soon," said John, shaking his head.

"The costs involved in ignoring all these issues can be significant. I once knew a manager who habitually turned each issue into a crisis. He would decide that a problem was either worthy of throwing all the company's resources at it or not critical enough to attend to at all. And it didn't matter if the problem was related to sales, marketing, R&D, quality control, production, or tech support. If he decided it needed solving, nothing else mattered until it got resolved so everyone had to stop what they were doing and work on it to the exclusion of everything else."

"Hmm," John interrupted, laughing. "That sounds familiar. Did someone tell you that's the way I do things?"

"My lips are sealed," Rick joked. "Seriously though, it's an all too common approach. Unfortunately, the world doesn't operate like that. You can't just focus on a single issue and ignore everything else. Constantly running from one crisis to the next is an inefficient way to solve problems and usually results in expending a lot of time and effort to resolve problems that could have been dealt with easily when they were small. By being more methodical, you can improve the probability that the best solution to each problem can be implemented."

"I sure hate to lose the ability we have right now to respond instantly whenever we need to," said John, "but I know what you're saying is right. So how should we set up this change-control team?"

"Well, it needs to be headed by an effective team leader, and based on what I've seen so far, Jerry is the only one who fits the bill right now. He's already familiar with the process and would probably welcome the additional control and can explain to everyone how the system will work. It remains to be seen whether he's the logical choice, though. A change-control leader who's also head of production may tend to give production issues priority at the expense of other important issues. That's why you should plan on attending frequently until you're satisfied that all the company's interests are being served. If Jerry has the right attitude, he might make a good general manager sometime in the future. This would be a good way to help him grow in that direction."

"Well, we'll see about that. But you said there were two areas that needed to be changed. What's the other one?"

"The screws need to be tightened around inventory control. It's not fair for Production to be responsible for inventory if they don't have the authority to control it."

"Jerry already has the authority to purchase anything he needs. What are you talking about?"

"Dan takes whatever he needs, from individual parts to finished boards. Jerry needs to have complete control over his stock. A tall fence around the inventory area might help," said Rick half-joking.

"Are you saying that Dan should order the parts he needs when Jerry already has them? That's stupid."

"If you expect Jerry to maintain a specific number of certain parts in order to achieve his production goals, he's got to know when he orders something that it will be available when he needs it. There's nothing wrong with Dan getting his parts from Jerry, as long as he places an order with Jerry and doesn't affect the rest of production. If Dan can't plan ahead, he should have to wait. And if he does take something in the middle of the night, it shouldn't be too much to ask that he leave a note telling Jerry what he's taken. That's not only proper procedure; it's common courtesy."

"Dan again, huh? All of our inventory problems are caused by Dan?"

"Of course not. But discipline is required for the systems to work properly, and Dan's mode of operation violates most standard practices. People like Dan can still thrive in more highly structured companies—they just need to be willing to follow the rules. You and I can talk to him and explain why the rules make sense. Right now, he's a loose cannon. The problems he's caused for Jerry should never have developed in the first place. That kind of behavior is hurting the company."

"For the first time in weeks, Dan and I just had a good conversation and cleared the air. Believe it or not, he's just as committed to the success of this company as I am."

"Well if he's really as committed to the company as you say he is, he'll start playing by the rules. But even if we get that taken care of, it would still be helpful if Jerry had the right software. The program that Ben wrote to control inventory is inadequate. Jerry should scrap it and purchase an inexpensive off-the-shelf inventory-control program to manage his parts. With the program and the proper discipline in place, he'll be able to stay on top of his parts needs and meet his production goals."

"How's this going to help our cash?" asked John.

"Consider this situation—you order parts, receive them, manufacture your products and ship them, all in one day. You would need only a single day's worth of inventory in stock to keep production running. Each day that's added to this process requires an additional day's worth of inventory. Purchase orders getting lost, vendors not shipping, parts disappearing—all these events cause Jerry to need more inventory to keep his assemblers busy. Minimize these inefficiencies, and you'll need less inventory. Less inventory equals more cash."

"As simple as that, huh?" When the problems were examined in detail, each solution became more obvious. To John, it seemed a bit like a magic trick that he'd seen when he was a teenager. When he bought the same trick at a magic store, he was disappointed that he'd been so easily fooled. It wasn't magic at all, not even sleight of hand. Once you knew how it worked, it was actually pretty straightforward.

"Okay," said John. "I'm convinced." Just then the phone rang. "Excuse me just a second. I've told Wendy to only interrupt me for emergencies when I'm in a meeting. Maybe my wife just won the lottery," he said as he picked up the phone. "Hello, this is John."

"John," said Herb, not bothering to identify himself. "I just talked to Leonard, and he's about finished with his review. I think it would be a good idea for us to get together Monday afternoon and discuss things. How about two o'clock at your place?"

"Two is fine. Do you mind if Rick Devereux sits in?"

"Doesn't matter to me. You and Dan are the only ones I want to talk to, but you can bring anybody else you want. See ya," he said, not waiting for a response.

"That was Herb," said John, hanging up the phone. "He's coming Monday at two to review Leonard's findings. A lot sooner than I'd hoped." John got up and started pacing.

"How did he sound? Conciliatory or loaded for bear?"

"Maybe a little more blunt than usual, which isn't a good sign. I'd better be prepared." He reached for the Tums in his pocket and popped two into his mouth. "Rick, I'll need your help to get ready for the meeting. Could you come back in a few minutes so we can plan a strategy? I need a few minutes to call Dan and to send an E-mail message."

"No problem," responded Rick. "I'll go get some fresh coffee. Want any?"

"Thanks," said John, as he swiveled his chair around to face his computer and began typing.

*r*ick and John worked until early evening on their preparations for Monday's meeting with Herb. As they were getting ready to leave, John suddenly said, "Want to grab something for dinner? I have a few things I'd like to discuss with you."

"Sure," said Rick.

They drove separate cars to a nearby seafood restaurant. Once inside and seated in a corner booth, they both ordered an icy draft beer—just the thing to help them relax after a long and stressful day. The beers arrived in frosty mugs. John took a long swig and said, "Ahh, I needed that." After they ordered, he told Rick, "It's easy to see that we've made a lot of progress this week toward getting things organized. But I'm the one that let things get out of control in the first place. How can I prevent it from happening again—assuming that I'm still in charge after Monday's meeting?"

Rick took another swig of beer before he responded. "People use several analogies when describing the way to manage a company properly. It's just like raising kids, because you need to be consistent, or like being captain of a ship or general of an army—it takes order and discipline to succeed. I've said many times that very few companies succeed by luck alone. They succeed because someone with a vision steers it properly.

It's also important to have competent workers, but if they aren't properly directed and motivated, their work can be ineffective.''

"I know it's my responsibility to make sure that each area is headed in the right direction, and I need to set the right course and make sure that everyone does their part and works together to get there—but what's the secret to doing that?''

"It's all pretty much common sense. It requires establishing your goals, using discipline and incentives to motivate your employees, and keeping track of what they're doing to make sure that none of them deviates from the desired course. There are no surprises or secrets.''

"That sounds too simple.''

"Well, the specific techniques often vary from manager to manager and take time to implement, but three principles work: Develop the goals together with your employees, monitor their progress frequently, and provide a suitable working environment for all of them. When people are involved in the decision-making process, they perform better and work harder than if they're just carrying out someone else's plan. It's important to get everyone to establish goals that are compatible with the overall company goal. That's why you and I didn't decide on our own that a procedure was inadequate and develop a new one—your employees did it.

"The procedures that have been set up this week here at Walpold Enterprises will be used by everyone and monitored to ensure efficiency and quality. And if someone comes up with an improvement, I think they'll be willing to do something about it, not just complain about the problem and watch money go down the drain. Monitoring their progress and offering frequent encouragement are also essential. A logical forum for that is the weekly operations meeting.''

"Every time we've tried that, we've been derailed by some minor issue that at the time seemed important but in retrospect was really just a distraction.''

"And that's the crux of the problem. It's within your power to control the direction of the staff meeting. It should be short, and you should stick to a predetermined agenda that you've set to accomplish a limited number of goals. When a peripheral issue is raised, table it for a separate meeting. And employees should come to every meeting prepared with a written report summarizing the highlights of his or her department's activities during the previous week and their goals for the coming week. Copies of these reports should be given to Joan to be kept in a notebook as a record of what everybody said they would do to be compared with what they actually do."

"I see. I could begin each meeting by making announcements—using it as a forum to highlight significant accomplishments and such. Then one by one, each person can deliver a report on his or her area, making sure to mention items that other department heads should be aware of."

"Right," said Rick. "Of course, the content of the reports will vary from week to week, but each department head should always provide information about certain fixed categories. You should sit down with each person separately to determine what those categories are."

"That's simple enough. Most of the data they'll be reporting on should be at their fingertips anyway," said John.

"You'll need to bring your own data summaries to every meeting, too."

"You mean the information in the report we prepared for Monday's meeting with Herb?"

"Exactly, but it needs to be constantly updated."

"Okay. Before each weekly staff meeting, I'll have Joan prepare an updated summary of the key operational items that will be reported on by each department head. Let's see," said John, writing notes on his napkin, "it should probably include our bank balances, the amount of outstanding purchase orders, aged payables, aged receivables with receivables collection rate, inventory level with inventory turn rate, and booked and shipped sales for the week, month to date, and quarter to date."

"You've got it," said Rick. "Consider the sheet to be your control panel, which will enable you to monitor everyone's performance and prescribe mid-course corrections, when necessary. For example, your receivables rose twenty percent last week. Why? Why is your inventory fifteen percent higher than it was last month at this time? You'll be in control, and you'll have the data you need to evaluate potential changes. You'll find that the more closely you monitor what's happening, the more efficient everyone will become."

As Rick was speaking, the waitress brought their dinner: giant plates of steaming seafood. John picked up a fried shrimp, dipped it in cocktail sauce, and took a bite. Then he said, "No wonder things seemed out of control—they were. From now on, I'll know exactly what's going on, but it won't appear like I'm micromanaging."

"I have to say that providing a satisfactory working environment for your employees is just as important as setting goals and monitoring your staff. I've said before that Walpold Enterprises is more than just a company, it's the people in the company, and its personality is a mirror of its people, especially you. The more inefficiency you accept, the more it will flourish, and the converse is also true. The example you set defines the character of the entire company, and it's time for you to evaluate whether you're satisfied with it the way it is."

"I guess you're referring to all the clutter and the dying ferns, huh?"

"Yes, but that's not all. Another indication of a professional environment is the demeanor of the workers. Are they courteous toward their fellow employees and customers, or are they rude or indifferent? Again, you can influence this. When you tolerate behavior that negatively affects the performance of the other employees, you're endorsing inefficiency. When you call a meeting and one person is ten minutes late, it'll disrupt the meeting, and you may even have to repeat what's already been said, wasting everyone else's time. If you don't make sure that it doesn't happen again, then you're letting that person behave as if they're more important than everyone else, and the others will resent it. But if you don't tolerate inefficiency, you'll find that it will disappear. If you don't tolerate rude or arrogant behavior, that too will disappear. And that attitude of professionalism will spread throughout all areas of the company. Employees will not just try to advance their own agendas but will work together to achieve a common goal and make Walpold Enterprises increasingly profitable."

John thought about all the inefficiencies that he had been tolerating and the slovenly environment he had grown accustomed to, all the excuses he had accepted and the way he had allowed meetings to turn into a waste of everyone's time. He felt that he had a road map now, and the course was clear. Everyone who wanted to help could get on board, and everyone else would have to get out of the way.

*t*hat night, John was lying in bed trying to read a detective novel next to Beth, who was also reading, but his mind kept wandering to the impending confrontation on Monday. He put the book face down on his chest and stared at the ceiling.

Beth had felt all evening that something was troubling John. She had waited for him to broach the subject, but he hadn't. "What's the matter?" she finally asked.

"I'm worried about Monday. We're meeting with Herb, and I'm afraid that he's going to pull the rug out from under us, just when we're getting things together."

"What do you mean?"

"I'm sure Leonard has been telling him all sorts of negative stuff about me, and unfortunately most of it is true. The problem for me right now is that the banks won't extend our credit, and I don't know of any other sources of funding other than Herb. So he's really in the driver's seat. Leonard has been telling everyone that he's going to replace me, so I guess he's probably already worked out a deal with Herb."

"Isn't there anything you can do?"

"Without another source of cash, I don't know. I'm going to try to show Herb that I'm still the right guy to run the place, but it won't be easy."

"But you've been working so hard this week—I thought things were going well."

"It's true. But Herb seems to have confidence in Leonard, and he's obviously lost confidence in me. I'm sure that Leonard has been talking to Herb on a daily basis, and I haven't, which makes things even worse. We're making a lot of changes to improve things, but they're all long-term things that won't solve our cash-flow problem right now. Looking at it rationally, it seems that my only chance is to be able to convince Herb that Leonard isn't right for the job. It won't be easy, especially since the only forum I'll have is that meeting."

"But Leonard has been working with Herb for several years, hasn't he? What would make Herb believe that Leonard isn't capable of running the company?"

"I didn't say *not capable*; I said *not right* for the job. I'm afraid Leonard being in charge could be the *real* ruin of Walpold Enterprises. His arrogance has alienated everyone. That type of self-serving behavior isn't good management. But my ace in the hole might be Herb's extremely high ethical and moral standards. I need to convince Herb that Leonard doesn't share his ideals."

"In the middle of the meeting? How can you do that?" Beth asked.

With a gleam returning to John's eye, he said, "Well, it might be a long shot, but I have an idea."

M
O
d
D
A
y

August 7, 1995

*h*urricane Erin had left Orlando relatively unscathed, and the only evidence of damage was being cleared away or repaired by highway crews and utility workers. Sunny weather had returned, and with it the heat and humidity of a Florida summer day, but Walpold Enterprises was engulfed in a pervasive feeling of doom. John asked Rick and Mike to join him for lunch to discuss the impending meeting with Herb.

As they were finishing lunch, John told Rick, "Incidentally, you were right about Jerry. I no sooner talked to him about being acting leader of the change control team than he put together some Engineering Change Notice forms and dropped them off for me to approve. They may be too rough to present at today's meeting with Herb, but I think they're pretty close to what we need. Most companies probably use something similar."

"Yeah," said Rick, "as I've said before, all it takes is common sense—like most management problems, when you get down to basics."

Mike asked John, "Speaking of getting down to basics—what's your backup plan, John, in case you can't convince Herb to leave you in charge?"

"I don't have one. I certainly can't go to anyone else for money, so if he decides against me, I'm screwed. I can only hope that he'll be impressed enough with the changes we've made that he'll feel a major change isn't necessary."

Rick couldn't help but recall one of Leonard's comments: "too little too late." John paid the bill, and they left. Mike went with them to the office to attend the meeting. When they got back, they put the finishing touches on their preparations and made multiple copies of several pages to be used as handouts, and by two o'clock they were all nervously awaiting Herb's arrival.

Herb strode into the office shortly before two with a look of resolve, followed as usual by Leonard and Phyl. As he approached John's office, John greeted him and said, "Herb, I'd like you to meet Rick Devereux. And you already know Mike Smith."

"Pleased to meet you," said Rick, extending his hand toward Herb, wondering if Herb would mention the fact that they had already spoken on the phone. Herb shook his hand and eyed him suspiciously but said nothing and then offered his hand to Mike.

As they entered John's office, Herb took the seat at the end of the long conference table, where John usually sat, and Leonard and Phyl sat down to Herb's left. John, Mike, Dan, and Rick took seats across the table from Leonard and Phyl, and Joan took a seat on Leonard's side of the table across from Rick, leaving the seat next to Phyl empty.

"The purpose of this meeting is to discuss the results of last week's review by Leonard and Phyl," Herb began. "Leonard, let's hear it."

Leonard opened a folder containing his report and quickly scanned the top page. Then, looking directly at Herb, he began. "Phyl and I reviewed Walpold Enterprises as though it were a potential new investment. We examined the financials, interviewed the key employees, and evaluated the status of the products in the marketplace. As to the financials, the most serious problem is that the company is heavily overleveraged. The payables are too high, and the vendors are getting very impatient and withholding shipments. Receivables and inventory are also too high. The cash position is critical, and with the recent financial performance, the possibility of any relief from a bank or new investor is virtually zero. In short, what we've found is a company on the verge of financial collapse. Now, as to the personnel issues, I'll let Phyl summarize what we've found."

John, feeling a combination of embarrassment and growing anger, opened his mouth to speak but reconsidered. Dan looked at John sympathetically.

Phyl also had a folder in front of her, which she opened, then looked at Herb and said, "I interviewed all the key managers. The prevailing theme is that they have lost confidence in upper management. This lack of confidence manifests itself in an enervating sense of frustration that is sapping the lifeblood out of the company. The department managers are all very competent, but they have been rendered impotent by the lack of direction from the top." She sat back and folded her hands together over her folder.

Leonard continued. "The company has been completely mismanaged. In fact, the current management can only be described as inept. In short, every department is running out of control, and everyone has lost confidence in the current management's ability to resolve any of the company's problems," Leonard said, looking directly at John each time he said "current management."

"That's a bit of an exaggeration, wouldn't you say?" said John, his face now red. "Who's this 'everyone' you're referring to?"

"All the department heads—they're all ready to jump ship," Leonard answered, with a cold stare at John. "You may be a good engineer, but you don't have a clue about running a company."

John again started to speak, but again reconsidered. Joan cast her eyes down as she felt the pain her good friend and boss must be experiencing.

"Leonard, what do you recommend?" asked Herb.

"An immediate management change. We can use the shake-up as a negotiating tool with the vendors to buy time while we collect the receivables to ease the cash shortage. A change will also be viewed as a positive sign by the key employees, and it will help ease their frustration so they can be productive throughout the transition."

"And you'll reluctantly agree to be the new CEO, I suppose," said John.

"I don't see anyone else that's qualified. I'll assume the position as acting president, and then we'll see what happens."

"And what if I refuse to step down?"

"Then we'll have to vote," said Herb, "and if Dan agrees with Leonard's assessment, he'll have to vote for a change of management. And John, it may not be so bad. After all, you'll still own thirty-four percent of the company, the value of which will increase with more professional management. You're not being fired—you could refocus your efforts on R&D, an area in which you've already excelled."

"And if I *don't* agree?" interrupted Dan.

"Let's get the issue of your new computer pager on the table," said Phyl. "Herb is prepared to fund a start-up operation, headed by me, to complete the development of the pager, perform a marketing study, and begin initial production. It will be a separate entity, but Dan will have total control of the development."

"And you'll have control of the purse strings, is that right Phyl?" asked John.

"I'll take care of the administrative duties, so Dan can concentrate on development."

"So you're offering Dan money to remove him from the picture?" John wanted to make sure that everyone understood the implications.

"I'm offering Dan a chance to venture out on his own," responded Herb. "You would be available to assume control of Walpold's R&D in his absence, so everybody wins. What's wrong with that."

"What about that, Mike?" asked John.

"It would violate the terms of Dan's employment agreement, number one," said Mike. "And number two, Dan and Herb would both be violating their fiduciary responsibility to Walpold Enterprises by stealing away its chief engineer. If that happens, I would recommend that John sue them both for damages. Enough precedents already exist to make it a virtual certainty that we'd win the lawsuit."

John said, "It would certainly be an effective way to solve our current cash shortage without further diluting the stock or borrowing more money. Good idea, Phyl."

Silence. Leonard and Phyl both looked slightly perplexed, but Herb forged ahead, asking Dan, "What do you think about this? Don't you want to develop your new product? Don't you think John has lost control of this company?"

"Look, I'm just an engineer," said Dan. "Sure I want to develop my new product, but the events of the last few days have caused me to reevaluate my priorities. I had totally forgotten about the terms in the employment agreement and that I have a fiduciary responsibility to the company. No, I'll stick with John, and we'll get the pager to market somehow. I want to see Walpold Enterprises succeed—with John at the helm."

"Wait a minute," said Leonard sharply. "Since everyone wants to talk about fiduciary responsibility, let's be realistic. The best thing for this company is for John to step down. He's displayed an inability to manage effectively, so anybody with a fiduciary responsibility would be remiss if they didn't address that problem. Herb, just for starters, why don't you ask John about the current receivables? How much obsolete inventory does Walpold have? What were last week's shipments?"

"I'm glad you asked," said John as he passed out copies of a report that had been on the table on front of him. "This past week has been an eye-opener for me and the rest of the staff. This is the first installment of a new report we will be preparing each week, which is a summary of the key operational information. In addition, each department head will prepare a weekly management report to be delivered at the weekly operations meeting. I'll admit I've been lax in the past, but when our sales volume was small, we could control everything without formal reports like this.

"We're now on our way to getting excellent control over every area." He then passed out copies of the next document. "This is a copy of our new purchase-order procedure, which will solve the problems we've been having with the payments to our vendors and give Jerry greater control over managing his parts inventory. Last week Marie completed the installation of a new software program to facilitate her payment of bills and give us additional information on purchasing commitments."

Without waiting for any responses, John passed out another document. "This is a copy of Scott's latest sales forecast." Again, without waiting for responses, he passed out the next sheet. "This still needs additional work, but it's a compilation of technical support calls prepared by Pete, sorted by category. Based on the information in this report, Pete and Dan are planning an addition to the documentation that should reduce the number of customer calls by more than twenty percent." John continued to direct his comments to Herb. "We are also in the process of evaluating new software to aid in the inventory-control process, and we're going to start maintaining a separate stock of parts for R&D, so that Dan won't be using parts already allocated for production boards. And last but certainly not least, we have established a change-control team, led by Jerry, that will provide a more effective way for us to incorporate all product modifications." John stopped for a moment to give Herb a chance to digest what he had said.

Herb looked at John and then at Leonard. If what John was showing him constituted his new approach to management, things might not be so bad after all. And John was right—he couldn't lure Dan away without leaving himself open to a lawsuit, in spite of Leonard's insistence that such a move would solve everything. Leonard seemed to have the knowledge required to run the company, but he had no experience in line management and, based on his performance at this meeting, was evidently lacking in "people skills." Herb finally said to John, "Very impressive. But what about these personnel issues?"

"Dan and I hired these people, and we developed the company to this level together. If I have to prove myself to them and earn back their confidence, so be it. But the situation certainly isn't irreversible."

"And what role do you see for Rick in all this?" asked Herb.

"Rick will be retained as an ongoing monitor of the company. He will review the performance on a monthly basis, and we will depend on his continuing advice to make sure that nothing falls between the cracks."

Leonard interrupted. "But what about your cash crunch? You can't wish that away with some hastily prepared reports."

"We have several proposals. The simplest might be for Herb to factor some receivables. Your return would be outrageously high," said John, addressing Herb, "but since it would only be a short-term solution, it might be the best way to ease the cash squeeze. Another approach involves Dan's computer pager. If you're really willing to fund it, then we might set up a simple debt arrangement, where the debt would be retired with a percentage of the revenue generated by the product. Last of all, Dan and I would be willing to accept a nominal dilution of our stock if you wanted to purchase more equity—say an increase to forty-five percent for you and a corresponding decrease to twenty-seven percent for Dan and twenty-eight percent for me. It's up to you."

"I can't believe you'll even consider this, Herb," Leonard protested. "This guy has run the company into the ground. And before you get too carried away here, Herb, you might be interested in hearing something about John's extracurricular activities. You want a happily married family man? John's pretty far from it, I'd say, and I've got proof."

"What the hell are you talking about," said John indignantly.

"To acquaint myself with the company as quickly as possible, I have been monitoring the E-mail every day."

"You've been reading everyone's mail?" asked Herb.

"Not their mail, just their computer E-mail. It's not illegal. As I said, I was just trying to get a sense as quickly as I could about what was going on in this company. And it's a good thing I did."

"It may not be illegal but only because a law hasn't been passed yet," said Herb, frowning.

John quickly added, "I think the information in those messages is just as private as mail delivered by the postal service, and it's a federal offense to violate the sanctity of someone's *mailbox*."

Leonard quickly said, "Let's not get sidetracked from the issue here. Listen to this message that John sent to Joan last Friday." He read from the printout he'd made of it:

Since you introduced me to Priscilla, I've experienced a new dimension to life. Even though Beth is a very understanding wife and is convinced that this will be just a fleeting relationship, she is becoming jealous and resentful of the time I'm spending with Priscilla. But I'm taking Priscilla to Vegas next month, and I don't care what anyone thinks about it.

"Do you deny sending this message, John?"

"Nope. That's the message I sent."

"And you're really taking this Priscilla to Vegas next month, like the message says?" continued Leonard.

"I'm taking her all right, but—"

"Herb," said Leonard calmly, "sometimes the end justifies the means, and this is clearly one of those times. Yes, reading the E-mail was unethical. But if I hadn't done it, we'd have never known about John cheating on his wife and taking another woman to Vegas."

"Woman?" said John. "What woman?"

"Huh?" said Leonard, confused.

"Joan," said John, "why don't you tell everyone who Priscilla is?"

"Priscilla is my cat. John has graciously agreed to take her to the annual Gumby Cat Show in Vegas next month," she said, grinning.

"What?" said Leonard, shocked.

"I suspected that Leonard was reading the E-mail, Herb," said John, "but I couldn't figure out how to get him to admit it without setting this little trap. And this ethical lapse is only *one* example of his unsuitability to run the company. As I was scrambling around last week trying to get things under control, Leonard was doing just the opposite. He attempted to derail our efforts by getting everyone stirred up—sometimes giving them the impression they would soon be replaced, other times by belittling them. He even plotted to steal away key employees, which in this case is illegal as well as unethical. My number one priority is making Walpold Enterprises successful; his is apparently making Leonard Wasserman successful. Is this a man you would trust to run your company?

"Wait a minute! I was set up!" Leonard protested.

"Leonard, you've said enough already," said Herb angrily. You and Phyl may leave now. I'll meet you back at the office."

On command, Leonard and Phyl stood up and left. The tension that had been hanging over the meeting was broken. Everyone was smiling and chuckling—except Herb.

"That was real cute," Herb said to John, "and I might have thought it was funny if it weren't my money at stake. However, your presentation indicates that you've recognized your problems and are taking the right steps to correct them. Only time will tell if you can overcome your crisis of confidence with your managers. You've convinced me to leave things as they are for now. But I want you to send me a copy of your summary report each week, and I also want Leonard to attend your weekly status meeting so I won't be blindsided again when a problem occurs. In spite of Leonard's gaffe, I still view him as a valuable asset. It will do you both good to learn how to work with each other." He paused and looked at Dan before continuing.

"I'll think about your funding proposals and call you in a day or so to discuss them with you. And now, John, if you're finished with your performance. . ."

"Sorry for the theatrics," said John apologetically, "but desperate times call for desperate measures."

As Herb stood to leave, everyone else stood too but waited until he was gone to say anything. Dan turned to John, and they slapped their right hands together in the celebratory "high five" gesture. "We did it," said Dan excitedly. "That was great. You actually had me believing you were fooling around!

"And two-time Beth? Never."

"The way the meeting started, I was afraid Leonard wouldn't be desperate enough to take the bait," said Joan. "He almost had me convinced you should be shot at dawn, John."

"Well, so far so good," said John. "Now we've got to do what we said we would. Rick, give me a few minutes to call Beth and give her the good news. Then we'd better roll up our sleeves and get busy."

Shaking his head, Rick said, "I need a few minutes to sort all this out anyway. That was, without a doubt, one of the most bizarre meetings I've ever attended."

E*p*ILoGU*e*
Monday, November 13, 1995

*O*ver the three months since the climactic meeting, John and Rick had worked out a budget for the next two years, and Walpold Enterprises was on the course that had been set. Rick now came into the office only two days a month, during which he updated the budget, calculated new trends and financial ratios, and discussed the results with John.

John had called and invited Rick to lunch, but he already had a commitment. John was obviously excited about something, so Rick agreed to stop by later in the afternoon. When he entered the office, he found Wendy busily typing. She looked up brightly and said, "Good afternoon, Mr. Devereux. How are you today?"

"I'm fine, Wendy. How are you?"

"Great. Mr. Walpold is expecting you. Let me take you to his office. Would you like some coffee?" She got up and started walking in the direction of John's office.

The front office had undergone a tremendous change. All the desks were neatly arranged and spotlessly clean, and the carpet even looked recently vacuumed. The fern that had been slowly dying on the filing cabinet had been brought back life and was joined by several other healthy looking plants.

Rick declined the coffee and followed Wendy to John's office. It, too, was noticeably tidier than before. Rick glanced at a chart on the wall that showed orders, shipments, inventory, receivables, and the number of support calls. Joan was in the process of updating the most recent numbers.

"Hi Rick," she said. "I was just updating the status board for our staff meeting. I'll be finished in a second."

"Rick, how are you?" asked John. He was checking over the agenda for the status meeting.

"I'm doing fine. The board looks good."

"Nothing like plastering the data all over the wall to keep everyone on their toes. Listen, thanks for coming by. We only have a few minutes before the staff meeting begins, but I wanted to give you a copy of the CompuPager business plan. Treating it as a start-up venture as you suggested has eliminated a lot of conflicts. I think we have a reasonable assessment of the costs and the additional operating income it might generate. But I'd like to hear what you think of the plan after you've had a chance to review it. We're excited about the possibilities." As John was explaining the details to Rick, people started arriving for the staff meeting, and Rick exchanged greetings with everyone. It was apparent that the gloom he had observed over the summer had been replaced by an air of contentment.

Just as Rick was turning to leave, Leonard entered the office. Rick greeted him and asked, "How are you doing these days? And how is Phyl?"

"Just fine," he responded, more reserved than the last time Rick had seen him.

John said, "Herb just appointed Phyl CFO of one of his companies. The general manager is about ready to retire, and she's being groomed as the replacement. Isn't that great?"

"Very impressive," said Rick. "I've got to go now, John. I'll review the business plan and call you later in the week."

As Rick left the room, Dan rushed by and greeted him with a quick hello. Then he heard John say, "Dammit, Dan, this is the last time you keep everyone waiting. Next time, the door will be locked five minutes after the meeting starts, and I won't let you in. I want you to promise . . ."

Analysis of Walpold Enterprises

for the Period

January 1995–June 1995

Report Prepared

by

Rick Devereux

The purpose of this report is to expand on the data provided in Walpold's financial statements and give you a better insight into your business. In addition to describing the historical trends of the various facets of your business, your operation is compared with the industry standards of other manufacturers of electronic components.

The purpose of any business, unless its charter is nonprofit, is to earn money for the owners. The focus of this analysis is twofold. First, Walpold's day-to-day operations are reviewed, and recommendations are made to increase the net profit and decrease the amount of necessary operating cash in order to increase the available cash for the owners. Second, the valuation of the operation is considered, and changes are recommended that will enhance the owners' sale price should you and Dan decide to sell the business.

Observations & Recommendations

1. Walpold's revenue trend is positive, but this positive trend doesn't carry through to the net profit, whose trend is erratic.
2. All of the revenue components display a positive or flat trend except the PC-OS2 component, which is slightly negative.
3. The operation is slightly more efficient than other, similar operations, based on the sales-to-assets ratio. However, asset management could be improved; reducing the receivables collection rate to 30 days would result in additional cash of over $190,000, and reducing the inventory turn rate to the industry standard value of 82 days would yield $172,000.
4. Not only is Walpold's net profit trend erratic, but its value is significantly below the industry standard. Curiously, the gross margin is significantly higher than the industry standard value, indicating a possible inconsistency in your reporting methods.
5. The primary source of cash for the period was the increase in payables; the primary use of cash was the increase in receivables.
6. The current ratio is only slightly higher than the industry standard value, so adding additional debt would not be logical. Payables aging is over 75 days, indicating a high likelihood of vendor dissatisfaction.
7. A sale of the operation at this time would most likely result in a net loss for the stockholders.

Trend Analysis

These graphs show the key operational items for the analysis period, with calculated trend lines where appropriate.

The top graph shows the consolidated revenue from all sources. There is very little variation from month to month and a slightly positive trend.

Cost of sales is essentially flat.

Operating expenses are slightly positive.

The bottom graph, showing the net profit for the analysis period, is too erratic to justify the calculation of a trend line, since the operating expense level is so close to the cost of sales level. This graph would be very worrisome to a banker, who gains comfort as an operation performs predictably.

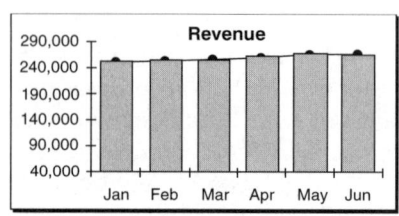

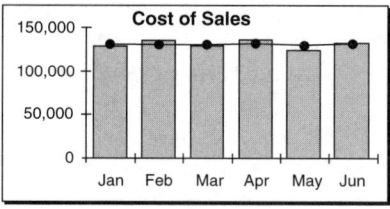

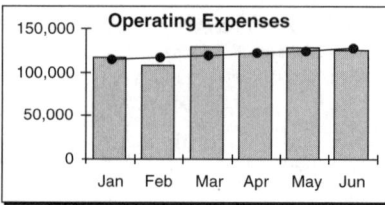

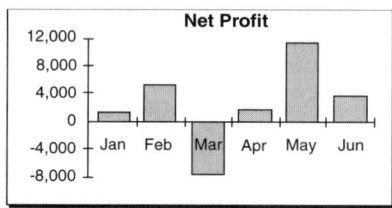

Revenue Composition

The pie chart shows the relationship between the various revenue components. The largest component, PC-DOS, represents 33 percent of the total; the second-largest, MAC, represents 21 percent; Sun and PC-OS2 each represent 16 percent; and Hewlett-Packard represents 8 percent.

The remaining graphs show the values of the various components for each month of the analysis period, along with the calculated trend lines. All components display a positive trend except PC-OS2, which is slightly negative.

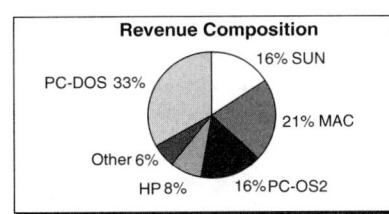

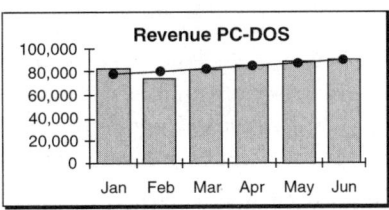

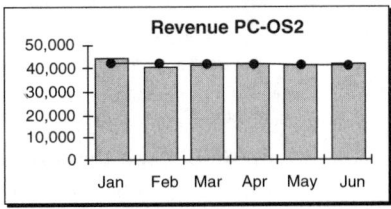

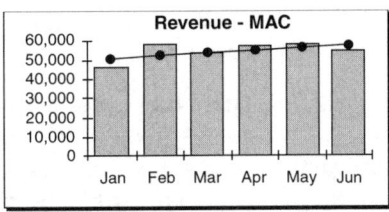

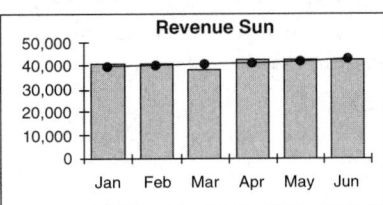

R*u*n a M o**k**

Asset Review

Proper asset management ensures that only a minimum amount of cash is being utilized for assets. The sales-to-assets ratio in itself is not an adequate indicator of proper asset management, since it can be low for a variety of reasons, only one of which is a high asset value.

Ratio of Sales to Assets = 2.02
Standard Ratio of Sales to Assets = 1.90

Walpold Enterprises is more efficient than other, similar operations by 6 percent, based on the sales-to-assets ratio.

Two factors that illustrate the management of the assets are the receivables collection rate and the inventory turn rate.

Receivables Collection Rate: Receivables collection rate is consistently above 30 days and by the end of the analysis period is equal to 52 days. With average monthly revenue of $257,000 and receivables of $451,000, each day represents slightly over $8,600. In other words, reducing the collection rate to 30 days would result in additional cash of over $194,000.

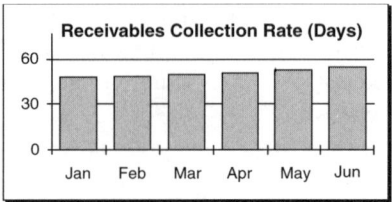

Inventory Turn Rate: The graph shows Walpold's inventory turn rate, with the straight line showing the industry standard value of 82 days. Reducing the inventory

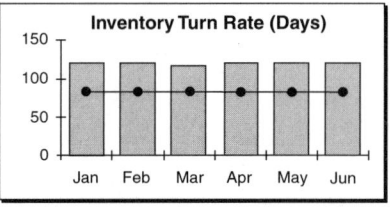

turn rate from the value of 121 days at the end of June to the industry standard value of 82 days would result in additional cash of $172,000.

Profit Review

Profit Margin = .98
Profit Margin = 6.60, industry standard

Gross Margin = 49.12
Gross Margin = 34.40, industry standard

The profit margin is defined as the net profit divided by the revenue. The value of 0.98 was significantly below the industry standard value of 6.6.

Gross margin is defined as the gross profit, or revenue, minus cost of sales, divided by the revenue. The value of 49.12 is significantly higher than the industry standard value of 34.4. It is possible that cost items classically considered as variable expenses are being reported as operating expenses, resulting in Walpold's gross margin being so inordinately high.

Cash Flow Report

In general terms, cash is required anytime an asset increases or a liability decreases. Similarly, cash is generated anytime an asset decreases or a liability increases.

A cash flow report is composed of two lists. One itemizes the sources of cash; the second itemizes the uses of cash. All of this information is tabulated from the balance sheet, which contains the values of assets and liabilities at the beginning of the indicated periods. (See balance sheet at end of report.)

A need for cash, indicated by the uses of cash exceeding the sources of cash, is not in itself bad, since growing businesses will continually need cash. The need for cash must be evaluated along with other data, such as the profit trend, asset management, and Walpold's ability to generate new cash.

Sources of Cash		Uses of Cash	
Item		Item	
Payables Increase	60,538	Receivables Increase	59,144
Owner Equity Increase	14,783	Inventory Increase	13,950
Total	75,321	Fixed Asset Increase	3,814
		Total	76,908

R*u*n a M*o*k

Leverage Review

Leverage involves the use of debt financing, which means funds for which the firm must pay a fixed cost. Examples of debt financing are bank or stockholder loans, trade payables, and the sale of bonds. There are two basic types of debt: short-term and long-term.

Short-term or current debt consists of debts that must be paid in the near term, usually within one year. A measure of a firm's ability to service its current debt is the current ratio, which is defined as the current assets divided by the current liabilities. The higher the current ratio, the more able a company is to satisfy its current liabilities. If the current ratio is higher than others in the industry and if the profit picture is bright, an increase in current debt could be considered to satisfy cash requirements.

Long-term debt relates to debts that do not require repayment in the near term. Owner's equity relates to the cash made available from operating profits and through the sale of stock. Invested capital is defined as the total amount of long-term debt (bonds, long-term loans, etc.) and owners' equity; the debt-to-equity ratio is a measure of the relationship between the two quantities. If all of the invested capital is derived from the sale of stock, the company is underleveraged and will provide a lower rate of return to the owners than if a portion of the invested capital were derived from debt. However, the higher the debt, the more interest will affect the net operating profit. It is logical to maintain a balance, with the goal being to maintain a debt-to-equity ratio similar to the others in the same industry.

Current Debt: The graph shows Walpold's current ratio, with a straight line representing the industry standard of 1.72. The amount of current debt is approximately 7 percent or $38,000 lower than others in your industry; therefore, only a slight increase would be logical.

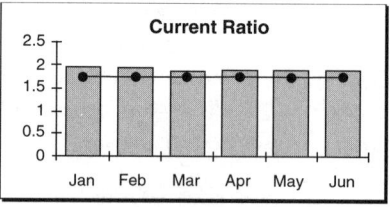

A major component of current debt is often trade payables. The second graph shows payables aging in days.

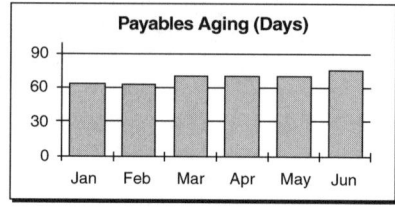

At the end of the analysis period, Walpold's average monthly cost of sales is $130,000 and current payables is $333,000, resulting in an average aging of 76 days. This means that each day of payables-aging translates to $4,300 or that decreasing payables-aging by 15 days would require additional cash of $64,500. It is likely that with payable aging of over 70 days, many of your vendors will become impatient to be paid, if they haven't already.

Long-Term Debt:

Debt/Equity Ratio = .76
Debt/Equity Ratio = .33, industry standard

Walpold's long-term debt is high compared to others in the industry. With long-term debt of $285,500 and owner equity of $371,000, a decrease in long-term debt of $162,000 would be required to realign your debt structure with the industry standard.

Valuation

The annual cash flow of $112,000 is sufficient to result in an investment payback. However, with positive cash flow, the sale price that would be returned in two years (i.e., a two-year payback of the investment with the annual interest rate of 12 percent) would be (considering cash flow only) $234,000.

The book value of $371,000 is above the investment that would yield a payback in two years.

RunaMok

Walpold Enterprises
Balance Sheet
($'s x 1)

	Jan 1995	Feb 1995	Mar 1995	Apr 1995	May 1995	Jun 1995
ASSETS						
Cash	23,829	22,565	36,832	26,177	35,728	22,242
Receivables	392,330	395,284	403,113	408,517	416,130	451,474
Inventory	516,756	525,929	508,141	524,535	519,562	530,706
Fixed Assets	239,052	239,052	238,581	231,297	231,297	231,297
Accumulated Depreciation	−47,218	−48,718	−35,077	−31,381	−32,881	−35,649
Total	1,124,749	1,134,112	1,151,590	1,159,145	1,169,836	1,200,070
LIABILITIES						
Payables	272,874	276,998	302,117	307,966	306,877	333,412
Current Notes	210,000	210,000	210,000	210,000	210,000	210,000
Long-Term Debt	285,000	285,000	285,000	285,000	285,000	285,000
Capital Stock	500	500	500	500	500	500
Paid-in Capital	200,000	200,000	200,000	200,000	200,000	200,000
Retained Earnings	955	6,194	−1,447	259	12,039	15,738
Prior Earning	155,420	155,420	155,420	155,420	155,420	155,420
Total	1,124,749	1,134,112	1,151,590	1,159,145	1,169,836	1,200,07C

Glossary of Frequently Encountered Business and Financial Words

Balance Sheet A snapshot of the financial position, showing that assets equal liabilities plus owners' equity. Where the income statement shows the operational results for a given time period (monthly, quarterly, annual), the balance sheet shows the status of the various accounts at a single instant, usually the end of the accounting period.

Cost of Sales (also COS, Cost of Goods Sold, or COGS) This relates to the amount of expense required to produce (or purchase) the items that appear on the income statement as revenue or income. A business with no product (one that derives its income from providing a service) may have no cost of sales, although sometimes this item can represent sales expenses. The expenses defined as cost of sales can vary from company to company. Within a given company, however, this definition must be consistent from one accounting period to the next. A rule of thumb that is sometimes used to determine which expenses should be considered direct (COS) and which should be indirect (operating expenses) is to assume income is zero, and consider all expenses that remain as indirect.

Current Assets The sum of all cash and other assets that are expected to be turned into cash, sold, or exchanged within one year. These include marketable securities, receivables, inventory, and current prepayments.

Current Liabilities All debts or other obligations that must be retired within one year, normally by using current assets.

Current Ratio Current assets divided by current liabilities. Bankers often use this ratio during loan evaluation. A banker will usually be comfortable with this part of his or her evaluation process if the current ratio of the potential borrower is greater than or equal to the industry standard.

Depreciation Amortization of assets: The process of allocating the cost of an asset to the periods of benefit. Purchasing a piece of equipment is not considered an expense, rather an increase in assets. If the life of the equipment is determined to be five years, then one fifth of the purchase price can be expensed (deducted) from the gross profit each year. Thus, its value is depreciated as it is expensed.

Expenses see **Operating Expenses.**

Financial Ratios (or Ratios) Calculated terms that can be used for a variety of purposes, mainly as a means to compare one operation's performance with another or with the industry standards. Many bankers subscribe to a service known as RMA (Robert Morris Associates) which provides information on industry standard ratios for over 350 industries by SIC (Standard Industry Category) codes. Dun & Bradstreet also maintains financial ratios and can provide them sorted by company size and geography. Trade associations for many different industries compile and publish financial ratios in literature that can usually be found in libraries.

Gross Profit Net sales minus cost of goods sold.

Gross Margin A percentage, computed as gross profit divided by revenue.

Income Statement The statement of revenues, expenses, gains, and losses for the accounting period, ending with the net income for the period.

Inventory Raw materials, supplies, work in process, finished goods.

Inventory-Turn Rate A calculated term that can be expressed either in days, to define the length of time the current inventory level will last at the current revenue rate, or as a ratio, defining the number of times per year the current inventory level will be completely depleted.

Leverage The act of acquiring debt to increase income. The additional debt results in increased income and has a cost—its interest—that is less than the resulting increase in income; thus, leverage.

Liquidity The availability of cash, or near cash, to satisfy the company's obligations.

Net Profit Net profit before taxes (NPBT) minus taxes.

Net Profit Before Taxes (also NPBT) The gross profit minus operating expenses.

Operating Expenses The sum of all indirect expenses or those expenses not directly associated with the production of items for sale.

Owner's Equity (also Book Value) Total assets minus total liabilities. In simplistic terms, if all assets are liquidated and used to retire all liabilities, the remaining funds belong to the owners.

Payables Billings that have not yet been paid but are not necessarily past due.

Payables Aging This term, calculated in days, represents how a company is managing its payables. It is defined as payables divided by cost of sales.

Quick Ratio Current assets minus inventory, divided by current liabilities. Bankers are often more comfortable looking at the quick ratio than the current ratio when considering a loan, because the current ratio includes inventory, which they've no way of evaluating; i.e., much of it could be obsolete. If only the current ratio is considered, they are correct. However, if the inventory turn rate and the sales-to-assets ratio are also considered, the current ratio represents a suitable indicator of the company's ability to satisfy its obligations.

Receivables Any collectible, whether or not it is due. For example, when a product is sold on terms, the amount to be collected is a receivable.

Receivable Collection Rate This term, calculated in days, illustrates how well a company manages its credit sales, or receivables. It is defined as receivables divided by revenue.

Revenue (also sales or income) The monetary measure of a service rendered. Sales of products, merchandise, and services and the earnings from rents, interest, dividends, and the like.

Sales-to-Assets Ratio Annual sales divided by total assets. This is a useful ratio when comparing one company to another, since it reflects the efficiency of the operation. That is, consider two companies with identical asset values. If one's sales are 20 percent higher than the other, it can be said to be operating more efficiently.

Key Financial Ratio Calculations

Current Ratio   Current Assets ÷ Current Liabilities
Current, in financial parlance, is anything that will occur within a single year. Current Assets are receivables, inventory, cash, and securities. Current Liabilities are trade payables, short-term notes, and any portion of long-term notes that will be retired within the year.

Quick Ratio   (Current Assets − Inventory) ÷ Current Liabilities

Debt/Equity Ratio   Long Term Debt ÷ Owners' Equity

Working Capital Ratio
Working Capital ÷ (Total Assets − Current Liabilities)

Gross Profit   Revenue − Cost of Goods

Gross Margin   Gross Profit ÷ Revenue

Profit Margin   Net Income ÷ Revenue

Inventory as Percent of Assets   Inventory ÷ Total Assets

Receivables Collection Rate   (30 × Receivables) ÷ Revenue
Where Revenue is a monthly average.

Inventory Turn Rate   (365 × Inventory) ÷ Cost of Sales
Where Cost of Sales is an annual value.

Investment Turn Rate   Revenue ÷ Invested Capital
Where Revenue is an annual value.

Working Capital   Current Assets − Current Liabilities

Return on Assets   Net Income ÷ Total Assets

Return on Invested Capital   Net Income ÷ Invested Capital

Return on Equity   Net Income ÷ Owners' Equity
For Return on Assets, Invested Capital, and Equity, Net Income is an annual value.